M000074496

JUSTICE OVERDUE

Rayven T. Hill

Ray of Joy Publishing
Toronto

Books by Rayven T. Hill

Blood and Justice
Cold Justice
Justice for Hire
Captive Justice
Justice Overdue
Justice Returns
Personal Justice
Silent Justice
Web of Justice
Fugitive Justice

Visit rayventhill.com for more information
on these and future releases.

Published by Ray of Joy Publishing
Toronto

ISBN-13: 978-0-9938625-4-0

JUSTICE OVERDUE

CHAPTER 1

Wednesday, 4:42 p.m.

VARICK LUCAS COULD hardly contain his excitement. He'd worked long and hard, finally landing a job in the prison auto shop. It took his mind away from life inside a federal penitentiary and allowed him time to formulate a plan.

Today, that plan would come to fruition and his hard work was about to pay off. In spades.

He glanced across the floor of the large workshop. The screw leaned against the wall in his usual spot, his arms folded, glaring at him. He was a cowboy, fresh out of training, and cowboys always wanted to show how tough they were. But he had a surprise coming. Lucas grinned at him and waved before turning his attention back to the grinder.

"It's all ready."

Lucas glanced up at the speaker and gave a short nod. "Got the tank in place?"

"Yup. We're all set to go."

"It better not fall off. I only got one shot at this."

"Don't worry. I know what I'm doing. It's totally secure and could take a pounding, if necessary, and never break loose."

Lucas switched off the grinder and straightened his back. As the machine hummed to a stop, he squinted thoughtfully at Rabbit. After this was all over, Rabbit would get the hole—and worse—for his part in this, but he was already doing an all-day sentence—life—and had nothing to lose. Lucas didn't really care what happened to his accomplice. Anyway, Rabbit could never have survived without him. He'd kept his scrawny little cellmate in line by threatening to withdraw his protection. Rabbit owed Lucas his life, and now he was about to pay. The warden would be heading to his cushy home in a few minutes and would need his SUV.

Rabbit wiped his greasy hands on a cloth and tossed it onto the workbench. "Let's do this."

Lucas nodded. "Ready," he said and gave Rabbit a push, shouting, "Get out of my face."

Rabbit stumbled and regained his balance. He drew back and took a wild swing, catching Lucas on the side of the head.

Lucas spat out a string of curses and sprang forward, bearing his opponent down. They wrestled on the floor, each trying to get the best of the other.

The screw shouted and hustled their way, anxious to break up the fight as he fumbled to pull the baton from his belt. The cowboy didn't see the thin wire stretched a few inches above the floor, and he didn't feel the meticulously fashioned metal arrow pierce his skull as the spring which held it let loose. He was too dead to care.

The scuffle, which had started so quickly, was over. Varick Lucas smiled grimly as he stood and brushed off his orange jumpsuit. "Good job, Rabbit," he said, giving his partner a hand up. "That went rather well, wouldn't you say?"

"Very smooth," Rabbit said. He glanced at the screw's body. Blood pooled on the immaculate floor, small streams breaking away and trickling dark red liquid across the concrete. He turned back and shook Varick's hand. "Good luck. You'd better get moving."

Rabbit turned his attention to the fresh corpse. Lucas watched him drag the body out of sight behind a pile of tires and then sprinkle sawdust over the puddle of blood. It would hide the stain for now, and the screw's body wouldn't be found until this was over and he was long gone.

He turned his attention to the SUV. Phase two.

He scrambled to the vehicle, swung the cargo area door up, and peeled back the carpeting. He pulled up on a small ring and a makeshift trapdoor swung open. It led into the now empty gas tank, barely large enough to hold him, but it was carefully tested, and if he lay in a fetal position, the newly customized thirty-one-gallon tank in the warden's SUV would more than suffice.

He climbed into the cargo area, eased into the tank, and curled up. The remains of the fuel made him choke, and he cursed Rabbit for not wiping it dry. But that was the least of his worries. Would they have enough gasoline? Rabbit had rerouted the fuel line into an eight-liter tank fastened underneath the vehicle, large enough to hold the tank unit and a small amount of gas, enough to get him safely away.

He chuckled to himself. He'd been in this hellhole for almost five years, and now was the day of reckoning. A day of rejoicing—for him at least—but not so much for anyone else. Certainly not for Rabbit.

His accomplice returned, the body disposed of, and as Lucas looked up, his fellow conspirator gave him the thumbs-up before closing the trapdoor. The carpet slapped in place, the rear door slammed, and Lucas lay still in the darkness.

It was all up to Rabbit now. They'd rehearsed this carefully and tried to imagine all possibilities. Rabbit had better not screw up or he'd have more to worry about than just the wrath of the law.

In a few minutes, he heard voices. As planned, Rabbit had summoned another guard to advise him the vehicle was ready. Lucas strained to hear.

"Where's Lucas?"

"He's gone to wash up. The screw's with him."

Silence a moment. If Anderson got suspicious, they had a backup plan. It meant Anderson would also die and things could get messy and rather uncertain. Not an optimum situation, and one he hoped to avoid.

Lucas breathed easier as Anderson asked, "Where're the keys?"

"They're inside."

Footsteps shuffled and faded. The front door opened, then slammed shut, and the vehicle came to life. The engine sputtered. Lucas held his breath until the motor roared and ran smoothly.

The large garage door rumbled open, the transmission clunked near his head, and the SUV backed up. It jerked to a stop, pulled ahead, and stopped again. The engine continued to purr as the driver-side door opened and closed. The garage door whined shut; he was halfway home.

4

Lucas adjusted his position to relieve the pressure on his leg. The tank creaked under his weight, but held.

The warden's voice. "Thanks, Anderson."

Anderson grunted something.

A door slammed and the SUV pulled ahead, then stopped. A gate rattled and the vehicle leaped forward and jerked to a halt. A second gate opened and the engine roared. Tires whined under his head as they picked up speed.

They were on the highway. He was going to make it. He *had* made it.

Phase three. Coming up.

Rabbit had timed it right. The engine of the SUV sputtered and died at what Lucas estimated to be a good two miles from the prison compound. Perfect.

He eased up on the trapdoor and squinted as the evening sun seeped through the crack. He carefully worked his way onto his back, tensed his muscles, and heaved up with his feet. The trapdoor burst open, the carpet flipped back, and Lucas climbed from the tank.

Warden Henry Parker sat wide-eyed behind the steering wheel, half-twisted in his seat, his mouth hanging open. Then one hand fumbled for the door handle, the other reaching for his pistol as Lucas dove from the cargo area into the backseat and wrapped his strong hands around the neck of the helpless warden.

The warden gasped for breath as he forced out the words, "Let me go."

"Can't do that. You're my ticket out of here."

"Please."

"Who's doing the begging now, Warden?"

Parker's eyes bulged as he fought for breath, clawing at the fingers that dug into his throat. The gun fell to his lap and slipped to the floor. His feet kicked wildly at nothing as his attacker held on.

"I am. I'm begging you. I'll let you go," the warden barely managed to say. "Just don't hurt me and I'll let you go."

"Sorry. No deal."

"Please." The warden gave a last gasp, then became still, unconscious but alive.

Lucas released his grip and slipped between the seats into the front of the vehicle. He retrieved the pistol from the floor, cocked it, and finished the job. The hole through the warden's head assured he would never breathe again. The bullet shattered the side window, bringing a spray of blood and human tissue with it.

Varick Lucas chuckled. He had four notches in his belt already. What was one more?

And now, to get out of here.

He scrambled to open the passenger door, stepped onto the gravel shoulder, and glanced around. Fields lined both sides of the rural road, and on the other side, a forest was visible a few hundred feet past a sturdy wire fence. There was no traffic in either direction, but he'd better hurry.

He spat out the foul taste of gasoline, then took a deep breath and went around the front of the vehicle and opened the driver-side door. Shards of bloodstained glass sprinkled to the ground at his feet. He kicked them aside, dragged the warden's body out, and removed the shirt, pants, jacket, and shoes from the corpse. The jacket was spattered with blood from the unfortunate incident, so he tossed it aside and changed into the rest. The clothes hung loose, some blood on the shirt, but they would do for now. The shoes fit him to perfection.

The warden's wallet held a couple hundred in bills. That should tide him over until he could round up some more cash. He left the credit cards and tossed the wallet onto the ground beside the body.

He gazed thoughtfully at the warden's remains a few moments, then turned his back, crossed the road, and climbed down into the ditch.

Leaving Parker's half-naked body on the side of the road beside the SUV, he hopped the fence and jogged across the open field toward the trees. He knew of a town a couple of miles away and he could use some food, fresh clothes, and transportation as far away from here as possible.

CHAPTER 2

Thursday, 7:45 a.m.

ANNIE LINCOLN watched her eight-year-old son poke the last bite of toast in his mouth, drop his plate in the sink, and dash from the kitchen.

"Thanks for breakfast, Mom," he called over his shoulder.

Matty had about as much energy as any kid his age. She wished she had his get-up-and-go, but the last few days had been so physically and emotionally exhausting, she wanted to sleep for a week. Chasing bad guys did that to you.

Jake, though, always recovered quickly, ready to tackle anything. Even now, as he sat at the table sipping his first coffee of the day, she saw the restlessness in his eyes. He was raring to go.

Jake set his cup down, leaned back, and looked at his wife. "We're going to have a great time this weekend. The weatherman promised us good weather. Are you sure you don't want to come with us?"

Annie shook her head and offered a weak smile. "Not this time. I'm just going to relax and maybe catch up on some reading."

"We'll miss you." He ran his fingers through his short-cropped hair and shrugged. "But we'll get by."

Matty dashed back into the room, his backpack slung over his shoulder. "I'm going over to see Kyle. I need to make sure he packed everything he'll need."

Their next-door neighbor, Chrissy, was a single mom and a good friend of the Lincolns. Her seven-year-old son, Kyle, and Matty were the best of friends, and Matty was elated when Jake had agreed Kyle could come camping with them.

Annie glanced at her watch. Matty still had enough time to run next door before he and Kyle needed to be off to school. "Don't be late."

"Don't worry, Mom."

"You forgot your lunch," Annie said as she stood, opened the fridge, retrieved a paper bag, and handed it to her son.

He grinned a crooked grin. "Yeah, I'm gonna need that," he said as he took the bag and stuffed it into his backpack.

Annie laughed. "Try to concentrate on your schoolwork today and keep your mind off the trip."

"Yeah, I will, Mom," he said, but Annie wasn't so sure.

Jake turned to Matty. "I want to leave as soon as you guys get home," he said. "I'll have everything packed and ready to go."

"Don't forget the bait," Matty said. "We can't catch any fish without that."

"We'll stop and grab some before we get there. There's a small town just a few miles from our camping spot."

Matty charged out, the front door slamming behind him. Annie sat at the table and leaned forward, her chin in her hands. "I've been thinking."

Jake took another sip of coffee and eyed her, waiting.

"This private investigation business we got ourselves into isn't exactly like doing the research we did before."

Jake chuckled. "You can say that again. Too many of our clients turn out to be criminals."

"That's my point exactly."

"Huh?"

"Doing research, we never had to get a retainer in advance because we did all of our work for established companies. We always got paid, but now … well, we'd better start."

Jake sat back, tucked his hands behind his head and stretched out his six-foot-four body. "Yeah, good idea."

"Which reminds me," Annie said. "We need to look into that possible fraud for the insurance company. We've been putting it off for a while. We don't want to lose a good client, and besides, we could use the money."

"I still have to pack for our trip," Jake said.

"I can do most of that. Do you think you can look into it today?"

Jake nodded. "I'll give it some thought and try to come up with an approach. I might have time."

Annie went into the office and leafed through a stack of papers, slipped out a page, and returned to the kitchen. She handed the report to Jake. "It's all there."

Sipping his coffee, Jake held the paper with his free hand and studied it briefly. "It shouldn't be a problem. I'll soon find out whether or not this guy has a bad back." He folded the paper and tucked it into his pocket. "I'll take care of it."

She knew he would. Due to a building slump, he had been laid off a short while ago from his job as a construction engineer. His crazy plan to expand Annie's part-time freelance research company into something more lucrative had worked, and when the company had wanted him back, he'd refused. Lincoln Investigations was a going concern and he was having too much fun.

And so was she. Unlike most private investigators, whose job usually involves little more than research, surveillance, or background checks, they'd had more than their fair share of frightening experiences. Sure, sometimes things did get a little dangerous, but Annie loved working alongside her husband and doing something they both enjoyed.

Sometimes their job forced them to work long hours, occasionally in the evening and weekends, but right now, she knew he wanted a little time off as well. The fishing/camping trip he'd promised Matty would be just what he needed.

And it would be great for Matty and his best friend as well. It would give the three of them a little guy time.

"I'll give Hank a call before we go," Jake said. "I haven't seen him for a couple of days and he might need us."

Annie laughed. "I'm sure the police can do without you for a while. But it's too bad he can't go with you. He needs a break as well."

"He said maybe next time." Jake pushed back from the table. "And now, I'd better get a move on. It's going to be a busy day."

CHAPTER 3

Thursday, 8:20 a.m.

THE SMALL TOWN of Haddleburg was gripped with fear. Many in the town had objected when the maximum-security penitentiary had been proposed to be built nearby, but the town councilors had won out. The new facility would bring much-needed jobs to the floundering community, and so it was built. But as far as anyone knew, though there were many attempts, there had never been a successful escape. Until now. The citizens had felt comfortable in their homes and were caught unawares by the brutal murder of one of their own.

Other than the name Varick Lucas, a name now on everyone's lips, authorities had released no other information, and the press was kept at bay. A massive Royal Canadian Mounted Police manhunt had the entire town in lockdown. Citizens were confined to their homes, the area cordoned off by the federal police.

The message was firm: people were ordered to stay in their homes, keep off the streets, and allow the RCMP to do its job.

The unofficial information that buzzed throughout the

close-knit community was that an unknown citizen had been accosted in his home late last night by an escaped convict, the victim then murdered and robbed. Nobody seemed to know who was killed and the sudden encirclement of the town served to intensify their fear.

In the early morning hours, teams of police officers had converged on their sleepy village, their weapons drawn. Some patrolled streets within the cordoned-off area, others employing K-9 units. Armored security trucks were also visible. Contingents of officers searched homes and businesses, street to street, door-to-door, no building left unsearched, every hole, nook, and cranny explored.

The Mounties had conducted the intensive manhunt through the night, and yet Lucas had eluded them.

Seasoned veteran RCMP Sergeant Lance Brewer was in charge and he made sure everyone knew it. Brewer leaned against his vehicle and cursed. He had hoped to end this right away. He bounced off the vehicle, turned, and uncrossed his arms as a corporal approached him.

"Report of a stolen vehicle, sir," the corporal said. "Could be Lucas. All forces province-wide have been notified to be on the lookout."

"This might be the break we need. We've about scoured this town clean. He's gone and that's going to make it even harder to track down this monster." Brewer raised one ragged brow. "Any way to track this vehicle?"

The corporal shook his head. "It doesn't seem like it. It's an older SUV." He consulted some notes. "It's a 2005 4-Runner. Black. No GPS."

"Anything else?" Brewer asked.

"That's not the worst of it, sir."

Brewer frowned. "Spit it out, Corporal Loy."

"We believe he's armed, sir. Neighbors confirmed the murder victim had at least one pistol in his possession. And that pistol's gone."

An intense frown took over Brewer's brow. He cursed again as he dug out his cell phone and dialed a number. "It's Sergeant Lance Brewer. Give me the commissioner, priority one."

"The commissioner is tied up at the moment," came over the line.

Brewer raised his voice. "Give me the deputy commissioner, then. And make it quick or I'll have your tail." Brewer glared at the phone. "Did you not hear me say priority one?"

"Just a moment, Sergeant Brewer. I'll see if he's available."

He waited a moment, kicking impatiently at the dirt. Didn't they know time was wasting and Lucas was slipping from their grasp? The volatile con would stop at nothing to get away and every second counted. He had to be stopped. Finally, he heard, "What do you have for me, Brewer?"

"I'm afraid he's gone, sir. He stole a vehicle and a pistol and now he's armed and dangerous. I want your okay to extend the manhunt. I need to block all the roads and search all vehicles within twenty miles of here."

The deputy commissioner talked fast, the words tumbling over one another as if in a hurry to spit them out. "Do it. I want this guy found. He's killed two already and we don't want more. Get on it. Whatever you need."

"I need more men, sir. This is a major operation and most of my people here have been up all night. I need some fresh troops and some fresh dogs."

"You can have every officer who's not doing anything vitally important. Our people put their lives on the line every day to protect our citizens and communities. This is what they're good at. We'll get him. Hell, we'll call out the army if we have to. They need some action."

"Thank you, sir," Brewer said and hung up the phone. He turned to Loy. "I want every piece of information you can get on Lucas. I want his mother's maiden name and I want to know what he eats for breakfast. Got it? Everything."

"Right away."

"What about his cellmate?"

The corporal shrugged. "They've finished with him. They've been at it all night but can't get anything from him. He's a lifer with nothing to lose. I just talked with the deputy warden. He's pretty convinced the guy has no idea where Lucas is headed."

Brewer sighed. "Lucas ain't stupid enough to give him that information, but I bet he knows something he doesn't know he knows. What's the guy's name?"

"His name's Stephan Padre. They call him Rabbit."

Brewer bit his lower lip thoughtfully. He had almost thirty-five years on the force with a stellar record, almost ready for retirement with a maximum pension. He couldn't afford to lose this one. He wanted to go out with a bang, not a whimper.

Brewer pointed a long finger at the corporal. "I want him

put in a four-piece suit, and let him cool in the hole awhile. He's an accessory to murder and I don't care what it takes. He killed the warden and a guard, and that makes it very personal. He knows something and I don't want him to eat, drink, or take a dump until he spits up something useful." Brewer leaned in and glared at the corporal. "Got that?"

Corporal Loy grinned up at Brewer. "Got it."

CHAPTER 4

Thursday, 9:59 a.m.

JAKE PULLED THE piece of paper from his pocket, unfolded it, and studied it. A small black-and-white photo of a man's face appeared at the top left of the page. Nothing outstanding about his features, but clear enough to be recognized. The information on the single-page report was sketchy. The insurance company hadn't given a lot of details regarding the alleged scammer.

The report stated Maynard Hughes had been involved in an auto accident a little more than a month ago and complained about severe back and neck injuries. According to his doctor, the patient also experienced shooting pain down his legs. Apparently, he was in so much agony he couldn't walk, confined to a wheelchair, taking a regular regimen of painkillers.

Typical story.

Sure, it happens, and insurance companies don't suspect foul play every time, but this guy had a pattern of prior claims. No information was given on what the claims had been or how they were settled.

Annie had already done some research on Mr. Hughes,

and through her online magic had discovered he'd lost his job a few months ago and was behind in mortgage payments—all indicators of a dubious claim. Hughes also lived alone, having been recently divorced.

Jake had worked with Richmond Insurance several times in the past and they had been right in their suspicions every time. He suspected this time would be no different.

Jake went into the office and scanned the shelves. He grabbed a pair of binoculars off the top shelf and, of course, a video camera—high-definition. He flicked it on and checked the battery. Lots of power, and the memory card was far from full. He dropped them both into a shoulder bag.

He wasn't exactly sure how to proceed or if he had enough time. Sometimes it took a few attempts and lots of patience to get the evidence the insurance company needed, and he only had a few hours before Matty got home and they had to leave. The trip north would take them four or five hours and he wanted to get there and set up camp before nightfall.

But he would do what he could. He might get lucky.

He went into the living room, where Annie was curled up in her favorite chair. She looked up as he approached.

"I think I'll take your car if you don't need it," he said. "The Firebird will stick out like a sore thumb and I don't want to announce my presence."

She nodded. "The keys are in my bag—in the kitchen."

Jake looked at his watch. "I should be back by two."

Annie closed her book and set it on the stand beside her chair. "I'll have just about everything ready for you to pack by then."

Jake leaned over, gave her a quick kiss, and strode from the room. One minute later, he pulled Annie's Ford Escort from the drive.

Maynard Hughes lived clear across the city, so Jake scooted north, took the bypass, and shortly pulled onto Orleans Avenue. He scanned the street numbers until he found number 338, a squat bungalow three or four decades old, rather in need of repairs.

He pulled the Escort to the curb across the street from the house, shut off the engine, and, with great difficulty, climbed over the console to the passenger seat. From there, it would be difficult for anyone in the house to see him. He leaned his back against the door and trained the binoculars on the front window of the house.

He assumed Maynard Hughes was at home. Hughes made occasional trips to the doctor via the city-financed disabled transit system, but unless he had a vehicle outfitted to take a wheelchair, it was unlikely he ever left the house for any other purpose. That was, unless he felt so secure in his fraud, he went out and left his wheelchair at home.

As far as he could tell, no one was in the front room. A few books sagged in an otherwise empty bookcase, a dusty picture hung haphazardly on the far wall, and an unoccupied couch sat halfway in view at the other end of the dimly lit room.

Half an hour later, nothing had changed inside the house and Jake felt restless. Stakeouts weren't his thing; he'd much sooner be just about anywhere else. He set the glasses in his lap and yawned as he dug a bottle of water from his bag. His hand stopped short, halfway to his mouth. Someone was heading up the driveway toward the house.

Jake dropped the bottle and grabbed the glasses, focusing them on the newcomer. It was a young guy, twenties maybe, stringy hair dripping down from under a dirty baseball cap. He wore a leather jacket despite the warm day, his right hand stuffed inside the pocket. He strode up the drive, climbed the steps to the front door, took a quick glance in either direction, and knocked. Then he turned his back to the door, stuffed his hands into his jeans, and waited.

In a few minutes, the door swung open and the newcomer spun back around. Jake trained the glasses on the doorway but all he saw was a pair of feet resting on the footrests of a wheelchair. The visitor entered and the door closed.

Jake swung the glasses back on the window of the front room and, in a moment, the pair entered the room, one sauntering in like he owned the place, the other wheeling his way. The wheelchair stopped and spun around to face the punk, and for the first time, Jake saw Hughes's face. He was middle-aged, greying at the temples, with short hair and unsmiling features. In fact, the face frowned as Hughes waved his hand toward the window. The young guy stepped over and swooped the drapes closed, completely blocking Jake's view.

CHAPTER 5

Five Years Ago

VARICK LUCAS WAS having the time of his life. Otis had made sure there were lots of females at the party. Varick suspected most of them were hookers, but he didn't care. The women were loose and the booze was free and that was all that mattered. Until now, that is.

"We're almost out of booze," Otis shouted over the blaring music as he approached Varick, his arm around a well-painted lady.

Varick cursed and yelled back, "The party's just getting started. Where'd it all go?"

"I didn't expect so many crashers." Otis glanced around. "I don't even know most of them. We gotta get some."

"How? The stores are closed, idiot. It's almost midnight."

Otis grinned. "That never stopped us before. We'll open one up."

Varick frowned. They'd almost gotten caught last time. The police had just happened to be patrolling the neighborhood at the wrong time. They'd managed to get away okay, but it was close. He wasn't too hot on the idea of a repeat performance, but they needed booze. "Can't you get the Bulewell brothers to do it?"

"The Bulewells are fools. We have to do it. We can be in and out of there in no time."

Varick sighed and climbed from the couch where he was settled in between a pair of scantily clad girls. One of them grabbed his hand and asked, "Where you going, Varick?"

He turned back. "Just a little business to take care of, Modesty. We won't be gone long."

Modesty pouted and looked at him through drunken eyes. "Can I tag along with you?"

Varick pulled his hand away. "Not this time."

"Hurry back, then." Modesty gave him a seductive smile, then settled into the couch, took a sip of booze, and chatted with the girl beside her.

"All right. Let's go," Varick said and followed Otis into the bedroom. The room happened to be occupied but they paid no mind to the couple on the bed. Otis slid open the closet door and dug around on the floor behind a pile of shoes. He stood and turned back, brandishing a pistol and a pair of ski masks.

"I'll take the gun," Varick said, reaching for it.

Otis frowned and held on to the weapon. "We're not going to plug anyone. It's only for effect if we need it."

Varick laughed and wrested the pistol from his friend's hand. "I'm not going to use it. The place'll be empty anyway," he said as he shoved the gun behind his belt and pulled his shirt over it. "Let's go."

They left the apartment and climbed into Otis's Jeep. Varick frowned as the roar of the vehicle broke the quiet night air. "You need a new muffler. They'll hear us coming for miles."

22

Otis shrugged. "We'll park a couple blocks away. Don't worry so much."

They drove without speaking for several blocks, and then Otis pulled the Jeep over in a dark alley behind a tenement. He shut the engine down, opened the back door, and removed a bolt cutter. "My key," he said. "Guaranteed to open any door." He produced a gym bag and handed it to Varick with a snicker. "This should hold our purchases."

They donned the ski masks and kept to the shadows as they made their way down the alley and out to the main road.

Varick pointed across the street to the large liquor store and whispered, "There it is. Refreshments."

They ducked low, waited until a car idled by, and then crossed the quiet street and circled around behind the brightly lit building.

"Remember," Otis said as he gripped the bolt cutter and slapped the free end against his palm. "We got two minutes max after the alarm blows."

Varick nodded. The last time they'd attempted this, they'd overestimated the response time of the police. It wasn't going to happen this time. "Just open 'er up and let's do this."

Otis took a last look up and down the alley before approaching the door. The bolt cutter occasionally served as a crowbar while he worked, mangling the hinges until the door sagged, ready to cave. He looked at his friend, then gave one last wrench. The door fell forward with a crash, narrowly missing Varick.

An inner door was made of bars, held by a padlock, and as the alarm screeched, Otis gave the lock a quick snap with the cutter and the door swung inward. They gazed at aisle after aisle of gleaming bottles—enough to last them forever.

"Nice of them to keep the lights on for us," Otis shouted as they stepped inside. He held the gym bag open while Varick scooped bottles from the shelves, filling the bag.

Over the clanging of the alarm, Varick heard a shout, then, from the corner of his eye, saw a sudden movement. Otis went down, clobbered by a baton. A bottle of vodka hit the floor and broke into a million pieces, the expensive liquid splashing at Varick's feet.

He cursed and jumped back. It was a security guard. There had been no guards last time, and he didn't expect one this time. Probably due to one too many break-ins. He swiped the pistol from his waist, raised the weapon, and glared at the uniformed man.

The guard raised the baton and shouted over the din of the alarm. "Drop the gun."

Varick squeezed the trigger. The guard went down, blood soaking his uniform, his heart pierced through by a single bullet. Varick knelt by his motionless friend. Otis still breathed, but he wasn't moving. He would have to leave the booze and drag him out of here.

Then a second guard appeared brandishing a pistol, pointed directly at his head. "Don't move."

Varick dropped to the floor, raised his gun, and began to squeeze the trigger. His hand trembled. It was a woman. He rolled to his feet, glanced at Otis, then the bag of booze, then the guard, and stumbled from the store. Behind him, the guard continued to yell for him to stop. He tripped over a bag of garbage, hit the ground with his right shoulder, and ended up on his back.

"Put your hands up." She pursued him relentlessly, coming up fast from behind, her gun ready.

He gripped his weapon, and again, he contemplated shooting the guard. He couldn't do it. He rolled to his feet, ducked behind an industrial-sized garbage bin, and then clung to the wall, out of sight of his pursuer.

The police would be here any moment. He hated to leave Otis in the lurch like that, but he had no choice. His knew his friend wouldn't squeal on him and the female guard would never recognize him. The ski mask made sure of that. He would be okay.

He tugged off the mask, stuffed it into his jacket pocket, and raced down the alley to the street beyond, leaving the guard behind. He had better not go back to the party. He would head home and lay low until this whole thing blew over. Maybe get out of town if things got too hot.

It was the first time he'd killed anyone. It didn't really bother him; the fool guard should've known better anyway. Maybe he should go back and finish the job, kill the other guard and help Otis get out of there. But no, he knew he could never kill a woman. Otis was screwed and there was nothing he could do about it.

CHAPTER 6

Thursday, 10:35 a.m.

JAKE GRABBED THE shoulder bag and jumped from the vehicle. Something was up inside Maynard Hughes's house and he had to see what it was.

He darted across the road, then the lawn, digging out the movie camera as he ran. When he reached the window, he smiled with satisfaction. There was a gap between the curtains, near the bottom of the window, just big enough to see inside.

Jake fumbled with the camera, got it working, and filmed through the space. With perfect high-definition clarity, the camera caught the action as Hughes stood to his feet, crossed the room, and bent over in front of a small table.

Jake grinned. Hughes had made a miraculous recovery.

The former invalid pulled open a drawer in the table and removed two plastic bottles. Jake could see a label on the side of the containers. They were pill bottles—prescription drugs. This was getting interesting.

Hughes straightened his back, turned around, and handled the bottles to his visitor, who examined them a moment and then stuffed them into his jacket, producing a roll of bills as he removed his hand from his pocket. Hughes took the money and flipped through the bills. An exchange of words took place, and then the purchaser spun around and moved out of the camera's view. Jake watched Hughes pocket the money with a look of satisfaction on his face.

He flipped off the camera and hurried across the lawn to the sidewalk, where he hid behind a large tree, stuffed the camera back into the shoulder bag, and waited.

He didn't have to wait long. Thirty seconds later, the front door of the house opened and the purchaser stepped out, glanced left and right, and then strode down the walk toward the street.

Thanks to the new Canadian law, it was now legal to make a citizen's arrest if one saw a crime taking place, and that's exactly what Jake planned to do. Of course, the pill bottles might contain M&Ms for all he knew, but he bet they didn't.

Jake stepped from hiding and onto the sidewalk. The hood went the other way and Jake followed, not too fast, but his long legs narrowed the lead with each step, now just twenty feet away.

The punk glanced over his shoulder, frowned slightly, and stepped up his pace. Jake walked a little faster. His prey took another look back and broke into a jog, and then a full-out run.

Jake chuckled. Nothing spells guilt like running away.

His quarry took a sudden dash into the street in front of an oncoming car. Tires squealed, a horn blared, and the driver yelled something unintelligible accompanied by a hand gesture. Jake lost a little ground as he waited until the vehicle skidded past, nipping at the runner's heels, then roared away.

His quarry took a glance back as he pounded up the sidewalk. Jake crossed the road at an angle and regained his ground. Ten seconds later he had his prey by the collar of his leather jacket.

The hood squirmed and squealed, "Let go." His pedaling feet gained no traction as Jake raised him off the ground and held on.

Jake laughed. "Afraid I can't do that. You're under arrest."

"What for?"

"Possession of a controlled substance."

"Are you a cop?"

Jake twisted one of the punk's arms behind his back and pushed him to the ground. He dropped a heavy foot on the hood's chest. "Nope."

"Then let me go. You have no right to hold me."

Jake pulled out his cell phone without answering and touched speed dial. In a moment, he heard, "Hey, Jake, what's up?"

"Hank, I've got an arrest here for you."

"An arrest?"

"Yeah, a drug purchaser, probably a dealer. I'm holding him."

Laughter came over the phone, then, "I'll send a car and I'll be right there. Where are you?"

"Orleans Avenue. You can't miss it. We're on the sidewalk. You better send a couple cars. I've got a seller and a buyer and video to back it up."

"See you soon."

Jake knew drugs weren't Hank's department. He'd been a close friend with the head of robbery/homicide for almost as long as he could remember, so the notch might as well go in Hank's belt. Besides, Jake owed him one. Well, he owed him a lot. Hank had often told him that Lincoln Investigations and the police department were on the same side, and had never hesitated to be helpful to them in their investigations.

Captain Diego wasn't always too happy with the Lincolns' involvement in police matters, but Hank got the job done and Diego didn't put up much of an argument. Hank's success was his success, and made him look good in front of the mayor.

The punk on the ground looked at Jake and pleaded, "Listen, Buddy, if you let me go I have a whole wad of cash in my pocket. You can have all of it."

"How much you got?"

"Couple of thou."

"A couple of thou, huh. That'll come in real handy, I bet—when the police confiscate it."

"Come on, man. This is the first time I did anything like this. I swear."

Jake looked at the pathetic hood on the ground. "We'll let the law decide that." He glanced down Orleans Avenue as a pair of cruisers turned onto the street. "And here comes the law now."

Jake waved the cars down and they pulled to the curb. A moment later, Hank squeaked to a stop behind them.

One of the officers stepped up to the squirming prisoner. "This is the guy, I assume?"

Jake nodded. "Yup."

The officer took control of the prisoner, cuffed him, and read him his rights.

"Where's the other one?" Hank asked as he stepped onto the sidewalk.

Jake pointed down the street toward number 338. "Down there." He pulled the camera from his bag. "It's all on here." He cued up the video and handed it to Hank, who watched with interest as Jake explained the story behind it.

When it finished playing, Hank reached into the punk's jacket pocket, removed the pill bottles, and squinted at the labels.

"It's oxycodone," he announced. "Possession without a valid prescription is a crime."

"And selling it without authorization is illegal," Jake said. "I'm sure Hughes is not a pharmacist."

"And not an invalid either." Hank chuckled and turned to the second officer. "Let's go get him."

CHAPTER 7

Thursday, 1:24 p.m.

VARICK LUCAS had a plan formulating in the back of his mind. He knew the RCMP would be relentless in their pursuit of him and he wasn't about to get himself caught. That just wasn't an option.

Haddleburg had welcomed him with food, a fresh change of clothes, a nice pistol, and a bit of spare cash. How wonderful of them. Too bad about the dead guy though.

He'd left the town far behind hours ago. The cops would be looking high and low for him—Haddleburg being an obvious first stop for anyone on the run. All the cons knew that, and none of them would be dumb enough to hang around there if they were lucky enough to be in his shoes.

Lucas headed east, keeping to the back roads, ducking into the long grass that filled the ditches on either side, when traffic happened by. He had family back east. He was originally from Nova Scotia and he knew the cops knew that. That would be the obvious place for him to go and he was going to make sure they followed the obvious trail.

He'd made a good twenty miles since leaving Haddleburg, close to where he wanted to be. The 401, a major cross-provincial highway, ran just a minute or two north of him, a truck stop for weary travelers his destination.

Five minutes later, he strode across the truck stop lot and into the building. He selected a private booth in the refreshment area and ordered a cup of coffee. The waitress brought it right away and he savored it, sipping it slowly. The best coffee he'd had for a good long time.

He laid his head back and closed his eyes a moment. He could use a little sleep but couldn't afford to rest yet. Hopefully, the coffee would keep him awake until he could. Soon.

Lucas finished his drink, ordered another to go, and then stood and glanced around the restaurant. Travelers had stopped to refuel and grab a bite to eat while they had the chance. Lucas could be polite when he wanted to, charming even, and as he approached the booth of a young couple he sported a pleasant smile.

"Good afternoon, folks. I'm sorry to bother you, but …" He paused and tried to look embarrassed. "My old beater broke down and, well, I need to get home and I could use a lift if you're heading east." He held up his hands, palms out, as if in surrender. "But it's okay if you can't do it. I understand."

The man looked up at him, his prematurely bald head exaggerating the frown on his high brow. "We can't—"

Lucas expected a negative answer. He glanced at the woman, gave her his best smile, and interrupted. "I really want to see my kids. It's been a very long time and I miss them every day."

The woman placed her hand on her companion's arm. "It's okay, Ben. We can give him a lift."

Ben's frown turned into a look of resignation and he sighed lightly and shrugged. "Whatever you think, Sal."

"I'm Sally Ann Draper," the woman said, holding out a delicate hand.

Lucas shook her hand, gave a slight nod, and offered another smile. A cute little thing, perhaps twenty-five or so, she looked rather out of Ben's league. Some guys had all the luck.

Sally Ann motioned across the table. "And this is my husband, Ben, and we'll be happy to give you a ride. We're going to Ottawa and we could take you east until the cutoff."

"That would be a great start," Lucas said. "I thank you both."

"Where's home?" Sally Ann asked.

"Nova Scotia. I've been on the road awhile, but I'm heading home to stay."

Ben frowned and looked out the window. Sally Ann took a last sip of her beverage and pushed her plate away. She smiled again. "We're just about ready to leave."

"Let me get the bill," Lucas said as he pulled a twenty from his thin roll and tossed it on the table.

Lucas followed the Drapers outside to a brand new Toyota Corolla, a good family car, and one Lucas would enjoy. Later. He got into the backseat, adjusted the gun tucked behind his belt, and settled back for the long ride.

Ben pulled onto the highway and sped up, merging into traffic. Sally Ann turned halfway in the seat and peppered him with friendly questions Lucas had no answers for. About his kids, his home, his wife. He gave fictitious answers, trying not to contradict himself.

Finally, he laid his head back and closed his eyes, tired of the questions. Besides, he felt exhausted, running on adrenaline for the last thirty or so hours. "I wouldn't mind a little nap if it's okay," he said.

"I'll wake you when we get to the cutoff to Ottawa," Sally Ann said with a smile. She turned back around.

Their murmured conversation and the soft sounds of the radio faded away as Lucas drifted into sleep.

A gentle shaking startled him awake and he forced his eyes open. Sally Ann leaned over the seat, her hand on his arm. "We're there," she said. Her pretty blue eyes reminded him of his mother, a long time ago. It seemed a shame to have to do to them what he was about to, but he had no choice.

The vehicle slowed abruptly and the tires ground onto the gravel shoulder. The car eased to a stop.

Lucas lifted the front of his shirt and slipped out the pistol. Sally Ann's eyes popped open and her mouth dropped. He waved the weapon. "I'm afraid you'll have to get out now."

Ben's narrowed eyes stared back at Lucas from the rearview mirror. He spun to face the would-be car thief.

"So, this is how you treat people who're kind enough to help you?"

Lucas shrugged. "I'm afraid so. I'm very sorry." He raised his voice and waved the pistol as a warning. "Now, get out." He opened the passenger-side door, stepped out, and opened

Sally Ann's door. She gave him a disdainful look and stepped onto the shoulder, her high heels catching on the loose gravel. Lucas caught her arm until she regained her balance. She pulled away and stepped back.

Ben came around the front of the car. "Leave her alone," he shouted and raised his fist, then stopped short when Lucas brandished the gun.

"Stand back," Lucas demanded.

"You'll never get away with this," Ben said through gritted teeth.

Lucas laughed. "They always say that." He took a step forward and swung the weapon, the heavy butt end catching Ben on the side of his head.

Ben staggered back but retained his balance. He touched his fingers to his head where a trickle of blood flowed from a nasty cut. He looked at his stained fingers, then at his attacker, hatred burning in his eyes.

Lucas looked at Sally Ann. "I'm sorry I had to do that." Then he bowed, went around the vehicle, and got inside. Without looking back, he pulled the shifter into gear and spun onto the highway, leaving the angry couple behind.

CHAPTER 8

Thursday, 2:33 p.m.

ANNIE STRAIGHTENED her back when she heard her car pull into the driveway. Jake had called her with the results of his stakeout and she felt relieved to have the task cleaned up and out of the way before the weekend. Their client would be pleased with the positive outcome, and catching a pair of criminals was a bonus.

She'd spent the last few hours packing up for the guys. All the things she knew they would need but would never think of themselves. Like raincoats, extra blankets, sunscreen, and clean underwear. She'd also put some sandwiches and fresh fruit into a cooler for their long trip north.

The front door opened, banged shut, and Jake came into the kitchen. "Another job well done," he said. "Two more bad guys off the street."

Annie leaned back against the counter. "You look pleased with yourself."

Jake chuckled. "Why not? It's more than I expected. Hank got the arrest and now Captain Diego owes me one." He frowned at the boxes on the floor. "What's all this?"

"Just stuff for your trip. We'd better start loading up. The boys'll be home soon."

Jake had borrowed an SUV from Annie's father, Andy Roderick, who ran a small local trucking company. The 2009 Toyota RAV4 would be perfect for their weekend trip and her father didn't need it back until Monday. One of his drivers had dropped it off a couple hours ago and it was backed up to the garage, ready to load.

Together they carried the boxes through the door leading from the kitchen to the garage. Jake pulled the third-row seats from the SUV and in twenty minutes the cargo area bulged with gear.

Jake turned to Annie. "Are you sure you don't want to come? It's not too late."

Annie shook her head. "I'll be okay here. I just want to relax and catch up on a little reading."

"Suit yourself."

"By the way," Annie said, "I heard on the news this morning someone escaped from Haddleburg Penitentiary yesterday."

Jake raised a brow. "Oh?"

"Lucas something or other. Apparently, it's the first escape they've had from there in a long time. None successful so far. The RCMP is all over it but no luck yet."

"They'll get him," Jake said. "The Mounties always get their man."

"Yeah, I've heard that. I'm not sure how true it is, but it sounds good."

Jake pulled out his iPhone. "I want to call Hank and see what happened with our two drug dealers." He hit speed dial, and in a moment, Hank answered.

"Detective Hank Corning."

"Hank, what's the verdict with our druggies?"

Hank's chuckle came over the line. "It didn't take long for both of them to cough up the truth. Hughes had been selling his prescriptions to the dealer ever since his pretend injury."

"Those go for twenty or thirty bucks each on the street, don't they?"

"Yup, and a lot more than that in some places. A lot of kids are abusing them. And adults too. Diego didn't say much when I told him you were responsible for the arrest. You know how he is. I think he's a secret fan of yours but doesn't want to admit it."

Jake laughed, then said, "He'll have to do without me awhile. We're about to head north as soon as the boys get home."

"I'll talk to you when you get back," Hank said. "Maybe I'll go with you next time but I'll have a busy weekend and Amelia hasn't seen a whole lot of me lately. She's made some plans and I can't afford to stand her up. You know how it is."

Jake looked at Annie and replied, "Yes, I know what you mean."

Hank laughed. "Have a good time."

Jake assured him they would and hung up just as Chrissy stepped into the garage. She carried a huge duffel bag which she handed to Jake. "Here's Kyle's stuff." She paused a moment and looked at him with concern. "Make sure he brushes his teeth and takes his vitamins every morning." She pointed to the bag. "They're all in there."

Jake smiled. "Don't worry, he's in good hands." He

packed the bag in the SUV and slammed the rear door. "That should be everything."

"Do you have the bear spray?" Chrissy asked. "Just in case?"

Jake grinned. "Why do we need bear spray? Black bears won't hurt you … as long as you don't threaten them."

Annie slugged Jake on the shoulder. "Don't let him worry you, Chrissy. The bear spray is in there."

"And the bug spray?"

"And the bug spray."

"Hey, Dad. Hey, Mom." Matty charged into the garage, Kyle close behind. They panted for air and had probably run all the way home. He tossed his backpack into a corner of the garage. "Are we ready to go?"

"All ready," Jake said.

"Is my other backpack in there?"

"It is."

"Come on, Kyle," Matty said, and the two boys climbed eagerly into the backseat.

Jake gave Annie a quick kiss. "I'll call you before we leave civilization. There won't be any cell reception where we're going." He got into the vehicle and gave a quick wave, and the two mothers watched as the guys pulled onto the street and disappeared from sight.

Annie turned to Chrissy and chuckled. "Peace and quiet at last. I think I'm going to enjoy this."

CHAPTER 9

Thursday, 3:24 p.m.

VARICK LUCAS could just as easily have stolen a car and headed out without any witnesses. Or he could've killed the Drapers, dumped their bodies somewhere, and taken their car with no one the wiser.

But then, that wouldn't suit his plans. He needed witnesses—someone who would tell the cops he was heading east. Because of course, the cops surely suspected he was heading toward home and family, and the Draper's testimony would serve as more proof of that.

But he wasn't going to go east. He was going to head north.

He had a little unfinished business to take care of, and then he would lie low awhile before deciding what his future held. And his future didn't include life behind bars. He'd had enough of that and wasn't going back no matter what.

He drove for about a half hour before coming across the next rest stop, where he pulled off. Time for a switcheroo.

It wouldn't take long for the cops to find out about this vehicle and search for it. He had to ditch it—now, and this twenty-four-hour joint would be just fine.

Lucas pulled around to the side of the restaurant and into the busy parking lot. He found an empty slot in the middle of the rest of the vehicles, pulled into the spot, and got out.

Hidden in plain sight. It might be weeks before they came across it here.

He took a chance and went inside the restaurant. He felt famished, so he ordered a hamburger, then bought a pack of cigarettes from a vending machine and went back to the vehicle.

He leaned against the hood of the car and munched his meal, watching as hungry travelers came and satisfied ones went. He crinkled up the empty foil, tossed it under the car next to him and belched. Slipping a cigarette from the pack, he lit it and blew the smoke upwards. He watched it dissipate high above his head, free and untouchable, just like he would be soon.

A stern-looking man with a long, somber face and high forehead was coming his way. He looked like an accountant or something. And he was alone. Just what Lucas was waiting for; he should be easy to take care of.

Lucas sauntered leisurely between the cars, not looking at his mark, but timing it so their paths would meet just as his intended victim reached his vehicle.

He took a glance around. All clear. As he drew closer, he slipped the pistol from his waist and held it behind his back.

The man had his keys out, pointed toward his vehicle. As he pressed the fob, Lucas heard a distinct beep as car doors unlocked. Beautiful. It was another good family car, a brand new Honda Accord, an inconspicuous vehicle that wouldn't attract any attention.

He waited until the man reached his car before ambling over, and then he gripped the gun tighter and approached his target as the vehicle door swung open.

The man looked up, his dark eyes wide, curious. "Can I help you?"

"I hope so," Lucas said and swung his right hand, the pistol catching his prey full on the side of the head. The victim's eyes bulged, a soft moan escaped his lips as the air shot out, and then he went down. But not out.

Lucas straddled him and raised the pistol. The man's arm came up and grabbed Lucas by the wrist, warding off the blow. This guy was tougher than he looked. His victim opened his mouth, no doubt about to call for help. Lucas's other hand clamped into the man's throat and squeezed, cutting off his vocal cords. He really wanted to shoot the guy but that wouldn't do. He needed to be as discreet as possible. For now, anyway.

The man cursed him with his eyes even as his breathing grew shallower. The grip on Lucas's wrist weakened, his hand fell away, his eyes fluttered, and he was as good as done.

It took a few more swings with the butt end of the pistol before Lucas felt satisfied the job was finished. The man had stopped breathing, would never breathe again, but blood soaked the pavement and had spattered onto his own shirt. He hadn't wanted to make a mess, but it couldn't be helped.

Lucas ducked as a pair of lovers passed a row away. The idiots only had eyes for each other but Lucas stayed low and waited until they were gone.

All clear. Time to clean up and get out of here.

He dragged the body to the rear of the vehicle, flipped the trunk open, and heaved it inside. The guy wore a t-shirt—thin, but it would be better than nothing. He ripped it from the body and sopped up as much of the blood from the pavement as he could, and then spread the rest around. That would have to do. He hoped no one would notice, but even if they did, he would be long gone and the police would be hard pressed to figure out what happened until he was safely away.

He tossed the stained clothing into the trunk, slammed the lid, and took another look around. Nobody.

He hummed to himself as he climbed inside the vehicle and started the engine. His plan was working well.

Another couple with a pair of brat kids left the restaurant, heading his way. Lucas pulled down the sun visor, rested his elbow on the edge of the window, and covered his face. They were two spots away, but they didn't pay him any attention as they packed their kids inside, climbed in their vehicle, and drove off.

And now, it was his turn to be gone. He backed carefully from the spot, crossed the lot, pulled onto the on-ramp, and merged into the eastbound traffic.

CHAPTER 10

Thursday, 4:03 p.m.

MATTY AND KYLE wrestled in the backseat as Jake pulled the SUV onto Highway 11. He flicked on the radio and settled in for the long ride north to Algonquin Provincial Park.

The park—more like a nature reserve, really—was located about two hundred miles north of Toronto. Larger than dozens of countries throughout the world, it covered almost three thousand square miles of lakes, trails, and forest, much of it uncharted and untrodden by humans.

Jake knew the wilderness waters of the isolated and unspoiled habitat contained plenty of brook and lake trout, as well as smallmouth bass. He had found a special spot near Wendigo Lake a few years ago, deep in the interior, and he had shared it with Annie and Matty a couple of times in the past. He and Hank had been up there last year as well, and it was one of his favorite getaways.

He leaned forward and turned up the radio as a news story caught his attention. Apparently, Varick Lucas, the escaped killer they had heard about earlier on the television, had still not been apprehended. An RCMP spokesman assured the listeners they were hot on his trail and expected Lucas to be taken into custody soon.

"Are we almost there?" Kyle asked, his voice impatient.

Jake glanced in the rearview mirror and laughed as Matty answered. "Not yet, dummy. We just left home. It's gonna be at least a couple hours, maybe more." Matty spun around, reached over the back of the seat, and undid the strap of his backpack. "Here, I brought some comics." He removed them from the pack and turned back, handing one to Kyle. In a moment, the boys had settled into reading about their favorite heroes.

Just over two hours later, Jake yawned and slowed the vehicle as he approached the small town of Sanridge. They were less than fifteen minutes from the northern park entrance but the boys needed a bathroom break and so did he. Besides, this was the best place to grab those last-minute supplies before leaving civilization for the next couple of days.

He turned the SUV into a small gravel lot that served as the parking area in front of an old-fashioned general store, the kind of place that sold just about everything. A sign beside a single pump out front offered gasoline and a free window wash. Another sign boasted they sold live bait and sandwiches.

The boys jumped from the vehicle as it ground to a stop, happy to have a little freedom. Matty dashed across the lot, Kyle behind him.

"Don't go too far, guys," Jake called. "We're not staying long."

The proprietor of the store sat out front, slouched back in an old wooden chair, his arms crossed. As Jake approached, he eased himself to his feet, a welcoming grin on his face, and a twinkle in his friendly eyes. His furrowed features and grizzled hair showed the years behind him.

"Welcome." The old man's voice crackled with age as he extended a hand. "Going campin'?"

Jake nodded and shook the offered hand. "Just for the weekend."

"From the city, are you?"

Jake nodded again.

"Get lots of city folk here. Fact is, more city folk than locals. Busy in the summer time. Not so much now in September." The old man took an uncertain look toward the sky. "Gonna be an early winter this year. It'll be cold afore long. Couple more weeks or so. Maybe another month, maybe two, it'll be all snow 'round these parts."

Jake followed the man's view and decided the old-timer knew what he was talking about, even though the warm afternoon sun beating down belied the claim that cooler weather waited just around the corner.

"Where you headed?" the man asked.

"Wendigo Lake. I've been there before. A couple of times, actually, and it's a nice quiet spot."

"I know the place. A few miles in, but well worth the trip. You won't likely be disturbed much there. Just bears and birds to keep you company."

Jake chuckled. "And mosquitoes."

"You might want some spray fer them." The old man

squinted. "Yer skin looks kinda tender." He nodded toward the door. "And them boys of yers are gonna need it. Skitters like young blood and tender skin."

"We have some already, but I might get more, just in case."

"Got bear spray too? You never know when one of them critters is gonna come at you. Best be safe than sorry. I got the best spray they make. It'll stop 'em in their tracks every time."

Jake smiled at the eager merchant. "We have bear spray, thank you."

"Best come inside," the elderly man said, motioning toward the open doorway.

Jake stepped inside the antiquated building and was greeted by a homey aroma. Rows of shelves, stacked high with merchandise, covered the worn hardwood floor.

"What can I get for you?"

"I need some bait. Maybe a few snacks for the boys." Jake glanced around. "I could use a new coffeepot, if you have one."

The man cracked a smile. "We got everything. Just help yerself and I'll take care of you."

A bell rang at the front of the store. Jake glanced toward the sound. A Honda Accord had pulled up to the gas pumps, waiting for service.

"I have to look after a customer," the old man said. He pointed a crooked finger toward the door. "Restroom's outside round the corner if you need it 'fore you go."

"We will," Jake said and pulled out his cell phone. He

dialed Annie's number, and as he waited for her to answer, he wandered up and down the aisles collecting necessities.

When Annie answered, Jake said, "We're just here in Sanridge. I'm not going to have any cell reception soon, so I wanted to let you know we're okay."

"Glad you called," Annie said. "How are the boys?"

"Couldn't be better. Just a little anxious to get there."

Annie laughed. "Oh, I'm sure you are too."

Jake dropped an armload of items on the front counter. "Any news?"

"No, nothing new here. You haven't been gone that long. What did you expect to happen?"

Jake chuckled. "Nothing, really. Just wondering." He paused. "I'll call you again Sunday afternoon on our way home."

"Have fun," Annie said.

Jake hung up and went to the counter where the old man had returned and was ringing in the purchases, packing them carefully in a box. He paid in cash, bid farewell to the friendly storekeeper, and lugged the box to the SUV.

Matty and Kyle sat on the grass nearby, laughing, worn out and panting. Jake beckoned them over and in two minutes, the SUV was speeding up the road on the final leg of its journey.

CHAPTER 11

Thursday, 4:18 p.m.

VARICK LUCAS had done about all he could to convince the cops he was heading east. And he was pretty sure he'd be okay with this car for now; it would be awhile before anyone reported its driver missing. It would get him to his destination, and then he would have to ditch it.

The body would be okay in the trunk for a few more minutes. If he got stopped by the law, that would be the least of his worries. He let up on the gas pedal and brought the Honda down to the speed limit. He'd best drive carefully. Of course, he could always kill any nosy cop dumb enough to pull him over, but he'd come so far now it'd be a shame to take any unnecessary chances.

He touched the gun at his waist, a backup weapon if necessary. He'd already left a lot of bodies in his wake and he only had firm plans for one more before he settled into his life of ease and freedom.

His plan had necessitated going east, and that meant he was many miles out of his way. Fortunately, traffic was sparse on this stretch of highway.

He glanced in his rearview mirror. Satisfied no one was behind, he hit the brakes hard, spun onto the shoulder, jumped from the vehicle, and popped the trunk. Dead eyes stared up at him as he dug in the pockets of the victim and found a wallet. Lucas flipped it open. It contained the usual stuff. Credit cards, driver's license, and a couple hundred in cash. Lucas could use the cash. He removed the bills, stuffed them into his pants pocket, and tossed the wallet back into the trunk.

He hoisted the body out, dropped it onto the shoulder of the road, and rolled it into the ditch. It would be found there before long. Someone in a passing car would be sure to see it. Just what he wanted.

He glanced down the road. No traffic in sight. He jumped in, spun back onto the highway, and sped away.

Time now to head north, then back west to get to his destination. He took the next off-ramp, circled around the cloverleaf interchange, and entered a northbound two-lane highway.

Ottawa stood pretty much north of him, an hour or so away, but he wanted to avoid it. He would take the side roads until he reached the city, and then head west.

He thought back to more innocent times. He couldn't put a finger on exactly when his life had changed. Despite his out-of-control father, Varick had been known as a peacemaker in school. Always the last to fight, and the first to make up. He had been the teacher's pet, and the pride of his mother. Then everything had changed. He'd changed.

But for better or for worse, he was what he was, and he was going to make the best of it. No use dwelling on what could have been—what came next was all that mattered.

Two hours later he was just about where he wanted to be as he approached the small town of Sanridge. A red light on the dash told him the vehicle was dangerously low on gas. He didn't have far to go now, but he would never make it. Wheels ground and snapped on gravel as he pulled in front of a gas pump at a small general store. In a moment, a wizened old man came out.

Lucas wound down his window, keeping his face covered by the sun visor. "Five dollars' worth."

"Just five?"

"Yup."

As the man pumped the gas, Lucas glanced around. The only other vehicle in sight was a Toyota RAV4 parked in front of the building. A couple of boys ran around in front of the store. He could vaguely make out someone moving around inside the shop.

"That's five dollars, sir."

Lucas handed a bill through the window without turning his head, pulled away, and turned back on the highway. Soon, he left the little town behind. Forests lined both sides of the road and everything looked pretty much all the same to him. But he'd been here before and knew the place he was looking for was just ahead.

He kept an eye on the left side of the road and in a few minutes, he breathed a sigh of relief. There it was. A narrow lane, and no traffic around. He pulled into the lane and up to a chain-link gate. Paying no heed to a large "Danger/No Trespassing" sign, he swung open the unlocked gate, drove inside, and then closed the gate.

He jumped back in the vehicle and took a rarely used lane in about a quarter mile. There it was. He smiled grimly and pulled the vehicle to within a few feet of a large quarry. He climbed from the car and eased up to the edge. It was filled with murky water, still and quiet. A perfect place to hide a vehicle. He couldn't afford for it to be found and possibly connected to him. That would ruin all his plans.

He glanced around, found a sturdy stick, broke off a piece about eighteen inches long, and returned to the vehicle. The engine roared as he wedged the stick between the seat and the gas pedal. That should do it. He opened the driver window, jumped out, closed the door, and then reached in and pulled the gearshift into drive. The tires whined on the grass and spat up gravel as the vehicle sped ahead, spun sideways, and then toppled into the quarry.

Lucas watched with grim relief as the car filled with water and slowly sank. Bubbles rose for a few minutes, and then all was still again.

He turned his back on the scene and walked toward the highway. He didn't have far to go now and he could easily make it the rest of the way on foot. He walked down the shoulder of the road, keeping an eye out for traffic in either direction. He ducked into the ditch and lay low as the SUV he'd seen at the general store came into view and breezed by.

He estimated he'd walked about a mile when he noticed a familiar landmark—a large outcropping of rock. This was the place. He hopped the fence, made his way into the forest of Algonquin Park, and wound his way among the trees. He wished he had a compass, but it was too late for that now. He felt pretty sure he knew where he was going. At any rate, he was in no hurry now, being well out of danger.

An hour later he topped a knoll and smiled at the sight of a log cabin.

"Ah. Home at last."

CHAPTER 12

Thursday, 7:02 p.m.

JAKE PULLED THE vehicle into the parking lot and stepped out. Of the several vehicle entry points to Algonquin Park, the North Gate was nearest to where they were headed.

Matty and Kyle tagged along behind as Jake entered the rustic building that offered visitors a small snack bar, public telephones, restrooms, and other amenities.

He approached the counter, where a smiling young woman rose from her seat behind a desk and approached him. She dropped her arms on the counter, leaned forward, and asked in a cheerful voice, "You been here before?"

Jake nodded. "A couple of times."

"Where you headed?"

Although there were numerous drive-in campgrounds in Algonquin, the park was better known for its interior camping accessible only by canoe or hiking in the summer, or plodding through snow in the winter. Jake preferred something in between—something remote and quiet, but accessible without a lot of hiking.

"Wendigo Lake," he answered.

The woman waved a pencil at him. "That's a long way in.

Things might look civilized right here," she said. "But the further you proceed from this point, the wilder the park becomes. It's possible to spend several days in there without seeing any other people."

"That's okay," Jake said and offered a smile. "That's why we're here."

The woman looked down at the boys. "You guys watch out for bears, now. They're probably more afraid of you than you are of them, but don't get too close if you see one."

Matty grinned up at the woman. "Don't worry. We've got some bear spray."

"I'm not afraid," Kyle put in.

Jake paid for a three-day permit and grabbed a brochure from a display rack. He flipped through it. It contained basic information on the park as well as tips and protocol. The last section warned against approaching bears and other wildlife. Jake folded it and tucked it into his back pocket.

"Here's a map of the area." The woman handed him a sheet of paper. She tapped at one spot with her pencil. "Here's Wendigo Lake." She moved the pencil down to the bottom of the page. "And here's a list of all the trails. Please keep your vehicle on the main road until you reach the lake." She smiled and added, "There might be some rough terrain, so drive carefully."

Jake assured her they would and stuffed the map and permit into his shirt pocket. "Let's go, boys."

They got in the car and drove to the main gate, where he showed his pass. The attendant gave it a cursory look and handed it back. "Have a good time now."

The road was smooth going for the first couple of miles, then deteriorated into a bumpier ride as it became narrower. According to the vehicle's compass, the trail wound south for several miles, and then west. As they topped the final rise, the sparkling lake waters came into view.

"There it is," Matty shouted.

Jake drove a few hundred more feet and then pulled the SUV onto a lush, grassy area between two towering maples. He looked around at their private getaway, nestled in a forest of mature pine, maple, and hemlock trees. To the right, masses of blueberries grew near smooth rock outcrops. Everywhere, the goldenrods were in full bloom, a reminder autumn was not far away.

"Don't wander off," Jake said as they climbed out. "I want to get the tent up before dark and I'll need your help."

It took them half an hour to erect the shelter, the boys possibly being more hindrance than help. Matty and Kyle unloaded the rest of the gear, lugging it to the tent.

"Not the food," Jake said. "Bears are constantly looking for food and they'll smell it a mile away. Our tent will be a shambles if they dig for it, and they'll keep coming back. We'll never get rid of them. Leave all the food inside the vehicle, as well as soap, toothpaste, and anything they can smell."

In a few minutes, they had everything organized and Jake dropped into a lawn chair and stretched his legs in front of him, enjoying the quiet, unspoiled calm. A small woodpecker worked in the tree above his head. A flock of geese honked as they flew over, heading south.

"Hey, Dad. We're hungry."

They spent a few minutes scrounging for firewood. The wild forest around them was littered with dead branches and trees and soon they had a fire going, wieners sizzling over the flame, and buns toasting nearby.

When they finished eating, Matty asked, "Can we go look at the lake now?"

"And go swimming?" Kyle added.

"Sure."

The boys changed into their swim trunks and soon the three of them snaked their way through the heavy grass and down to the water's edge. A moose fed in the shallows a hundred feet away. It reared its head when they approached and lumbered into the thick foliage.

Off to their right, a mother loon taught her lone chick the finer arts of fishing. It paid them no attention, safely out of reach of the intruders. To the east, where the large bay on the edge of the lake met the western sky, a natural rock dam forced a river into a torrent where it dumped into the lake. This was nature at its best.

Matty and Kyle had wandered into the water, the shallow beaches of the lake allowing them to wade out fifty feet where the still water was only waist deep.

Jake sank down onto a rock, enjoying the serenity of the spot, entranced by the majestic beauty. The evening sun painted the sky as it dropped over the western horizon. It would be dark soon.

CHAPTER 13

Thursday, 7:12 p.m.

VARICK LUCAS leaned against a towering pine and observed the cabin. It perched in the middle of a small clearing, surrounded by weeds, and everything appeared to be undisturbed, just as it was when he was last here, several years ago. Back then, he and the guys had been more interested in whatever bass and lake trout they could pull out, maybe a little canoeing up and down the rivers, and of course, to see how much beer they could drink in a weekend.

Today was a different matter, however. He was looking for a place to lie low awhile—maybe for years—and this would be the perfect spot. He could always trap some game and steal other necessary supplies from the nearby town. And there were always unsuspecting campers a couple of miles east he could rob. He'd done that before as well, and never gotten caught.

He stood upright, eased down the knoll, waded through the weeds, and approached the cabin from the rear. He peered in through a small window, dead center of the back of the building. The interior was dim, the surrounding trees keeping out most of the light. A few rays shone through a side window and lit up one end of the room, revealing a small cot.

It appeared someone had been here recently, and perhaps was close by. That was pretty much what he expected.

He crept around toward the front of the building, stopped at the corner, poked his head around, and grinned. His old friend, Otis, lounged in a tattered hammock, a beer in one hand, a smoke in the other. He'd changed a lot, but there was no mistake about it; it was Otis. He was gonna be in for a surprise.

"Otis," Lucas shouted, stepping into clear view.

Otis shot upright. The hammock teetered and spilled him onto the ground, his beer draining away onto the trodden-down weeds and soil surrounding him. He sat in the dirt and peered at his old friend, a dumbfounded look on his face. Finally, he sputtered, "What the ... Varick Lucas ... how the—"

Varick interrupted and took a couple of steps forward. "Happy to see me, Otis?"

Otis made it to his feet, stuck the smoke in his mouth, and stood glaring at Lucas. "Varick, you're out already? I thought—"

"Thought what, Otis?"

"I thought ... they put you away for good."

"They tried to. Couldn't hold me. I found my own way out." Varick settled into a lawn chair, leaned back, and crossed his arms. He looked disapprovingly at his friend, at his ragged beard, his tattered clothes, his uncombed hair straggling down over his ears. He looked like a tramp, and smelled like he could use a dip in the lake. "So, you didn't answer my question, buddy. Are you happy to see me?"

"I, uh … yeah, sure. Why wouldn't I be?"

Lucas squinted at Otis. "Maybe because if it wasn't for you, I wouldn't have spent the last five years rotting behind bars."

Otis looked uneasy and spoke in an almost pleading voice. "Come on, Varick. You know that wasn't my fault. I had no choice."

"There's always a choice, Otis. You could've kept your mouth shut about that night."

"But you left me there to hang. And the woman saw you plug the guard."

"I had a ski mask on, Otis. They never saw my face."

Otis ground his cigarette into the dirt, stuffed his hands in his pockets, and kept his eyes on the ground a moment. Finally, he raised his head and spoke firmly. "They had me cold; it was either me or you. I was going to go down for murder and they offered me immunity if I testified against you."

Varick uncrossed his arms, leaned forward, and glared. "And so, you gave up your old friend to save your own hide. What kind of a friend does that?"

Otis's voice came out as a whine. "A frightened one." He paused, cleared his throat, and spoke more firmly. "I couldn't do time like you, Varick. I wouldn't survive in there."

"I survived."

Otis fidgeted with his hands, an uncomfortable look in his eyes as he avoided Varick's stare. He prodded the empty beer bottle with his foot and then kicked it across the clearing. It landed near a spray of goldenrods that had somehow managed to work their way up through the dirt.

Otis spoke slowly, quietly. "I ... I'm sorry, Varick. I really am." He looked at his friend earnestly. "If I could do it again, it would be different."

"Different how?"

"Just different, that's all. I wouldn't have squealed on you."

Varick nodded slowly as he observed Otis. His friend was a liar, and probably afraid. And he had every reason to be afraid.

Otis steadied the still-swinging hammock, sat back down, and dug his smokes from his shirt pocket. His hand trembled as he poked a cigarette into his mouth and flicked his lighter. He took a long drag, blew the smoke into the air, watched it rise, and then turned his attention back to the conversation. "What're you gonna do, Varick?"

"About you?"

Otis nodded uneasily, still twiddling his fingers.

Varick shrugged. "Nothing." Yeah right, nothing. He had to do something; his honor was at stake. "You owe me, Otis. I did your time. You owe me."

Otis spoke in a fervent voice. "Whatever you want, Varick. I'll do whatever you want."

Varick said nothing.

Finally, Otis broke the uneasy silence. "How'd you know I was here?"

"I might've been inside but word gets around. I heard you

had taken off somewhere. Figured it was here. I know how you always liked this place."

Otis nodded. "Yeah, it's quiet here."

Varick eyed Otis thoughtfully. "Figured I might stay awhile. You know, until things blow over."

"Sure, Varick. It'll be cool to have you here." The words tumbled out eagerly. "You can stay as long as you want."

Varick grinned. "I thought you'd say that."

CHAPTER 14

Thursday, 7:56 p.m.

THE CAR TIRES squealed as the driver hit the brakes and pulled onto the shoulder of the road. The vehicle came to a dead stop, backed up fifty feet, and stopped again. The driver leaned sideways, blinked a couple of times, and stared out the passenger-side window.

The driver-side door swung open and a man stepped out, hurried around the car, and gazed into the ditch. He scratched his head and frowned. The sight before him was not exactly what he expected to see today.

A body lay on its back in the ditch, nestled in weeds, feet pointing upwards, but there was no doubt about it; it was a dead person and it shouldn't be there.

He climbed down into the ditch for a closer look. The sight was gruesome and made him gag. He looked away and climbed back out of the ditch.

He glanced up and down the road, hoping to see another vehicle, perhaps someone else who could take responsibility for finding the body and all the headaches along with it. He didn't want to get involved in something like this.

There were no other cars in sight and he considered a

moment. Should he leave it alone and be on his way? Better judgment took over his thoughts and he sighed, reached for his cell phone, and called 9-1-1.

He decided not to give the police his name; then he could be on his way with no one the wiser. There was no need for him to stick around. It was a dead body and he didn't have anything to do with it. Besides, he had better things to do right now.

He gave the emergency operator a few details and the approximate location of the body, then got back in his car and continued on his way. He'd done his duty and that was that.

~*~

RCMP SERGEANT LANCE BREWER had barely finished interviewing Ben and Sally Ann Draper when he got word of the body that had been discovered.

The Drapers' car had been stolen at gunpoint by someone who perfectly fit the description of Varick Lucas. They had been kind enough to give him a lift, and he'd rewarded them by assaulting the driver, taking their car, and dumping them on the side of the highway. And now, a body had been found along the same highway, a little further east.

Brewer dropped his notes onto the passenger seat, hung up the radio, pulled the shifter into drive, and spun onto the road. This was no coincidence. That body was more evidence of the work of that scumbag, Varick Lucas.

First responders had already secured the area, a forensic

team at work when Brewer arrived on the scene. Four cruisers had pulled to the side of the road, red and blue lights flashing. A forensic van sat with its doors open, police milling about, unloading equipment. A cop was setting up orange cones by the side of the highway.

The sun was sinking low in the western sky and remote area lighting was set up in the immediate vicinity. The darkness would arrive before they were done here.

Brewer climbed down into the ditch, approached the investigator in charge, and offered his hand. "Sergeant Lance Brewer. RCMP."

The towering young investigator shook his hand and looked at him quizzically. "Inspector Bruce Sheldrick. Why're you guys involved in this?"

"I believe this is the work of Varick Lucas."

The other cop whistled. "The escapee?"

"Believe so. Our inspectors are on their way and we'll be conducting a joint operation with local law enforcement."

"Always happy to work with you guys, but there's not a lot to go on here."

Brewer glanced at the body. "Who's the vic?"

"No ID on the victim," Sheldrick said.

"No wallet? Credit cards?"

"Nothing."

"What about the witness? The guy who found the body?"

Sheldrick shrugged. "The guy who called it in didn't stick around. Didn't give his name to the operator."

"We'll find him," Brewer said. "It could've been Lucas himself called it in."

"Why would he do that?"

"Dunno. But if he killed this guy and stole his car, why dump him here? Why not leave the body where the deed was done?"

Sheldrick looked confused. Finally, he said, "He wanted to make sure the body was found."

Brewer nodded. "Makes sense to me."

"But why would he care?"

"That's the question. Why?" Brewer said and approached the body. "Maybe he can tell us." He crouched down and looked at the now whitened face. Blood had flowed from wounds inflicted to the top and left side of the head, now dried and turned a brownish hue. There was evidence of defensive wounds to the arms and chest. His mouth and jaw was banged up and the left jaw possibly dislocated, a real mess. "Maybe he can tell us," Brewer repeated as he straightened up and turned back to face Sheldrick.

The young cop looked bewildered but nodded as if he understood, then asked, "How can you be sure it was Lucas?"

Brewer observed the young cop, still green. He had a lot to learn. "Just my gut, son. It never leads me wrong." He waved toward the body. "Make sure they don't move him until we're done. Our first priority is to find out who he is, and then put a BOLO out on his car."

Brewer glanced toward the road as two RCMP cars pulled up. A forensic van stopped close behind. Officers and investigators streamed from the vehicles. They were going to take over this scene whether the local law wanted them to or not. As far as he was concerned, the scene had already been contaminated, but they would make do and sift through everything.

Brewer crossed his arms and stared up the highway. It looked like Lucas was heading east. The roadblocks that were set up earlier had netted nothing. Investigators would try to find out who the victim was as soon as possible; they had no choice but to do their job.

Brewer wasn't convinced that knowledge would give him anything. Lucas had probably killed this guy and stolen his car. He was changing cars all the time, and he had to be stopped.

CHAPTER 15

Thursday, 8:42 p.m.

VARICK LUCAS dropped down onto the bunk, leaned against the wall of the cabin, and stared across the small room. His former friend was cooking up something on a small wood stove they had lugged up here many years ago.

His eyes wandered around the room. The cabin was dirty. The wooden floor probably hadn't seen a broom in years. Spiders had spun their webs in the rafters and the entire place smelled of human sweat. There was no excuse for that, and that would change. Varick didn't like living in a pigsty.

Otis glanced over. "Want some bread with your beans, Varick?"

"Beans? Canned beans? Is that all you got here? No real food? Don't you have any meat?"

"I like beans," Otis said. "Sometimes I catch a rabbit, maybe the odd fish, or a duck, but I don't have a fridge here, Varick. How am I supposed to keep stuff fresh in the summer? Wintertime I can freeze it, but right now … it's beans and bread."

That was going to change too. Varick had no desire to eat beans every day. Steak. Now that was food. A moose or a deer would last him a long time. If he was going to stay here awhile he was going to be comfortable. And comfortable meant this small cabin only had room for one. Otis had to go.

"Haven't you been able to scrounge up any food from the campers?" Varick asked. "There should be lots of opportunities around here. Just like we used to do years ago."

Otis stopped stirring, set the spoon on a small table beside the stove, and turned away from the sizzling meal. "I gotta be careful. The game warden has been here a couple of times. I don't know how he found this place being it's so far from any roads and trails. He seemed like a decent guy, though. We're a long way from any campers, but if there are reports of stuff stolen …" Otis paused. "I just don't want him to report me being here, that's all. This is government land."

"What do you do here in the winter?"

"Only been here one winter. Mostly I just lay back, take it easy. Maybe do a little hunting, fishing." Otis laughed. "And a lot of sleeping." He glanced around the cabin. "I like it here. I have enough wood piled up for the winter and it'll be nice and toasty in here."

Varick thought a moment before asking, "Got any money, Otis?"

Otis dished out the beans onto plates. "I got a couple thousand stashed away. I don't buy much. Too hard to lug it back here so it oughta do me awhile."

That was good news. Varick's small stash had dwindled and he would need money if he wanted to make this place his home for a while.

Otis pointed toward the ceiling, where a toboggan rested

across the rafters. "In the winter I can bring stuff back here with that, but in the summer, it's not so easy. Besides, I would run out of money real fast if I bought steak and beer every day."

"What about in town?" Varick asked. "Surely there are some houses there you can liberate stuff from?"

Otis shrugged. "It's a small town. You can't be breaking into houses every day. Sometimes I rob their gardens, grab some corn, potatoes, and carrots from the farmers, but money's hard to come by. Folks ain't rich around here." He set the plates on the table, grabbed a loaf of bread from the cupboard, and removed four slices. He dropped two on each plate. "Food's ready."

Varick crawled off the cot and sat at the table. The food wasn't half-bad, likely because Varick was famished. He hadn't eaten for a while. He wolfed it down in silence. When they finished, he pushed his chair back and stood. "Gimme a smoke."

Otis pointed to a cupboard beside the stove. Varick found the cigarettes, lit one, and breathed the warm smoke in. It tasted good. They always tasted good after a meal. He'd already chain-smoked the pack he'd bought from the truck stop. Nerves, maybe. He didn't smoke much but he liked one now and then and didn't want to get in the habit now. Otis's money wouldn't last long at that rate.

Varick waved the cigarette in the air. "You have more?"

Otis pointed to the cupboard. "A couple more cartons. They need to last me awhile, so take it easy."

"No problem," Varick said, turning toward the door. "I'm going outside."

"Be right out soon as I wash up."

Varick stepped out in the bright moonlit evening, lounged back in the lawn chair, and closed his eyes. The weather was pleasant enough and he hoped it would stay that way awhile. He wasn't looking forward to the winter, but he'd survived enough of them in his life; what was one more? At any rate, he would have to make do until everything blew over. The future was open and changeable.

He opened his eyes a few minutes later when Otis came out and dropped into the hammock.

"Nice night," Otis said.

"Yup," Varick answered. He looked over at Otis, lounging comfortably. It was a shame. They were such good friends, but Otis had betrayed him. There was no way around that, and of course, there could be no forgiveness.

"Gonna get cold soon, though," came from Otis.

"Yup." Varick lifted the front of his shirt and wrapped his hand around the pistol. Yes, it would get cold real soon. Might as well get this over with. He stood, removing the pistol as he approached the hammock.

Otis turned his head toward Varick and opened his eyes. They popped as he stared at the weapon gleaming in the moonlight, now pointed at him. "What ...?"

"Sorry, old pal. You betrayed me."

Varick stepped back as Otis sprang to his feet. "I thought we were past that."

"Maybe you are. I'm not."

Otis dropped to his knees and raised his hands in a begging position. "Please, Varick. I'm sorry. Don't kill me. I'll make it up to you."

"What's done is done."

"It can be undone." He was pleading. "I'll do whatever you want. You can stay here for as long as you want and won't have to do nothing." Otis took his eyes off the gun and looked at Varick. "Please. We're friends."

"We were friends. You put an end to that."

"No, Varick. No."

Lucas tightened his finger on the trigger. He didn't have a lot of ammunition left, but at least this one would be put to good use.

"Varick, you're not going to—"

"It looks like I am," Lucas said as he squeezed the trigger.

Otis's eyes were still wide, but now staring blankly at nothing as he crumpled to the dirt, a hole in his forehead. Varick had waited years for this day and now it was over. Justice was done at last.

He looked down at the body and sighed. "Sorry, old friend. You know how it is."

It was time to dig a grave, and then find that money.

CHAPTER 16

Thursday, 9:45 p.m.

JAKE YAWNED and looked at his watch. He was getting tired and he expected the boys must be as well. They had been active earlier, swimming, chasing each other through the bush, and working off energy until they dropped. Right now, they toasted marshmallows over the fire, having a grand old time.

He grabbed a bucket from the SUV and carried it down to the lake. Mist danced above the still waters, illuminated by the moonlight. He imagined the fish, just below the surface, waiting for some lucky angler to haul them in come morning. Fish for breakfast.

He filled the bucket with water and climbed back up the grade to the campsite. Kyle seemed to have grown tired of the sugary snacks and wandered around slapping at bugs with a tree branch.

Jake set the bucket down and dropped into the lawn chair. "We'd better settle in for the night, guys. It's getting late and I know you'll be up with the sun."

Matty popped a darkened marshmallow into his mouth and looked at his father. "We going fishing tomorrow, Dad?"

"We'll try it awhile. Then we'll take a run into town. I want to call your mother and maybe grab a newspaper."

Matty reluctantly packed up the snacks, stuffed them into a grocery bag, and tossed his toasting stick aside. "Let's go, Kyle."

Kyle took a final swing with his weapon, tossed it into the bushes, and followed Matty into the tent. Jake heard them scuffling about and giggling. Before too long, everything was quiet.

Jake thought about Annie. She had wanted some peaceful time at home, but how could it get any better than this? She didn't know what she was missing. They'd been so busy lately, they'd barely had time for family and relaxation. He was going to get lots of that this weekend, and be refreshed and ready to get back at it the following week.

He sat and enjoyed the night sounds awhile. The fire crackled and hissed near his feet while crickets continued to surround him with their steady trilling. Somewhere far away a wolf howled—or was it a dog? The leaves above rustled as a light wind blew through the trees.

Something snapped in the bushes twenty feet away. Was it a raccoon, or a deer, perhaps a moose?

Jake swatted at a mosquito that had perched on his arm, looking to draw sustenance from his veins. Not tonight. He flicked the dead pest away and yawned again.

Time to turn in. He doused the fire with the pail of water he'd hauled from the lake earlier, waited a few minutes until he was sure it was extinguished, and then headed for the tent.

The boys bunked together on a foam mattress, snuggled

up in separate bags. Jake lay on the other mattress, zipped up his sleeping bag, and closed his eyes, and soon the night sounds lulled him asleep.

He was startled awake sometime later by a whisper from across the tent. It was Kyle. "Mr. Lincoln, wake up." The voice persisted, repeating, and growing louder. "Mr. Lincoln. Mr. Lincoln."

Jake groaned and opened his eyes. Kyle was out of bed and crawling on his hands and knees toward him. The boy looked frightened as he leaned in. "Are you awake?"

"What is it, Kyle?"

"There's someone outside. I can hear someone out there."

Jake listened a moment. "I don't hear anything."

"There was a minute ago. I heard somebody walking around."

Matty rolled over and moaned. "What's going on?"

Kyle waved a hand at his friend. "Shhh. There's somebody out there," he whispered.

Jake continued to listen but heard nothing but the natural sounds of the forest at night. He unzipped the bag and tossed the flap aside. "I'll go take a look," he whispered, and then stopped halfway to his feet. He had heard the certain sound of a twig snapping outside the tent, close by.

Matty sat upright, his mouth and eyes wide. Kyle had retreated and buried himself in his blankets, only the whites of his frightened eyes visible.

Jake held up his hand in warning. "Stay here. I'll be right back."

He crept to the door of the tent, slowly unzipped the flap,

and stepped out into the moonlight. He glanced around the site. There was no sign of an intruder. Then, from the corner of his eye, he saw a shadow disappear behind a bush thirty feet away, too dark to make out a shape. Was it man or animal?

Jake took a step forward. "You there, stop," he called.

There was no response and no sound from the intruder.

"Who's there?" He took another step, then stopped to listen.

"Is someone there, Dad?" He turned to see Matty, his head stuck through the flap of the tent.

Jake waved a hand. "Get back inside," he said and then took a step toward the prowler. The bush swayed, and then came the unmistakable sound of running footsteps going the other way.

Jake went toward the sound and then stopped to listen. All was still again. He should've brought a flashlight. There was an electric lantern in the tent—not much good, but the flashlight was in the SUV. Should he go back and get it?

Again he heard running as if someone was trying to make a hasty getaway. Whoever or whatever it was, it was going fast, branches crackling underfoot. Jake heard the rustling of leaves and the thud of heavy footsteps.

He dashed into the darkness of the forest, fumbling his way through bushes and low-hanging branches, but the sounds ahead faded away. It was gone. He would never catch up now.

He stood still a moment, listening for further signs of the intruder, but was unrewarded. He returned to the tent and poked his head inside. "I think it was just a deer or a wild animal. Go back to sleep. Nothing to be worried about," he said, but he wasn't so sure. He had an uneasy feeling it was more than that. Possibly another camper had wandered into their camping spot, but that seemed unlikely.

The boys drifted back to sleep, content they were safe. Jake sat in the lawn chair and kept watch lest the interloper should return. Eventually he began to drift off, so he returned to the tent and lay down. He slept uneasily the rest of the night; he had a bad feeling.

CHAPTER 17

Friday, 7:15 a.m.

VARICK LUCAS rose early despite feeling exhausted from his adventures of the last couple of days. After a quick breakfast, it was time to get reacquainted with his surroundings.

It was several years since he'd been up here. A lot of the familiar trees that surrounded the cabin had grown taller, young ones popping up to take their place. Patches of shrubs and weeds took over the clearing around the cabin. Maybe he would pull them up later and clean up the area a little bit.

The uncharted wilderness where the cabin sat was at least a couple miles from anywhere, and anybody, in any direction—a long way for people to wander when faced with a dense forest. He had no fear of being discovered. And certainly the cops would never suspect he was so far north.

If he remembered correctly, the grandfather of one of his old friends had built this place eons ago; then the old man had died, and the place had gone unused for decades. He and his friends had resurrected it a few years ago, but according to Otis, none of the guys had come up here since then. And now, sad to say, Otis had passed on, and it was just him now.

He had wandered out briefly last night before going to bed. There was a guy—a big guy—who'd set up camp a bit east, in an area not often frequented by visitors. Varick had snooped around their campsite until he heard a kid whispering inside the tent. He'd been heard. As soon as he'd backed out of the site, the big guy had crawled from the tent and tried to follow him. Varick had had no weapons with him so he'd beat it out of there.

He planned to be more careful this time. That big guy could probably snap him in two given half a chance. But now he had his pistol stuffed behind his belt and Otis's hunting knife strapped to his leg. Otis had a rifle as well, and a good supply of ammunition, but he would keep that for hunting. He preferred a pistol anyway.

He locked up the cabin, dropped the key to the padlock into his pocket, crossed the clearing, and headed into the forest. He gave a quick salute as he passed Otis's grave. *Sleep well, old pal.*

It took him just over an hour to reach the campsite he'd visited the night before. This time, he made a more careful approach, walking slowly and stopping often to listen.

The site was quiet. Their vehicle was there, but no sign of life. Could they still be sleeping? Not likely. People didn't come all the way up here to sleep in. More than likely, they were out tromping through the woods, or perhaps fishing.

The faint sound of laughter caught his attention, coming from down by the lake, a hundred yards away. He headed toward the sound and in a moment, he saw them. There were two kids with the big guy—not just one. The boys splashed around in the lake but the big guy was somewhat further to the left, perched on an outcropping of rock.

No women around anywhere. Probably just as well. From his experience, women were always trouble, always nagging, always wanting you to do this, do that. Other than for one thing, women didn't serve much of a purpose—except for his mother, of course. She was a saint. She'd put up with the old man for a long time, until the drunken skunk had finally dropped dead. Varick had only been twelve at the time, but it was liberating. His mother had smiled more after that.

In spite of his father's death, or perhaps because of it, he had excelled in school, usually scoring near the top of the class.

And then his mother had died as well. Probably the result of one too many beatings the old man had given her. Well, she was better off now. It was then that he'd dropped out of high school, vanquishing all thoughts of a higher education. He just didn't care anymore.

Varick shook himself out of his unpleasant memories and watched as the guy on the rock cast a line and slowly wound it in. He knew from experience, the waters were deeper in that area. He'd pulled a few lake bass from there himself in times past. He wondered how the guy knew about it. He must've been up here before as well.

He would have to get rid of them somehow. Would he kill them? He would find it hard to kill the boys, but he would have no problem with offing the big guy. Or perhaps he would scare them away. There had to be a solution. This was his backyard, not theirs.

He descended the grade to the tree line, hunched down out of sight, and watched them awhile. The kids still splashed in the water and the guy had caught a couple of nice-sized fish.

They were going to be awhile longer. The guy had cast out again and he looked like he was in no hurry to leave. Might as well go back up to the site and check it out.

He rose to his feet, made his way back up the grade, and entered the site. He looked into the tent. Not much there: some blankets, some sleeping bags, a lantern, and that was about it.

He backed out and looked around. There was nothing of use at the campsite at all except a lawn chair. Better not touch that. Too obvious. He didn't need it anyway.

He peeked in the window of the SUV. Too bad he didn't know how to break into these things. That's where they kept all the good stuff. There was a whole cache of goodies inside. He checked all the doors. Locked. If only he could get ahold of the keys, surely he could liberate some items they wouldn't miss. He returned to the tent, lifted the mattress, and checked under the lantern, but the guy must've taken the keys with him.

That would have to wait. There might be other campers further east where he could do a little shopping.

The morning's excursion hadn't netted him much—nothing, in fact, but it had killed a little time. He could always come back later.

CHAPTER 18

Friday, 9:20 a.m.

JAKE HAD CAUGHT a couple of nice-sized smallmouth bass. One would be enough for breakfast. He gave the smaller one back its freedom, packed up his gear, and wandered over to where the boys had tired of swimming and were building a sandcastle in a small sandy area of the beach.

"Let's go back up to the site, guys," Jake said.

Matty looked up and squinted away the sun. "Can we stay here a bit longer? We're almost done with this."

Jake looked at their work of art. Not bad. Maybe he would have to show them how to do it right a little bit later. "Okay, just a few minutes. And don't go back in the water without me around."

"We won't, Mr. Lincoln."

Jake left the boys and hiked up the grade to the campsite, cleaned the fish, and soon got it sizzling over a fire. In a few minutes, Matty and Kyle appeared, and they devoured a meal of roast fish and baked potatoes. When they'd finished cleaning up, they packed their cooking utensils and the leftover fish in the SUV, climbed in, and headed for town.

A couple of miles from the park entrance sat the small

town of Whaleton. It wasn't much to look at. The kind of town you might miss if you blinked, barely a dot on any map. The village consisted of a handful of houses, an auto repair shop, and a small convenience store that served the surrounding neighborhood. A liquor outlet and a grocery store, along with an outdoor shop, occupied a small plaza further on.

Jake pulled in front of the convenience store and they went inside. A pimply-faced man in his early twenties sat behind the counter, sucking on a popsicle and reading a magazine. He looked up as the newcomers entered, gave a nod, and buried himself back in his reading.

"Got any newspapers?" Jake asked.

The guy looked up, scratched at his cheek, and pointed to a rack near the door. "Yesterday's paper right there."

"You don't have today's paper?"

The guy shrugged. "Maybe tomorrow we'll get it. Maybe not. Might come Sunday."

"What about at the grocery store?"

"Nope. Same delivery guy. Same great service."

Jake went to the rack, picked up a paper, rolled it up, and tucked it under his arm. It would have to do.

He returned to the counter. "You have cell service in this town?"

"Most of the time. Not always." The clerk cocked his head and studied Jake. "You staying at the park?"

Jake nodded.

"Catching any fish?"

"A few."

"Don't catch too many. The game warden'll fine you."
The guy frowned. "You have a fishing license?"

"Why're you so interested?" Jake asked. "What's with all
the questions?"

The storekeeper closed his magazine, tossed it on the
counter, and stood. "The game warden is my uncle. I want to
be a warden someday." He grinned a crooked grin. "Just
practicing on you." He held out a skinny hand. "My name's
Bob. Bob Fletcher. My uncle's name is Andy. Same last
name."

Jake set the newspaper on the counter and shook his hand.
"Haven't seen him come around yet."

"He might not. You just never know when he's gonna
show. Depends on how long you stay." He looked down at
the paper. "That all you're buying?"

Jake pointed a thumb toward Matty and Kyle. "They'll
want something. Give us a few minutes." He pulled out his
cell phone and turned it on. "Not very good reception."

"Might be better outside," the guy said.

Matty and Kyle came over with a large bag of potato chips
and four cans of Coke. Jake paid for the purchases and they
stepped outside. A group of four teenagers—two boys and
two girls—had arrived and lounged near a bench outside the
front door. They carried backpacks and looked like they'd
been hiking all day. One lay on the grass nearby; another one
guzzled water from a glass bottle.

"Don't you guys go far," Jake warned Matty. "I'm just
going to call your mother." He stepped to a quieter spot and
checked his phone again. Four bars. Not bad.

Annie answered on the first ring. Jake grinned when he heard her voice. "Having a good time. Wish you were here," he said.

"You sound like a postcard."

"It's great up here. You don't know what you're missing."

"I'm doing all right," Annie said. "Chrissy and I are catching up. It's a little quiet without you guys around, though."

Jake laughed. "Yeah, I miss you too. We'll be back soon. Anything new there? Any business come in?"

"I'm not planning on checking my email or phone messages until Monday. I'm taking a holiday. Business can wait."

"Heard from Hank?"

"He called once. Nothing doing for him either. He's spending most of the weekend with Amelia. I bet he doesn't even miss you guys."

Jake chuckled. "It's just as well."

They talked for a few more minutes before Jake hung up and wandered over to where Matty chatted with the hikers. One of them, a girl of eighteen or so, was telling him how far they'd hiked. "We're going to jump the fence and spend the weekend in the forest."

"You have a tent?" Matty asked.

The girl nodded and smiled. "We have a couple of small tents. Just fit two people each."

"You do that often?" Jake asked.

"First time. We met online on a backpacking web site that puts hikers together who are in the same area. We hooked up yesterday." She giggled at Jake's worried look. "We've chatted online awhile, so it's not like I don't know them."

Jake furrowed a brow. He knew how impulsive teenagers could be sometimes. He had been one once. He glanced sideways at the two guys. They looked pretty normal. He was probably worried for nothing. "Just be careful," he said, hoping he didn't sound like an over-the-hill party pooper.

She giggled again. "We will."

Jake said goodbye, packed the boys in the SUV, and then made the long drive back to their campsite, deep in the wilderness.

CHAPTER 19

Friday, 10:35 a.m.

VARICK LUCAS flipped the top off his beer bottle and took a swig. It was warm but better than nothing. He flung the cap through the air. It spun away, soared awhile, smacked into a tree, and hit the ground.

There were only about a dozen beers left in the case. He should've sent Otis for more before he'd dispatched him to the great beyond. He was beginning to have second thoughts about that. Perhaps Otis could've been useful around here. He'd have been a bit of company at the least, and someone to do his bidding at best.

Ah well, what was done was done, and he preferred whisky anyway. It went down smoother, hit him quicker, and was easier to lug. Perhaps he would pick up some later on, but for now, this would have to do. Or maybe he could find some campers who had some alcoholic refreshments that he could steal when they weren't around.

He strolled outside and lay down in the hammock. Otis's supply of cigarettes wasn't going to last forever either, but he lit one, dropped the packet on the ground beside him, and nestled in deeper. The smoke wafted up and gradually dissipated among the pines.

Things were okay right now, but he began to wonder if he could make it through the winter. There would be some boring times, that's for sure. No TV, no radio, and he wasn't much of a reader. Maybe this wasn't such a great idea after all. He might give it a few weeks, and then head west, maybe Vancouver. From there he could dip down into the States. Nobody would find him there.

Half an hour later he wondered how he would make it through the day, never mind a few weeks or more. Perhaps he would take a little hike to drum up some excitement.

He finished his beer in one haul, tossed the bottle aside, and climbed from the hammock. Adjusting the pistol behind his belt, he started into the forest.

Halfway to the campsite where he'd seen the big guy that morning, he heard what must have been at least three or four people tramping through the woods, talking and laughing.

He cursed Otis. Otis had said people rarely came around this area, and yet the big guy was camped about a mile away, and now these people tramped on his territory.

He ducked behind a towering maple and watched the group pass by twenty yards away. It was a bunch of kids, backpacking. He could probably pick off all four of them in no time if he had the rifle with him. But that wouldn't be sporting. That would be too easy.

One of the girls looked pretty good, though. She reminded him of the times he and Otis used to have back before all this started. They'd had lots of women then. It had been years since he had been with a woman and he knew he could have a great time with this girl. But then if she recognized him, however unlikely, he would have to kill her after, and he couldn't bring himself to do that. Best leave them alone.

They were headed toward the lake anyway, away from his cabin. Maybe they'd keep going. He hoped they would drown in the lake and become fish food.

When they were safely out of view, he continued on and soon reached the campsite he'd visited that morning. The big guy sat in a lawn chair, the boys at his feet, talking about something. The guy had his shirt off and somehow it made him look even bigger. His muscles bulged even when relaxed. Lucas shuddered. He didn't want to have to tangle with him without a good dependable weapon.

He didn't dare get close enough to listen in. He hoped they would leave soon, get out of his backyard and not come back.

Perhaps he would have to kill them after all. It was something to consider. Something to help with the boredom. He'd gotten the taste of blood now, and craved more. He'd seen a lot of blood in prison—senseless blood, some shed in thirst for control, even more spilled for a pack of smokes or a minor grudge. It had bothered him at first, but he'd soon become accustomed to the sight. The power over others, brought by the shedding of blood, somehow fascinated him.

Prison had definitely matured him.

Lucas backed up a few feet, skirted around the site, went down to the lake, and sat on the rock where he'd seen the guy fishing. The morning mist still overhung the lake but would soon disappear as the sun grew hotter. He tossed a small stone into the water and watched it skip a time or two, then sink. Except for the newly formed ripple, the lake was calm, quiet, and peaceful. Somehow it reminded him again of his mother and he felt torn between anger and sadness. Things might have been different if she hadn't left him when she did.

He brushed away his feelings, climbed off the rock, and wandered across the beach. Somebody had built a rather lame-looking sandcastle there. Must be those boys. He kicked at it viciously until it was nothing but scattered sand. Yeah, that was his life right now—scattered sand, going nowhere, useless, and kicked around by circumstances beyond his control. He cursed his father bitterly and muttered to himself as he made his way back into the forest.

As he came closer to his cabin, he heard an unearthly scream, steadily becoming louder. It sounded like an animal, but shrieking like nothing he'd ever heard. He approached cautiously and grinned when he saw the sight. A rabbit had sprung one of Otis's homemade snares and hung three feet off the ground, fighting for its life and scratching uselessly at the noose around its neck.

Lucas watched it awhile, fascinated with the sight— fascinated with the dumb creature's struggle for survival, too stupid to realize it was all over.

Finally, Lucas found a branch the size of a baseball bat. He pounded at the rabbit, again and again, the helpless animal swinging freely in the air, the screams long ago having subsided. He continued to batter the animal's flesh until forced to stop, exhausted and panting. The animal hung limp, almost beyond recognition, a mass of fur, tissue, and blood.

Lucas tossed the branch aside, spat, and turned his back on the sight. He felt better now.

CHAPTER 20

Friday, 11:55 a.m.

MATTY KICKED THE soccer ball across the beach toward Kyle, then wandered under the shade of an old oak and dropped down. Kyle grabbed the ball and sat nearby. They had tired in the hot sun, their game of one-on-one soccer now over.

Matty wiped his brow on his t-shirt. "You want to take a hike?"

"Sure."

They climbed the hill to the campsite where Jake dozed in the lawn chair. He opened his eyes and suppressed a yawn as they approached.

"Dad, we're just going to take a hike, okay?"

Jake sat forward. "Okay, but don't go far and be back soon, and take your compass with you. Do you remember how to use it?"

"No problem, Dad. You're a good teacher, and we won't be gone long." Matty opened the door to the SUV, dug out his backpack, and returned. "Let's go, Kyle."

"You have bear spray in there, too?" Jake asked.

Matty nodded. "Yup." He put the pack on, went to the

tent and grabbed a couple cans of soda, dumped them into his pack, and headed into the forest, Kyle at his side. "See you soon," he called back.

The natural path between the trees soon petered out and the immense array of green became thicker. The forest floor felt soft under their shoes, a thick carpeting of soil, fallen leaves, pine needles, and moss. Sun filtered through the trees, producing an ever-moving dappled pattern.

They romped through the trees for a few minutes before the denseness of the forest opened into a natural clearing a hundred feet wide. The ground was rocky, with some patches of fertile soil producing a rich shade of grass. Small saplings grew at the edges of the clearing.

"Look there," Matty whispered and pointed.

Kyle's eyes grew wide as he gazed at the sight of a deer, quietly emerging from the edge of the forest to graze in the clearing. It raised its head in their direction; its nostrils flaring to catch their scent. In a flash it was gone, sensing danger.

Kyle's attention was drawn by a squirrel that darted in and out of sight. It raced across the clearing, Kyle following behind, and then disappeared.

Matty wrinkled his nose. He'd caught the faint scent of a skunk from somewhere nearby. He knew enough to steer clear of them if they happened upon one.

"We should be getting back, Kyle," Matty said. "I told my dad we wouldn't be long."

"Just a few more minutes?"

"Better not," Matty said as he removed his backpack. He was pretty sure he knew which way was the right way back, but he should check the compass to be sure.

Kyle was disappointed. "Okay, let's go." He turned, and then stopped short and pointed. A small bear cub stood ten feet away at the edge of the clearing.

Matty stopped digging in his backpack; the compass could wait. "Get back, Kyle. This way," he warned.

Kyle crouched and held out a hand toward the cub. "It's only a tiny one. It can't hurt us."

As if in answer, a black bear ambled out of the forest and stopped. It was the mother. It glared at them, tossing its head, and then emitted a low growl, huffing and blowing through its nostrils. The boys stood frozen as the protective female swatted the ground with its forepaws. Matty held his breath, watching, unable to move as the animal lowered its head and drew back its ears.

Kyle inhaled a sharp breath and jumped to his feet, ready to charge the other way. Matty reached out, grabbed him by the arm, and whispered, "Don't move."

The boys stood frozen a moment. "Back up, slowly," Matty warned, his heart galloping as he reached carefully in his backpack, searching desperately for the bear spray.

The animal took a step toward them and huffed again. That was enough for Matty. The backpack slipped through the fingers of the frightened boy as he tugged at Kyle. In three quick backwards steps they were at the tree line. A moment later they ran as fast as their legs could carry them.

Matty chanced a look back. The bear wasn't following, likely content it had scared off another predator. But he wasn't taking any chances. They ran for several minutes and finally collapsed on the ground, panting, frightened, and worn out.

"That was scary," Kyle whispered.

Matty nodded and swallowed hard. "Sure was."

"We'd better get back now, don't you think?"

Matty looked at the shivering Kyle, and then stood and glanced around, bewildered. Everything was the same. The dim forest went on forever, in every direction, as far as he could see. He'd lost his backpack and the compass was inside.

He stood still and listened to the sounds of the forest. Birds sang. A gentle breeze blew, causing the leaves on the trees to shift and sway. The sun stood straight overhead and gave no indication of which direction would lead them safely back.

"I think it's this way," Kyle said, pointing to his left.

Matty shook his head. "I don't think so."

Kyle's lower lip quivered. "Are we lost?"

"Don't worry, Kyle," Matty said as he put a small arm around his friend's shoulder. "We'll find our way out of here. It can't be far."

He picked a direction that seemed correct and Kyle followed. Matty led the way over rocks and around thick roots that went on forever. They had run so fast he wasn't sure what kind of ground they'd covered, but he didn't remember seeing any of this before.

He stopped, lifted his face, and let the light shine across his features. The sun hadn't moved. It still wasn't going to be of any help. If he could find the clearing again, he could use the compass and make their way back. As long as the bear wasn't hanging around, they would be fine.

"We're going the wrong way, Kyle." Matty pointed and

headed in another direction. "It's got to be this way." But he wasn't so sure.

The friendly forest had become threatening and unfamiliar. The trees stood as statues around them, unwilling or unable to lead them home. Eyes glared from twisted tree trunks while the howl of a lone wolf mocked them from far away.

Matty stopped, sat on the leaf-covered ground beneath a tree, leaned back against the gnarled trunk, and took a deep breath.

They were lost.

CHAPTER 21

Friday, 12:35 p.m.

JAKE GLANCED at his watch, concerned the boys hadn't returned yet. They'd been gone longer than he'd expected. When Matty said they would be back in a few minutes, Jake knew he fully intended to be. He also knew it was easy to lose track of time, especially when you're a boy and having fun.

He hoped that's all it was. Matty was responsible, as dependable as any eight-year-old boy could be, and they would be back soon.

He gathered some wood from the surrounding forest, chopped it into manageable-sized pieces, and stacked it neatly by the fire pit. He would make a fire and heat up the leftover fish for lunch. The boys would be hungry when they returned and he felt peckish himself.

As he worked, his worry deepened, concern seeping into his mind until he could no longer concentrate on what he was doing. He straightened up and made a decision. Something wasn't right and he needed to still the sense of foreboding that had overtaken him.

He had to find the boys. He went to the SUV, found a piece of paper and a pencil, and wrote a note, fastening it securely to the flap of the tent. If they returned while he was gone, they would be sure to see it.

Everything should be safe enough here. He made sure the vehicle was locked up and took a look around the site. There's an unwritten code among campers—you don't tamper with another camper's belongings. Bears and other animals aren't bound to that code but, satisfied everything would be safe from wild creatures, he headed into the forest the way the boys had gone.

He looked for any signs that indicated exactly which way they'd gone. The forest floor of rotting leaves and pine needles yielded no help, no visible footprints, and the trees and bushes that surrounded him grew wild, seemingly untouched by any passersby.

He stopped often to call Matty's name, listened intently a moment, then continued on, uncertain he was going in the right direction. They could have wandered anywhere in their excitement to discover what the forest had to offer.

This wasn't like Matty at all. He had his compass, knew how to use it, and could surely find his way back. Any danger out here was unlikely to come from wild animals, and he had the bear spray in case they ran across one.

Something dreadful might have happened to them. He never should have let them go off alone. He thought about the prowler at the campsite the night before. Had there been one, or was it just his imagination? He wasn't so sure now.

He continued to call but the only answer was the chattering of squirrels and the squawking of birds.

He dashed ahead, searching frantically in all directions, and finally stumbled into a clearing. Something familiar lay on the grassy surface. It was Matty's backpack; perhaps they weren't far away. He crouched down and examined it. The straps were undone and hanging loose, the compass and bear spray still inside.

He studied the ground around the area but saw no signs of a struggle or any other indication of why the backpack had been left in the clearing. He picked up the pack, tossed it over his shoulder, and chose the most likely direction the boys might have taken.

He tried to think straight, logically. They couldn't be far away. Matty knew enough to not wander aimlessly, and he knew his directions, and how to follow the stars at night, and the sun by day. Surely they would return soon, safe and unharmed.

He circled through the woods, around the clearing, making wider and wider circles each time. He combed the uneven ground thoroughly, looking for signs, tracks, or footprints in the undergrowth.

After several more minutes of frantic searching, he stopped, hoping desperately they'd returned to the camp. Hesitant to leave in case the boys were just out of reach, just out of the sound of his voice, he called their name awhile, waiting and praying for an answer. None came and he reluctantly returned to camp, hoping to see the boys laughing, giggling, and just being boys.

His heart dropped when he saw the note, still fastened to the tent, the site undisturbed. He dashed down the grade to the lake in case they'd returned and wandered there. He stopped where the sandcastle used to be, perplexed it was gone. It didn't make a lot of sense for them to destroy it. Perhaps it was an animal? That made no sense either.

He crouched down and examined the spot. Faint, yet distinct footprints were embedded in the sand. A man's footprints. He felt certain now someone else was in the area, maybe close by.

Finally, he sagged into the lawn chair and leaned forward, his head in his hands, his mind imagining the worst. He blamed himself. He never should have let them wander off like that. He was so certain they would be safe, and now … he wasn't so sure. He felt irresponsible and fully to blame.

He stood and paced the camp, turning at the slightest sound or movement from the otherwise still forest surrounding him, begging the wilderness to give back what it had taken away.

He couldn't give up the search. They could be in danger and he felt helpless as he stood in quiet desperation, hoping to come up with a plan, anything.

CHAPTER 22

Friday, 12:56 p.m.

MATTY CAME TO a quick stop and pointed through the trees. "Look, Kyle. There's a house over there."

Kyle stopped and squinted. "I don't see it."

"Right there. Look beside that tree. You can see the roof."

Kyle grinned. "I see it now." He looked at Matty, his grin growing wider. "That means we're not lost anymore."

"Let's go." Matty tore through the trees, dodging stumps, clumps of bushes, and fallen logs. Kyle followed close behind, and in a minute, they charged into a clearing.

"It's a cabin," Matty said. "It looks like it's about a thousand years old. Let's see if anybody's home."

He hurried forward, banged on the wooden door, waited, and banged again. There was no answer. "Hello. Is anyone there?" he called, but still no answer came.

Kyle pointed. "There's a padlock on the door. I don't think anyone's there."

Matty stopped pounding, stepped back, and eyed the lock. "It looks like a fairly new lock. I'm pretty sure somebody lives here." He glanced around and noticed a hammock hanging between two trees. A beer bottle lay beside the hammock.

Cigarette butts were ground into the dirt. "It sure looks like it, anyway," he said.

Kyle went to the side of the building, stood on his tiptoes, and peered through a small window. "I think you're right, but there's nobody there right now."

Matty followed Kyle, stood beside him, and looked through the window. The small cabin was dim, lit only by the sunlight that made it through the small windows. There was no one inside but one thing seemed certain, somebody lived there.

"Maybe they went hunting or something," Matty said.

"I think we should wait until they get home. They must know their way around here and can help us find our camp."

Matty frowned. "Dad's going to be mighty worried if we don't get back soon."

"But we don't know the way."

"Stay here. I'll look behind," Matty ordered and then circled around to the rear. He waded through the overgrown weeds and wild shrubs behind the cabin and made it to the far side, then back to the front, where Kyle now waited for him. "There's nobody there."

"Do you think there's a road around here?" Kyle asked.

"Nope. We're way too far in. And even if there was one, I don't know which way it would be. The closest road is probably miles from here."

"Then the people who live here, how do they get here?"

Matty shrugged. "Maybe they never leave. I've heard about that before. Old hermits just living off nature, catching rabbits and eating berries. Maybe that's who lives here. An old hermit."

"Then maybe he's not very friendly," Kyle said. "Maybe he's an ogre or something who likes to eat little kids."

Matty ignored his friend and squinted thoughtfully at the sky.

"What're you looking at?" Kyle asked, following his gaze.

"The sun."

"The sun?"

"Yeah, look." Matty pointed. "It's moved over that way a bit. In the morning, it comes up right behind the SUV, and at night, it sets over the tent." Matty whirled around and pointed. "That means the camp is straight over there. All we have to do is keep our eye on the sun and make sure it's always straight behind us."

"And that'll get us back?"

Matty slugged Kyle on the shoulder. "Guaranteed."

~*~

VARICK LUCAS approached the cabin cautiously. He'd heard the sound of voices—kids. He dove behind a wide cedar tree just off the trail and listened intently.

He couldn't make out what they said, but that didn't matter. What did matter was, they'd found his cabin. This was beginning to be a nightmare. He was so deep in the forest, and yet this area was becoming a major thoroughfare.

He pressed his face against the bark and peered around the trunk. He recognized those brats. They were the ones he'd seen hanging around with that big guy. Could things get any worse? He had to do something about this.

But what? He should skin them alive and feed them to the squirrels, that's what. No, he could never do that. They were just dumb little kids and didn't deserve it.

He would have to play this one smart and somehow scare the three of them off. Or he could kill the big guy and maybe the kids would leave him alone. He would have to think about that awhile.

He pulled back from the trunk, turned, and retreated, dodging from tree to tree until he felt certain he was safely out of sight, then sped up to jogging speed, slowing only when he had to dodge a fallen tree or a patch of wild brambles.

He came close to the big guy's campsite in a few minutes and approached slowly. The camp seemed vacant. He listened awhile in case the guy was nearby, or maybe in the tent. All remained still, so he crept in, his attention drawn to a piece of paper fastened to the flap of the tent. He edged over, peered at the note, and grinned. So that was it. The boys were lost and their father had gone to look for them.

And if the guy found them, Lucas couldn't let them leave. Not yet, anyway, and maybe not ever. He hadn't fully formulated a plan yet. He would work at it as he went along. There were so many possibilities.

He scurried over to the SUV and tried the doors. They were still locked up. Never mind; he had learned a thing or two in the prison auto shop.

What he really wanted to do was hot-wire the vehicle, drive it out of here, and hide it in the forest somewhere. But he didn't know how to do that; he would do the next best thing.

If he couldn't drive it, he would make sure nobody else could either. He could slash the tires, but that would be too obvious. He wanted to keep them guessing.

Lucas slipped the hunting knife from the sheath fastened to his leg, lay down in front of the vehicle, and rolled underneath. He reached up under the engine, carefully working the blade into the right position, and began a sawing, hacking motion. He heard a snap, then tugged with his hand until the drive belt lay on the ground, chewed in half by Otis's knife.

That would keep them here for now. It was too far to walk out and they'd be at his mercy. It would give him time to determine his best course of action.

He left the belt where it lay and headed for home.

CHAPTER 23

Friday, 1:24 p.m.

JAKE HAD SEARCHED through the forest on the opposite side of the camp from where the boys had wandered off. He thought it possible that, after dropping the backpack, they had circled around in confusion and gotten lost.

After several minutes of frantic searching, he returned to camp. He would have to go for help. He hated leaving the boys out here alone but he had no choice; he was out of ideas. A more experienced tracker would have a better chance than he would.

He got in the van and started the engine. It idled a moment, then rattled, shook, and died. Jake frowned and turned the key again. The engine cranked, the starter whined, and the SUV hummed. He dropped the shifter into reverse, backed up a few feet, and turned the steering wheel.

Something was terribly wrong. The power steering was stiff and unresponsive. He shut the SUV off, popped the latch for the hood, and climbed out.

The drive belt lay on the ground in front of the vehicle. It must have been worn out and finally snapped. He picked it up and examined it. Although the ends were frayed, the rest of it appeared to be in good condition. It was unusual for a belt to wear in one spot and snap with no warning. The RAV4 had been running perfectly when they'd arrived.

If he was at home he could patch it up long enough to get some help. He had every tool you could need in his garage, but that didn't do him much good out here.

He stood with the belt in his hands, uncertain what to do. The vehicle wouldn't get far in this condition. The engine would soon overheat and shut down without the water pump circulating coolant. He was miles from the main gate, and probably just as far from other campers.

Out of desperation he turned on his cell phone. No reception. He didn't expect there would be.

What a mess this weekend had turned out to be. The unusable vehicle was repairable, given time, but the missing boys were his prime concern right now, and without the vehicle, he would have to find another way.

He spun around at the sound of rustling leaves and snapping twigs. Someone was coming. He stepped closer to the sound, held his breath, and strained to see.

He expelled his breath in a whoosh, overwhelmed with relief as Matty appeared at the edge of the tree line, Kyle directly behind.

He dashed toward them as they entered the site, knelt on one knee, and spread his arms wide. "Matty, where have you been?" He pulled them both close, overcome by emotion.

Matty hugged his father's neck, his voice quivering as he spoke. "We got lost, Dad."

"There was a bear," Kyle put in.

Jake held his son at arm's length, his brows knitted in a frown, and looked at Kyle. "A bear?"

"We got away," Kyle said.

"I can see that," Jake said with a hint of a smile. He stood and leaned over. "But what happened?"

"We saw a bear cub," Matty explained. "And then the mother came and she was angry and we ran. The bear didn't follow us, but we kinda forgot which direction we were going."

Kyle bit his lip and looked at the ground. "It was my fault. I wanted to pet the cub."

Matty put his arm around his friend. "It's okay, Kyle. Everything turned out fine."

Kyle looked up and smiled. "I sure won't be doing that again."

"What about your backpack?" Jake asked. "What about the bear spray?"

"I tried to get the spray out when we got scared. The backpack fell and we ran as fast as we could out of there." Matty pointed over his shoulder. "It's back there somewhere. Sorry, I lost it, Dad."

A smile touched Jake's lips. "It's all right. I found it."

"You were looking for us?"

"For a while. I was pretty worried."

"Sorry, Dad." Matty paused, then added, "The compass was in my pack too, so we didn't know which way to go."

"Then we saw a cabin," Kyle said.

Jake looked at Kyle. "A cabin? In the forest?"

"Yup. We thought maybe they could help us get back here, but there was nobody home."

"How did you find your way?" Jake asked Matty.

"We followed the sun. At first it was straight up and didn't help much, but it moved and we followed it."

Jake grinned and messed up Matty's hair. "You've no idea how worried I was. And I guess I had no need to be."

"If it makes you feel any better," Matty said with a playful look, "we were a little worried too."

Jake chuckled and asked, "Where's this cabin you saw?"

Kyle turned and pointed. "It's that way."

"Probably about a mile away," Matty added.

"Are you sure somebody lives there?" Jake asked.

"For sure," Matty said. "There were cigarette butts and beer bottles lying around."

"And I saw stuff on a table in the cabin," Kyle added. "And the weeds in front of the cabin were all trampled down."

Jake gazed into the forest, his brow wrinkled in thought. He wondered if the owner of the cabin was the person on the beach, the one who destroyed the sandcastle, and the prowler at the camp the night before. If so, perhaps he was a harmless squatter checking out those who had intruded into his territory.

And now he had the problem with the SUV to worry about. They had to head back on Sunday and he didn't know whether or not they would see another human being by then. If not, they would have to leave everything here and hike back; a long way to go if they took the same route they'd come in by. They could always hike through the woods to the highway, less than five miles away. Surely they could get some help then.

He decided if no one came around, they would start hiking early Sunday morning and get some help, and they should be on their way home by noon.

CHAPTER 24

Friday, 2:55 p.m.

THE BOYS WERE hot and tired from their experience and
wanted to go swimming. Jake agreed, so the boys changed
into swimming trunks and the three of them went down to
the lake.

Matty and Kyle ran straight into the water while Jake
wandered to the left and perched on the rock where he'd
fished that morning. He watched the boys awhile. Jake had
taught Matty how to swim a few years ago and he had taken
to it immediately. Kyle knew how to stay afloat, and Matty
was helping him with some of the finer points of swimming.

He turned his attention to the calm lake in front of him,
tranquil and undisturbed by the boys splashing twenty yards
away. The water displayed countless hues of blue, reflecting
the bright sky. He gazed into the depths of the clear water.
Minnows swarmed just out of arm's reach. A fish broke the
surface a few yards away, ripples widening out.

At the far end of the lake, to his left, a flock of geese
caught his eye, and then his attention was drawn to a moving
patch of red. Someone was over there. More than one. He
could make out three or four people at the edge of the lake.
He cupped his ear and heard voices, laughing, talking.

He glanced over at the boys. They were back on the beach, rebuilding their sandcastle. He went over and watched them awhile. Finally, he spoke. "If you guys are done swimming for now, I'm just going to go down to the other end of the lake. There're some people there and I want to see how they're doing."

Matty looked up and scratched his cheek with a wet, sandy hand. "We'll stay right here."

"I'll be able to see you from there," Jake said. "Just don't go in the water until I come back."

"We won't," Kyle said. "We'll stay here and work on the sandcastle." He grabbed a plastic pail, went to the edge of the lake, filled it with water, and then returned to where Matty sat.

Jake watched the boys a moment and then made his way toward to the end of the lake, walking through knee-high grass and wildflowers and over rocks jutting from the sandy soil.

As he drew closer, he recognized the girl he'd talked to in Whaleton the previous day. The other three stood in a group, talking and laughing. A pair of small tents was set up a little further back, just inside the front line of trees.

He looked around the site and narrowed his eyes in disgust. The previously unspoiled area was littered with papers. Beer bottles and empty cups were scattered around.

The girl smiled as he approached. "It's nice to see a friendly face," she said.

Jake grinned and nodded his head toward the others. "They aren't so friendly?"

She crinkled her nose. "Not exactly what I expected." She held out a small hand. "My name's Holly, by the way. Holly Churchill."

Jake's big hand smothered hers. "I'm Jake Lincoln. I just wanted to drop by and see if everything was okay here."

Her face took on a rosy hue at his touch. "Everything is great," she answered, but she didn't look so sure.

She glanced toward her companions. Jake dropped her hand and followed her gaze. The two guys eyed them, the other girl coming their way, a paper cup in one hand.

"Hi," she said. "I'm Rosie." Her voice was slurred and Jake suspected something other than water was in the cup. She smiled at Jake. "Do you want a drink?"

Jake politely declined.

"Okay," she said and wandered away.

Holly watched her go, then turned back. "They're not much fun to be around today."

"Certainly not my idea of communing with nature," Jake added. He glanced back toward the beach where he'd left the boys. They were still there.

He smiled gently and continued, "I don't want to sound like a stick-in-the-mud, but the game warden might come around any time. He won't be too happy if he sees this. You're planning on cleaning this place up before you go, right?"

Holly sighed. "It's not my mess, but I'll clean it up." She shook her head. "It's the last time I go backpacking with strangers."

A thought formed in Jake's mind. "Were you camped here last night?" he asked.

She nodded.

He cocked a thumb over his shoulder. "Do you know if any of these guys visited our campsite? I saw someone last night."

"I have no idea," Holly said. "But I wouldn't put it past them. It seems like they've been drinking and wandering around ever since we got here." She glanced toward the group, who had now turned their attention elsewhere.

"Did you ever consider leaving?"

"Yes, I did at first, but I think I'll stick it out another night. Maybe head back tomorrow." She giggled. "I don't think they'll even miss me."

"Probably not."

Holly nodded her head toward Matty and Kyle. "Are those your boys?"

"One of them is. The other one is a friend of my son's."

"Are you three here alone?" she asked cautiously.

"My wife didn't come with us this time."

"Oh," Holly said and looked away, her face turning color again.

Jake held back a smile and flicked something off the front of his shirt. "My vehicle is broken down right now or I'd offer you a lift back to civilization."

"What'll you do with no vehicle? Can you fix it?"

"I'm hoping someone will come around before then, maybe the game warden. If not, we'll hike back early Sunday."

Holly widened her eyes. "Perhaps you could give me a lift if I'm still here?"

"Sure could. Whether we're walking or driving out of here,

you're welcome to come with us. I'll check back before we leave. We're not far away. Just up the grade from where the boys are playing."

Holly laughed. "If I can survive that long."

One of the guys lay against the trunk of a large tree, passed out, his drink beside him. Jake turned back to Holly. "Will you be okay here?"

Holly cocked her head toward the other two. "Oh, they're okay. They're just boring and annoying, but I'll be all right. Maybe I'll go for a hike by myself. That'll cheer me up a bit."

Jake considered asking her to stay with them but soon thought better of it. He took a brief look to where the boys wandered around the beach. "I'd better be getting back. I'll drop by early Sunday morning, if not before."

Holly sighed and said goodbye. When halfway back, he looked over his shoulder at her, still watching him. She waved a hand, turned, and headed toward the forest.

He hoped she would be okay. He chuckled to himself. She'd probably learned a good lesson this weekend.

CHAPTER 25

Friday, 4:11 p.m.

VARICK LUCAS finished off his plate of beans and dumped the dishes in the washbowl. He was going to have to do something about the menu in this place. Maybe he shouldn't have beaten that rabbit to a pulp; a bit of rabbit stew would go down good. He would have to remember to reset the snare.

He dumped a dipper full of water in the bowl and carefully scrubbed the utensils. It would be easier with hot water, and some soap, but he had no desire to fire up the stove on such a warm day. There were no clean towels anywhere, so he set the now spotless dishes in a draining tray and stood back. He still hadn't swept this place yet. He would make a point of doing it later today.

Perhaps he would mosey into town tomorrow and see what he could find. There was a problem with that, however; he might be recognized. That would never do. He might have made a serious error in judgment when he decided to set up home in this place, but then, no matter where he went, there was always that danger.

He had little in the way of a wardrobe, nothing but the

clothes on his back, and he felt grimy. He sniffed a ripe armpit and grimaced. Otis didn't have many extra clothes either. His ex-friend must have lived in that getup he was wearing since he'd come here a year or two ago. Alas, his dearly departed friend had no suit to wear to his final resting place.

He dug inside a small cabinet and came up with a razor. He tested it with his thumb. It was sharp. He doubted if Otis had shaved for a while. That mangy beard he wore was proof positive of that. He dug some more but couldn't find any soap. A bare razor with water would have to do.

Not far from the cabin, a small stream which supplied his washing and drinking water, curved gently through the forest. The water was always fresh and seemed clean, and he needed a bath.

He took the razor and a rag and journeyed down to the stream that burbled and gurgled over limestone rocks and smooth stones, making its way to Wendigo Lake. A family of ducks played upstream, paddling on the water. He wished he'd brought his rifle. Alarmed by his presence, they splashed across the surface and took to the air as he drew closer.

Footprints lined the edge of the stream—telltale signs of rabbits, raccoon, deer, and even a fox, which had come to drink. He didn't mind sharing with them. They belonged there. Other humans didn't.

He walked up the bank a few yards to where a naturally formed pool beckoned him, then stripped off his clothes, stepped into the cool water, and rested on a smooth rock that was half-immersed.

Without soap, it was hard to remove the grime from the clothes, but at least he could scrub the smell from them, and from his body. When he'd removed as much dirt from the clothes as he could, he climbed out and spread them on a rock. They would be dry soon.

He got back in the pool and shaved—something he hadn't done in years; he had sported a full beard for as long as he could remember. He rubbed his smooth face with the back of his hand and admired his reflection in the water. He looked, and felt, like a new man.

He soaked awhile longer, scrubbing the filth from his skin, then lay on a patch of grass on the bank, leaned his head against a rock, and closed his eyes, enjoying the late afternoon warmth of the sun.

He dozed off and was startled awake by the sound of something coming up the bank, from downstream, heading his way. He sprang to his feet, gathered up his clothes, and dashed up the bank in the opposite direction, where he hid behind a large cedar. He peeked out from behind the ragged bark and waited for the intruder to come into sight.

It was a girl—the same girl he'd seen that morning, the pretty one, and she was alone.

Boy, would he be glad when the weekend was over and all these trespassers would get out of his hair.

He struggled with his clothes and managed to get them on without making any sound that would betray his presence. They were still a little moist, but they would do. At least they were clean, and he felt much better.

The girl took off her running shoes, rolled up her pant legs, and sat on the bank of the river. She dipped her feet in the water, splashed them around awhile, and then leaned forward, dropped her elbows on her knees, and gazed into the bubbling stream, her chin in her hands.

He heard her singing softly to herself. He couldn't make out the words, or recognize the tune, but could tell she had a nice voice—a sweet voice, and it seemed to fit in well with the beauty of this place, a place filled with both loveliness and ugliness. It was life and death at their best, survival of the fittest, and a place that guaranteed him his survival—if he was careful, and smart.

He continued to admire her. She looked young and innocent—not like the other girl he'd seen her with earlier, and not like the ones he'd known when he was growing up. He felt somewhat ashamed for his earlier thoughts of having his way with her. This girl didn't deserve that. Maybe the other one, but not this one.

But he had no time for that now and no inclination. He just wanted to be left alone.

His eyes popped a moment later as he watched the girl stand and undress, then step into the water and begin to bathe. He fought with his earlier decision to leave her alone. He hadn't seen a sight like that for a good long time and it stirred his memory of better days.

He watched awhile, entranced and unable to move, unable to make a decision whether or not to act on his instinctual desires.

He chose not to, and before he could change his mind, he fled from the spot and arrived at his cabin, panting for breath, unsettled and confused.

CHAPTER 26

Friday, 8:00 p.m.

ANNIE FLICKED OFF the television and tossed the remote control onto the coffee table. She yawned. She wasn't tired, just bored—and lonely. Sure she was having the quiet, peaceful weekend she'd planned, but she missed the guys, and missed the quiet noise that always surrounded and comforted her when they were here.

It was too much of a good thing.

She couldn't even call them on the phone. She glanced at her watch. They wouldn't be home for two more days, and at just about this time of the evening. She might die of boredom by then.

She made herself a cup of coffee, sat at the kitchen table, and picked up her phone. She dialed her mother's number; there was no answer. Her parents had probably gone out somewhere for the evening, something they often did on a Friday night.

It didn't matter anyway. She didn't care to talk to her mother all that much. Their conversations usually devolved into a one-sided discussion about Jake, about what a bad example he was, and what a lousy father. And then she realized, she must be bored to consider it.

She yawned again, and as if on cue, an idea popped into her head. It was a crazy idea to be sure, but so what?

She would leave early in the morning, drive up north, and surprise them. Maybe bring them some real food. They'd probably be ready for it by now.

She'd spent the afternoon with Chrissy, gossiping, laughing, and catching up. Perhaps Chrissy would like to come north with her. That would give her someone to drive home with as well.

She picked up her cell phone from a basket on the counter and dialed Chrissy's number. "I'm going north early tomorrow to surprise the guys and wondered if you want to come with me," she said when Chrissy answered.

"Gee, I'd like to, Annie, but I'll be busy for the rest of the weekend. I'm taking the time to drive out of town to visit an old friend while Kyle's away."

"That's okay," Annie said. "It was just a thought."

"Have you talked to them today?"

"Not since this morning. No cell coverage where they are and it's a bit of a drive to town."

"I'm sure they'll be glad to see you," Chrissy said.

"Jake, maybe. The boys probably won't care much either way."

Chrissy giggled. "I thought Kyle might be a little reluctant to go away for the weekend without me. Boy, was I wrong. He didn't hesitate a moment."

"When those two are together, they forget all about us."

"Guys might stray for a while," Chrissy said with a laugh. "But they always come running back."

"That's true enough," Annie said. "And now I have a few things to do here. I'll talk to you again when I get back."

She ended the conversation and hung up. She had to get ready for tomorrow's excursion and she wanted to get at it.

She spent the next hour putting together a homemade macaroni-and-cheese casserole, one of Jake and Matty's favorites. They could easily heat it up by the fire and have a nice lunch tomorrow.

She wasn't all that tired but she went to bed early, setting her alarm for 6:00 a.m. She wanted to be there before noon.

~*~

THE SUN HAD SET some time ago, but the full moon lessened the blackness of the night, shining on the water like a pale band of silver, dimming the stars that speckled the summer sky. The fire on the beach had died to a bed of glowing embers.

Jake glanced across the darkened waters. The backpackers at the far end of the lake had a campfire blazing as well. He could vaguely make out figures moving about, lit up by the glow. He felt concerned that the lack of respect for nature they'd exhibited earlier might result in a brush fire, or worse, a raging forest fire.

He and the boys wanted to do a little hiking in the morning, heading out after an early breakfast. He planned not to wander too far away in case someone came by with a vehicle. He preferred to get the RAV4 fixed up and running the next day if possible. That would save a lot of headaches.

He stretched and yawned, tired and ready to hit the hay. Whether they knew it or not, the boys would be worn out from the day's events as well and welcome the early retirement.

Much of nature had calmed down. The occasional wolf howled far away. Somewhere, an owl screeched, hidden and rarely seen during the day, now announcing its presence by night. It was echoed by a soft, low hoot, perhaps a mate calling her answer.

Jake looked over at Matty and Kyle, sitting on the sandy beach a few feet away. They giggled and scared each other, telling spooky stories in whispered tones.

"Are you boys ready to pack it in?" he asked.

"Can't we stay just a bit longer?" Matty asked.

Jake stood. "I'll go pack up the campsite and be right back. That'll give you a few more minutes." He pointed to the dying campfire. "You can douse that while I'm gone."

"Okay, Dad." The boys went back to their storytelling and Jake climbed the slope.

He wandered around the campsite, gathering up anything that might attract wild animals, especially scavenging bears. He put any leftover food and snacks in a plastic bag and packed them into the SUV.

By then, the boys had wandered up on their own and in a few minutes, the camp was asleep.

CHAPTER 27

Saturday, 6:00 a.m.

WHEN ANNIE'S ALARM clock startled her awake, her plans for the day rushed in to fill her thoughts. She rubbed the sleep from her eyes, stretched, yawned, and rolled out of bed. She padded to the bathroom, eager to get started as soon as possible.

She had a quick shower, fixed her face, pulled on her favorite blue jeans and a t-shirt, and went downstairs. After a soothing cup of coffee, she felt fully awake and ready to get the day under way.

She reheated the casserole she'd made the night before and put it in a small cooler, suitable for not only keeping food cold, but keeping it warm as well. That way it would be easier to reheat it and feed her hungry guys.

She found another cooler, a larger, empty one, and then grabbed her keys and packed everything in her car. She pulled from the driveway, pleased she'd made this decision.

Traffic was usually light on Saturday mornings, and at this time of the day, it was even lighter. She liked to drive and made it to the main highway leading north in no time flat, Randy Travis's easy, mellow voice keeping her company.

An hour later she pulled into a truck stop, filled up with gas, and went inside the restaurant for a light breakfast. As she ate, she watched a big-screen TV perched on a nearby wall.

Her attention was drawn by a news story about the escaped convict, Varick Lucas. The police booking mug shot of Lucas sporting a full beard, taken when he was arrested, appeared on the screen. His head was raised in a cocky, rebellious manner, dark, expressionless eyes watching her from the TV screen.

The view switched back to the commentator, on the scene of the hunt. Police officers and emergency vehicles could be seen in the background.

"Law enforcement officials have picked up the trail of Varick Lucas, the fugitive accused of killing three people in a murderous spree.

"Lucas, twenty-seven, who escaped Wednesday afternoon, allegedly killed a guard along with the prison warden. At least one other murder since has been attributed to him as authorities continue to track his movements. He's considered armed and dangerous, and a massive RCMP manhunt across Ontario and to the east has ensued.

"Lucas was serving a life sentence at Haddleburg Maximum Security Penitentiary when he escaped, allegedly with the aid of a fellow prisoner."

The commentator continued, giving some history of the case and the facts surrounding his arrest. A video of a craggy, rugged man appeared on the screen and a banner at the bottom introduced him as RCMP Sergeant Lance Brewer.

His voice was grim, yet he spoke with a calming tone that inspired confidence.

"I want to assure you we will track down and apprehend this dangerous criminal. We've brought in aerial support as well as troops on the ground, and the search will continue as long as necessary. He may or may not still be in the area, but until he's found, we urge residents not to answer their doors except for people they know or uniformed law enforcement.

"Lucas is still out there and we don't know what he's going to do. We know what he's capable of doing, and we won't stop until we find him. This hardened, convicted felon being on the loose causes me great concern, and I pledge never to give up the hunt until he's back behind bars. As Lucas is on the RCMP's most wanted list, police have been authorized to use deadly force if they identify Lucas and he refuses to surrender.

"We're interviewing those who assisted in his escape, and along the way we'll be looking closely at those who may have helped or harbored this fugitive."

The commentator came back on the screen and the view switched to an overview of a pretty little town, nestled in a lush valley, proud Victorian homes lining the streets.

"Sources have confirmed Lucas has ties to the eastern part of the country, specifically, this small town in Nova Scotia. The search remains a topic of conversation for residents. In this small

community, most people have friends or relatives affected by the manhunt, and many said they know the Lucas family.

"We were unable to gain access to any of the family members but have been told by certain sources they are staying away from the public eye, declining to comment, apparently not leaving their home. Friends of the family are shocked a man many of them knew since his childhood is now the subject of this massive manhunt.

"Police said they could not provide information about possible sightings, but he had allegedly told witnesses he was heading home to stay. Authorities are considering that information but will continue their nationwide manhunt, now in its fourth day. We'll continue to bring you breaking news as this story unfolds."

Annie finished her coffee and the waitress brought her the bill. "Been watching that most of the day," the waitress said, pointing a finger toward the television. "I'm glad he's not in this neighborhood." She shuddered. "I hope they get him before he hurts anyone else."

Annie nodded and smiled. "I hope so too." She'd had enough of killers lately and didn't want to hear any more about murderers and criminals right now. This was her weekend off and Varick Lucas was not going to spoil it for her.

She left the friendly waitress a nice tip, paid the bill, and left the restaurant. Traffic had increased somewhat but it was still easy going as she turned back onto the highway.

She looked forward to seeing the guys and realized how much she'd enjoyed their camping trips in previous years. This one would be short, at least for her, but it would still be a good, relaxing time away.

CHAPTER 28

Saturday, 8:25 a.m.

THE BOYS MUST have been exhausted. Jake had gotten up without waking them, grabbed his fishing equipment, and went to his favorite perch by the lake, allowing them to sleep.

He returned to the camp with a large bass, gathered some wood, and started a fire. He cleaned the fish, wrapped it in tinfoil along with an onion and some lemon juice, and buried it in the hot embers of the now dying fire. He shoved a couple of foil-wrapped potatoes in beside the fish.

Matty poked his head from the tent, glanced around the site, and ducked back in. Jake heard him waking Kyle, and in a few moments, both boys came from the tent, rubbing their eyes and yawning.

"Fish for breakfast," Jake said.

"Again?"

They talked about the previous day's events as they ate their meal. As they finished, the sound of a vehicle caught Jake's attention. He set his plate on a stump beside him and stood as a white 4x4 pickup came closer, bumping over the trail. In a moment, it pulled up and stopped. An emblem on the side of the vehicle said, "Conservation Officer."

The officer stepped from the pickup and approached them. "Morning, folks. Just wanted to stop by and see how yer keepin'."

Jake glanced at the gold badge pinned to the game warden's loose-fitting tan shirt. His matching pants sagged down to his rugged boots, a belt full of equipment at his waist. A gun hung on his right hip, secured in place by a leather holster.

"Good morning, Officer," Jake said. "Am I glad to see you."

The officer raised his brows and looked over his Ray-Ban sunglasses. "That's not something I usually hear."

Matty and Kyle came over and gazed up at the officer. Matty tucked his hands in his pockets, his head twisting back and forth as the two men talked. Kyle seemed more intent on the officer's equipment, staring at the gun at his waist.

Jake motioned toward the RAV4. "I'm having a bit of trouble. The drive belt snapped on my vehicle and I can't go anywhere. I would appreciate a lift into town."

The officer stared at the SUV and looked thoughtful a moment, then turned back to Jake. "I can send a truck in here to tow you, if that's what you want."

"I can fix it myself as long as I can get to an auto shop and get a replacement belt."

"Sure. Won't be a problem. We'll get you fixed up and outta here afore the day's out." The officer paused. "I have a few stops to make out here. A few places to check out, you know how it is. But I'll stop by later and give you a lift."

"I'd appreciate that," Jake said.

"You ever use that gun?" Kyle asked, still in awe.

The officer looked down. "Not often, son. Mostly just to shoot a rabbit caught in a trap or some other animal needs help in his dying misery."

"You ever shoot anybody?"

The officer laughed loud and long, his laugh a deep guttural sound, ending in a chuckle. Then his voice turned serious as he looked at Kyle and said, "Can't say that I have. Can't say that I ever want to."

Matty and Kyle seemed to lose interest after that and wandered away.

"How long you folks staying?" the officer asked Jake.

"We had plans to go home tomorrow." Jake glanced at the SUV. "I hope we make it in time."

"Oh, you will." The officer glanced over at Matty and Kyle, sitting by the fire. "Gotta get those little guys home safe."

Jake examined the badge again. No name tag. "Are you Andy Fletcher?" he asked.

"One and the same. Just call me Andy."

"Nice to meet you, Andy. I'm Jake." He offered his hand. "We met your nephew in town yesterday. He said you might come around."

Andy shook Jake's hand. "How is my nephew?"

"He didn't complain. He told us he wants to be a game warden like you some day."

Andy laughed. "That'll be awhile." He turned more serious. "You been doing any fishin'?"

"A bit," Jake said. "Just enough for breakfast."

The officer pursed his lips and nodded slowly. "While I'm here I guess I should check your fishin' license. Just something I'm required to do, you understand."

Jake removed his wallet, flipped it open, and removed his fishing license. Andy squinted at it briefly and nodded. "Good enough. Just make sure you stay within the limit, no problem."

"I intend to."

Andy narrowed his eyes. "You got any firearms?"

Jake shook his head. "Nope."

"You been doing hunting of any kind?"

"Just fishing."

"Okay, sounds good. What about alcohol? Any alcohol?"

Jake answered, "No," and thought about mentioning the group of teenagers, then decided not to be a busybody.

Andy shook his head slowly as if considering Jake's answer. "Ain't nobody come around bothering you while you're here, I hope. We want our visitors to have a good time."

"There seemed to be somebody poking around here last night." Jake scratched his head. "I wasn't sure though if it was man or beast."

"Could be a bear," Andy said, his eyes roving around the site.

"I don't think so."

"Maybe just a coon, then," Andy said and moved over toward the SUV. He looked in the back window and then circled the vehicle slowly as if examining it thoroughly. He came back and approached Jake.

"Everything all right?" Jake asked curiously.

Andy glanced around thoughtfully. "Yeah, it looks like things are fine here. Except for your vehicle, of course." He paused a moment, then added, "Nice to meet you folks." He turned around, headed to leave, and then stopped. "Afore I go, do you know if there's anyone else camped in this area?"

Jake hesitated before pointing vaguely to his right. "There are some backpackers camped down at the end of the lake. Four of them. Two boys and two girls."

The warden pursed his lips. "Guess I should go see how they're making out afore I go." He turned and strolled to the pickup. "I'll be back this afternoon," he called and then got in the pickup and backed out.

Jake watched the vehicle until it disappeared from sight over a knoll. The game warden was somewhat of a strange man, a bit like his nephew. It must run in the family.

He looked forward to getting the SUV fixed up so he could enjoy the rest of the weekend.

CHAPTER 29

Saturday, 10:10 a.m.

ANNIE FELT RELIEVED when she saw the sign heralding her arrival in the small town of Whaleton. She didn't have far to go now, just a few miles until she reached the park entrance.

She pulled over in front of a small convenience store and went inside. A young man, stocking shelves near the front of the store, straightened his back and gave her a friendly grin.

"Can I help you?" he asked, his wide grin growing even wider, splitting his youthful face.

She smiled back. "I just want a couple bottles of soda."

He pointed to the back of the store. "Right back there, in the cooler. Help yerself."

"Oh, and do you have any ice?"

He waved the other hand and squinted one eye toward the front of the store. "Right there by the door. Lots of ice. A buck a bag."

Annie went to the back of the store, picked out three large bottles of soda from the floor-to-ceiling refrigerator, and brought them to the front, placing them on the counter.

The clerk squeezed through a small slit between two

showcases and approached the cash register. He sat on a stool, crossed his arms, and relaxed.

"You look like city folk," he said. "Where you headed?"

Annie laughed. "And what do city folk look like?"

The clerk shrugged. "Well ... like you."

"Yes, I'm city folk," she said.

"From?"

"Richmond Hill. Not far from Toronto."

"Nice place ... Toronto."

"I guess so." Annie snapped open her wallet. "How much do I owe you?"

"You want ice?"

"Oh." Annie glanced over at the case, stacked high with bags of ice behind a frosted-over glass door. "Two would be fine."

The clerk slipped off his stool and rang up the purchase. "By the way, my name's Bob. Bob Fletcher." He held out a smooth palm.

Annie shook his hand. "I'm Annie." She paid for the soda and thanked him.

"So where you headed?" Bob asked.

"Wendigo Lake."

"Been a lot of folks headed there lately."

"My husband is there," Annie said as she tucked a bottle under each arm and struggled to carry the other one.

"Here, let me help you with that," Bob offered. "You still got ice to get yet."

Annie relinquished the third bottle to Bob, who came out from behind the counter, grabbed two bags of ice from the freezer, and followed her outside.

He stood watching her as she flipped up the trunk lid, dumped the ice in the empty cooler, and placed the soda on top.

She shut the trunk, stepped back, and looked up at Bob, still watching her. He rubbed at the thin array of bristling hairs on his chin and squinted at her.

"Is your husband a big guy? Like tall, and tons of muscles?"

She nodded.

"His name Jake?"

Annie raised a brow. "Yes," she said. "How do you know that?"

Bob folded his arms and grinned. "Him and them boys was in here yesterday. Said they was campin' at Wendigo Lake."

Annie moved to the driver-side door of the car, unlocked it, and climbed in.

Bob leaned over and looked through the open door. "Tell Jake I said hi."

Annie forced a lackluster smile. "I will. Nice to meet you," she said as she closed the door. She backed out and drove away, amused at Bob's small-town friendliness.

The entry point to the park was five minutes away. She pulled into the lot, went inside the building for a few minutes to refresh herself, paid the fee for a two-day pass, and then proceeded through the North Gate.

The traveling was easy going for several miles but soon turned into a much narrower trail as the rough terrain became almost unmanageable. Her Ford Escort cruised smoothly on the highways, but it wasn't designed for driving over the rough terrain of some of the deeper trails found throughout Algonquin Provincial Park.

She didn't remember the track being so littered with potholes and protruding limestone rocks the last time they were up here. Occasionally, she had to slow down to a bare crawl. She would make a point of strongly suggesting Jake find a more accessible spot next time.

She breathed a sigh of relief when the RAV4 finally became visible through the trees. She pulled up between a pair of towering pines, shut off the engine, and peered through the woods to the lake beyond. It was a breathtaking sight, a sight she'd missed. She looked forward to taking a dip in its cool waters before long.

She half-expected the boys to come running when she first pulled up. They didn't, and she laughed at her expectation. Why would they hang around the camp when they had a whole forest around them, just waiting to be explored?

They were bound to be surprised when they saw her here—and pleased, or at least, Jake would be. She got out of the car, opened the trunk, and carried over the items she'd brought, packing them in the tent.

She went to the fire pit, leaned down, and poked at the coals with the same sturdy branch Jake had used as a makeshift poker. The fire was out but some glowing embers remained at the bottom of the pit. Wherever the guys were, they hadn't been gone long.

She looked at her watch. It might be awhile before their hunger called them back to camp. Perhaps she would take a quick swim and get back before they return.

She dug her swimsuit from the bag and changed in the

tent, and then wrapped a towel around her shoulders and picked her way down the incline to the lake.

The warm sun felt good on her back as she stood and gazed out over the water. The idyllic scene took her breath away. Unruffled by wind or rain, the waters were still and restful.

A small woodland creature, a rabbit, drank at the edge of the lake a hundred feet away. Annie watched it raise its ears, sensing danger, then dash into the forest.

She had missed this place and was glad she had come. Maybe—just maybe—she would forget about asking Jake to find a different spot. This place was heavenly.

She dropped her towel and removed her watch, leaving them in a heap on the beach. She moved closer to the lake, tested the water with a toe, and then waded out fifty feet where it was deep enough to swim. Several minutes later she reluctantly stepped from the water and wrapped the towel over her shoulders. She would have time to come back later, maybe with the boys, but she wanted to get back to camp before the guys arrived.

CHAPTER 30

Saturday, 11:30 a.m.

JAKE AND THE BOYS had hiked through the forest much of the morning, exploring the area west of their camp, watching the wildlife at play and at work. The boys grew weary, their steps dragging, and they decided to return and rest up awhile.

Jake stopped, consulted the compass, changed direction slightly, and continued on. The camp was close by and they were exhausted, ready to cool off with a dip in the lake before lunch.

He stopped short and stared as the tail end of a blue car came into view. Someone was parked at their campsite. The boys ran behind as he strode closer. A grin split his face. It was Annie's car.

"Your mother is here, Matty," he announced.

"Mom? What's she doing here?"

"Let's find out."

Annie sat under a wide tree near the tent, leaning against the rough bark, reading a paperback.

"Mom," Matty called, surging ahead.

Annie set the book in her lap and looked up as Matty knelt

beside her and hugged her neck. "What're you doing here?" he asked.

"I missed you guys," she said. "So here I am."

Jake stopped and looked down at his wife. "Hi, honey," was all he said, but his huge grin revealed his pleasure at seeing her. He held out a hand and helped her to her feet.

Matty rolled his eyes at Kyle as Jake gave his wife a prolonged kiss.

"I brought you guys some food," Annie said.

Matty turned back to face his mother. "Food. I'm about ready for that if you guys are done saying hello."

Jake chuckled. "We're done. Let's eat."

Annie went to the tent and returned a moment later, lugging a cooler. She popped it open and revealed the meal she'd prepared. Jake liked fish and potatoes, but he was ready for something different.

"Mom, do we have five minutes to go swimming?"

"Yes, but no more. Lunch will be ready right away."

The boys changed quickly and then disappeared down the slope.

The casserole was still warm to the touch, and a few minutes on what was left of the embers brought it up to serving temperature.

Matty and Kyle had returned, wrapped in large beach towels, and plopped down on a hollow log near the fire pit.

"So what changed your mind about coming here?" Jake asked when they had sat down to eat.

"I got bored," she said. "Things were nice and peaceful at home, but too quiet."

Jake nodded as if he understood. "Well, I'm glad you came," he said, then added, "There's a problem with the SUV. The drive belt has snapped."

"Does that mean it won't run without it?"

"Not for long. I was hoping somebody would come along."

"It was rough getting in here with the car," Annie said. "But here I am."

"Yes, here you are, but it's all right now. The game warden came by awhile ago. He said he'll stop by and give me a lift into town on his way back."

~*~

VARICK LUCAS was more careful this time. As he crept towards the big guy's campsite he carefully avoided twigs and fallen branches, attempting to stay on the packed soil or mossy areas.

As he drew closer, he heard their murmured conversation and he trod more carefully. He had no desire to be seen. He stopped behind a bush, knelt down on one knee, and gazed through the branches toward the interlopers.

The woman he'd seen swimming a few minutes earlier sat with the guys now, eating and talking. He couldn't make out what they said and he dared not venture any closer. It was vital to his plans that he not be seen.

He'd admired her smooth, lithe body as she stood on the beach. Through the modest swimsuit she wore, he could imagine what was underneath. With her midlength golden hair, and her perfect poise, she looked a vision. But good, and somehow wholesome—not like the women he'd known, and certainly not anyone he cared to harm.

He had watched her take to the water and swim gracefully awhile before returning to the beach. He saw her gather up her towel and climb the hill toward the campsite, and then disappear from his view. That was when he'd turned away and left before he did something stupid.

He realized she must be the big guy's wife and those were their kids. They seemed like a family—a happy family—not like he'd known. He wondered why she'd come here now. Perhaps she had to work earlier, but what bothered him most was the invasion of more and more people into his territory.

He regretted cutting the vehicle's drive belt, but then, he had a lot of regrets in his life. This was just one more. He wasn't sure if he wanted to get rid of them or keep them here and kill them. The big guy anyway, not the kids or the woman. Or maybe he would just play with them awhile longer.

And then kill them.

Or not.

He pulled his head a little further back behind the thick bush as the woman stood and walked toward him. He held his breath, shifted his weight, and prepared to run. He relaxed and breathed freely again when she stopped, flipped open a cooler, removed a jug of soda, then returned and sat down again.

She certainly was beautiful—like the young girl he'd seen bathing in the stream, but a little older, more mature, more like how his mother had looked before she took sick and died.

Sometimes he wished he could have it all over again—a new life, new friends, a new everything. Lucas squeezed his eyes shut and wished away the haunting thoughts of his mother, the anger he felt for his father, and the way life had treated him. He didn't want to erupt again—at least not right now.

Watching them eat, enjoying a home-cooked meal, made him hungry. There wasn't much of anything in the cabin, but he would go back, see what he could scrounge, and then after he ate—who knows. He'd had an interesting morning and the day was young.

He turned, crept away quietly, and headed toward his cabin, devising a plan of how best to handle the situation.

CHAPTER 31

JAKE AND ANNIE followed as Matty and Kyle led the way through the trees. The boys had recovered from their morning jaunt and were eager to explore more of nature.

The fresh air was filled with the scent of pine, soil, and nearby streams. A lizard dashed up a tree, his feet scratching as he clamored up the rough bark, barely heard over the sounds of crackling footsteps on the rustling leaves.

Kyle kicked at the forest floor, leaving a flurry of leaves in his wake, while Matty chased a squirrel through the bushes and returned panting and empty-handed.

Jake was content to follow behind, enjoying the beauty of nature, the sounds of forest life, and the simple pleasure of being with his family.

Over to his right, a clump of bushes rustled as a rabbit dashed out and away, gone to safer territory. Jake stared, stopped short, leaned in, and squinted. He took a step closer to the bush and crouched down.

His mouth dropped open in disbelief.

The face of a man could be partially seen, one eye visible, the rest of his body covered with soil and rotting leaves. It was unmistakably a man—and he appeared to be dead. Freshly dead.

Jake glanced up. The boys had continued on but Annie had stopped. She was turned around, watching him and waiting for him to catch up.

"Are you coming?" she asked.

Jake stood, took a step or two, and beckoned her over.

She came toward him and her eyes narrowed when she saw his face. "What is it?" she asked. "What's wrong? You look like you've seen a ghost."

"It's a body," he whispered, nodding his head toward the bush. "In there."

"A body?"

"Of a man."

Annie inhaled sharply and held her breath, staring at Jake through bulging eyes. She finally exhaled and managed to say, "A man?"

Jake nodded and looked toward the boys. They'd stopped several yards ahead, waiting for the stragglers to catch up, taking the time to roll around in some maple leaves that had blown into a natural pile.

Annie looked around as if expecting danger to be lurking close by and moved instinctively closer to Jake. She seemed unable to speak and stood open-mouthed, staring toward the bush.

"Take the boys and go back to camp," Jake said. "I'll be along shortly."

"What're you going to do?"

"See if I can find out who it is."

Annie took another glance toward the body. "We can't leave him here."

"We have no choice. I can't carry him back that far and I don't want the boys to see."

Annie observed him a moment, as if considering it. Finally, she nodded and whispered, "Okay." She hurried toward the boys. "We have to go back now," she said.

"Aw, Mom, can't we stay a bit longer? We just left."

"I know. We can come out again later, but right now we have to go back."

"Why?" Kyle asked.

Annie hesitated. "We just do, that's all. Mr. Lincoln will be back later." She herded them back the way they'd come.

The boys reluctantly followed her. Jake stood between them and the bush, preventing them from catching a glimpse of the body.

Matty walked past and looked at his father, a curious look on his face.

"I'll be there soon," Jake said to Annie. "Go in the tent and stay there."

"Is something wrong?" Matty asked.

"I'll fill you in later, Matty. Please go with your mom and don't complain."

Matty shrugged and continued on, Kyle trudging behind his friend.

He watched them until they were out of sight, then returned to the body and pulled the bush aside. Scavenging bugs and insects had begun to gather. He swept away the dirt, revealing the rest of the man's face. It was unfamiliar.

He brushed at the leaves and soil until the body was clear of debris, and then rolled it into the open.

The body of the middle-aged man wore a pair of dress pants, a button-down shirt, and sturdy shoes. His dark hair was cut short and matted from the damp soil.

The front of his shirt was soaked with blood, now dried and turning a reddish-brown hue. He appeared to have been shot, or possibly stabbed. Jake didn't bother checking. He would leave further investigation to the proper authorities.

Being careful not to disturb anything, he felt in the man's pockets. They were empty. No wallet, no cash, no keys. He checked around his neck and wrist. No jewelry, no watch.

Jake was no expert, and he knew he should leave everything to the real experts, but he calculated the man had likely been dead for less than a couple of hours. The joints of the man's arms and legs were still easily manipulated. Rigor mortis had not yet begun to set in.

He explored the forest floor around him and then moved around behind the bush and crouched down. He lifted his gaze, his eyes following a vague trail of disturbed leaves, as if something had been dragged through there.

He followed the indistinct tracks a hundred feet and came upon what appeared to be a seldom-used trail. Not a footpath, but wide enough for a vehicle to pass. The tracks ended abruptly at the trail.

He examined the ground for tire marks and footprints. Neither were visible, not unexpected considering the terrain. He examined the trail for fifty feet in either direction and still no evidence of the method of transport could be found.

It was possible the body was carried here from somewhere else, and then dumped and dragged. It would have to be a strong person if that were the case. The body of the victim looked to weigh close to two hundred pounds, maybe a bit less.

He returned to the body and stood awhile, contemplating what he knew, and what he didn't know.

He concluded someone had driven or carried a body here, dragged it to the bushes, burying it with soil and leaves in an attempt to hide it. The type of vehicle—and it seemed inconclusive whether there was one—was unknown. The killer or killers were also unknown.

In truth, he didn't know much.

He recalled the cabin the boys had found. He was uncertain where it was, but knew it was somewhere this side of camp, perhaps a mile or so further on.

The boys were sure someone lived there, and if so, it was possible the person who lived in the cabin was the victim—or the killer.

He considered heading in the direction of the cabin in an attempt to find out what this was all about but soon changed his mind. His first priority was to ensure the safety of his family, and the second was to notify the authorities. There was nothing else he could find out here. He had to get back.

He rolled the body out of sight behind the bushes and set off toward camp.

CHAPTER 32

Saturday, 3:11 p.m.

HOLLY CHURCHILL wasn't getting the enjoyment she'd expected from this backpacking experience. She had hoped her companions would want to explore the area further, enjoying the wilderness. Instead, their only desire was to camp in this one spot, drink booze, and hang around.

She had enjoyed her little excursion yesterday afternoon. The stream she'd visited was beautiful, and she'd felt refreshed and clean after her improvised bath. Maybe she would take another solo trip this afternoon and get away from her fellow hikers.

She slipped off her shoes, hung her legs over the edge of the limestone rock, and dangled her feet in the cool lake water. She didn't need the others around for her to enjoy the afternoon. Their purpose was only for security. She knew it wasn't practical or safe to hike long distances alone, especially in an uncharted area. Next time she would find someone more suitable to explore with.

She turned her head when, from the corner of her eye, she caught a glimpse of someone coming along the beach. He wore a tan-colored uniform, a beltload of equipment at his waist.

He approached her and stopped, a friendly smile on his face. "Good afternoon. Heard you folks were here."

She looked at the badge on his chest and beamed at the handsome ranger. "Good afternoon, Officer."

He pushed his sunglasses up on his nose and held out his hand. "I'm Andy."

Holly shook his hand, her smile growing wider. "Holly. Nice to meet you."

Andy waved vaguely across the lake. "I was over at another camp and they mentioned you were here. Thought I would drop by, see if all's okay with you folks."

"Everything is fine here."

"Staying long?"

"Just for the weekend. We plan to go home tomorrow afternoon. I have to work on Monday."

"I hope you're having a good time," he said. "You're a long ways in. Folks don't often get in this far, especially with no vehicle access to this area. I had to stop back a ways and walk in here myself." He glanced up the beach toward the trees and the pair of tents nearby. "You with them folks up there?"

Holly laughed. "I came with them but I spend most of the time by myself." She glanced toward her companions. She didn't see Rosie, but the two boys leaned against a tree, looking her way. "They're not very good company."

Andy pursed his lips and bobbed his head up and down several times. "I hear you. It ain't everybody likes the same thing. Guess we all have our own way to camp."

"They have theirs and I have mine," Holly said with a smile.

Andy's eyes scanned the beach. "Been making a bit of a mess here, I see." He pointed toward some debris that had blown up against a tree. Three or four bottles lay in a heap nearby. "I'd hate to have to hit you with a fine." He looked at Holly, his eyes narrowed. "Be sure and clean that mess up afore you go."

"We will."

"I best go and chat with the rest of 'em," he said as he turned his back and started up the beach.

Holly slipped her shoes on and followed him.

Rosie lay on a soft bed of pine needles and fallen leaves, propped up on one elbow. She sat upright and watched them as they approached.

Holly looked around but the two boys were no longer there.

Andy had stopped short, staring at the fire pit at the edge of the tree line. He crossed his arms, glared at Rosie, and pointed toward the pit.

"That's not safe," he said, his once friendly voice now taking on a gruffer tone. "Yer too close to the trees and you could start a fire." He moved over and kicked at the burned out coals. "Next time you light that on the beach where it's safe, or not at all. You tryin' to burn this whole forest down?"

Rosie ignored his question and stared at him blankly. "It wasn't me that lit it."

"Then see to it you get the message across." He turned toward the beach. "And clean this mess up afore you go. I won't have you coming in here and messing up my forest."

"Yes, sir," Rosie said in an insolent tone.

Andy gave her a black look. "You oughta learn not to be so disrespectful. Not just to me, but to everything around you," he said, with a sweeping motion toward the forest.

Rosie turned her head away and said nothing.

Holly touched the officer's arm. "I'll be sure the message gets across."

Andy looked at her as if deciding whether or not to believe her. His tone softened. "I might check back again later." He turned his head, pressed his lips together in a thin line, and squinted toward the trees. "Where're the other two at? I understand there was four of you here."

Rosie spoke up, her voice impatient. "They just went for a walk."

Andy shook his head at Rosie, frowned, and glared a moment. Then he turned to Holly and motioned across the lake. "I was at the Lincoln camp already. Is there anybody else 'round here you might've seen?"

"I haven't seen anyone else except Mr. Lincoln and the two boys with him."

"All right, then. Guess I best be moving on."

He turned abruptly and headed back the direction he'd come. He stopped after a few steps and turned around. "I'll be back." Then he strode down the beach and out of sight behind the trees.

Rosie stood, placed her hands on her hips, and scowled down the beach. "I don't like him."

"He's just watching out for the forest. That's his job." Holly laughed. "You have to admit, this place is a mess."

Rosie stuck her nose in the air. "Well, I still don't like

him." She dropped back down to her resting place and lay on her back, her hands behind her head, and closed her eyes.

Holly looked curiously at Rosie, a girl with a stubborn, rebellious nature. Holly thought the warden was fine. It was Rosie that Holly didn't like all that much.

She sighed, went to her tent, found a garbage bag, and set about cleaning up the site. None of this was her mess, but she didn't care. She would clean it up anyway. She didn't bother asking Rosie to help, already suspecting what the answer would be.

CHAPTER 33

Saturday, 3:18 p.m.

ANNIE WAITED ANXIOUSLY for Jake to return. They were in the middle of the wilderness, miles from anywhere, and there might be a killer lurking nearby.

The boys had pelted her with questions, wondering why their excursion was cut short in such an abrupt manner, and she didn't know how to answer.

She watched them, finally settled down and sitting quietly on the floor of the tent, working on a jigsaw puzzle she'd packed for a rainy day. They would be finished soon, bored, and eager to be active again.

She lifted her head and listened intently to a rustling sound outside the tent, then breathed in relief when she heard Jake's voice. "It's just me."

She warned the boys to stay put with a meaningful look and an upraised finger. They went back to the puzzle and she crawled from the tent.

She stood as Jake approached, a worried look on his face. "Everything okay here?" he asked.

She nodded. "The boys are in the tent." She scrutinized his face for a sign. "Did you find out anything?"

He moved away from the tent and she followed. They sat on a log by the fire pit and turned sideways, facing each other.

"There was no ID on the body," Jake said. "Nothing at all in his pockets, and he was nobody I've ever seen before."

"What was the manner of death?"

"I don't know for sure. There was blood all over his shirt. Probably a gunshot wound or maybe a knife. I didn't want to disturb any evidence."

She turned and stared into the cold fire pit, unfocused and frowning. Her detective skills usually kicked in and came up with a plan of action, but this time, all they had was the dead body of an unknown man, and not a clue in the world how to proceed. Besides, the boys were here and she couldn't bear to subject them to danger.

Jake spoke again. "The body hasn't been there long, maybe a couple of hours or so. It appears he was dragged there, possibly carried a distance first, and then dragged the rest of the way." He paused and held out his hands, palms up. "That's all I have."

She studied her husband's face. "We need to get out of here. Leave the SUV and take my car."

Jake nodded. "That seems to be our best plan of action— our only plan of action. We can notify the authorities at the gate and the police can take care of it. We'll get the SUV later, when it's safe."

Annie took a quick look around. "We'll leave everything else here as well—the tent, everything. There's nothing we need to take with us."

"Almost everything else is locked in the SUV anyway,"

Jake added. "And there's nothing much of value to worry about."

"I'll get the boys in the car," Annie said as she jumped to her feet. "You can get it started."

"I need the keys."

"They're in my bag. I'll get them."

She ran to the tent, found her handbag, and fumbled for the keys. She popped her head through the flap of the tent and tossed them to Jake. He caught them with a one-handed swoop and strode toward the Escort.

She pulled back into the tent and spun around. "We're leaving. Matty, Kyle, we have to go."

Matty looked at her in disbelief and disappointment. "I thought we were staying until tomorrow. Why do we have to go home now?"

"Change of plans, hurry. I'll explain everything to you later, but right now we have to move," she said. The boys reluctantly obeyed, crawled from the tent, and shuffled toward the car. Annie came behind, prodding them along.

Jake stepped out from behind the steering wheel and gave Annie a bewildered look. "It won't start," he whispered as she drew closer.

She cocked her head and frowned. "It ran fine when I got here." She turned and hustled the boys into the back seat and spun back. "I know it's not out of gas."

"No, it's not the gas. The starter turns but it won't spark." He had already popped the latch for the hood and he went to the front of the car, lifted the hood, and fastened it into place.

Annie looked around uneasily before following Jake to the

front of the vehicle. He had his head under the hood, poking around beside the engine. "Any idea what the problem is?" she asked.

He straightened his back, a grim look on his face. "I sure do. The spark plug wires are missing."

"Missing? How? Who?" Annie was at a loss for words.

Jake frowned at the engine. "How'd he get the hood—?" He stopped abruptly and turned his gaze toward Annie. "Did you leave the car unlocked?"

Annie's mouth dropped open. Finally, she said, "I didn't bother to lock it. Out here in the wilderness … I didn't expect—"

Jake interrupted, "You could never have anticipated that."

Annie glanced at the engine. "So, we're stuck here, then." She blamed herself. She should have locked up the car, but then, a determined person could find any number of ways to disable the vehicle.

Jake was deep in thought, his arms folded, his brow wrinkled.

"What about the SUV? Will the wires from it fit on here?" Annie asked, hopefully.

Jake's jaw tightened and he shook his head slowly. "They're totally different. They won't fit."

"What about the belt thingy that's broken?" She pointed to the front of the engine. "Will this one fit the SUV?"

Jake shook his head again. "Nope. Different length. Even if it would, I have no tools."

Annie was out of ideas. She looked uneasily at Jake. "Someone doesn't want us to leave here."

Jake was staring at the SUV. "I wonder ..."

"Wonder what?"

He didn't answer. He strode over to the RAV4, unlocked it, and opened the back door. He reached in, removed a belt from the floor and held it up, turning it over and over, examining the ends. He walked slowly toward Annie, still holding the belt, inspecting it closely.

"It looks frayed," he said, holding the ends out for her to see. "But even when I first saw it, I was curious about how it'd snapped in one spot and wasn't worn anywhere else." He stopped and looked intently at her. "It might've been hacked off, and didn't wear out at all."

Annie was struck with a sudden realization of what that meant. She spoke slowly, thoughtfully. "So if that's the case, even yesterday before I came, someone had plans to keep you here."

Jake raised his head and looked vaguely across the campsite. "That might be exactly what it means."

Annie turned and followed his gaze, her eyes scanning the miles of wilderness surrounding them. Now she knew for sure, someone dangerous was around, maybe close by, and whatever his plans were, it made her very afraid.

She looked at her husband. He stood unmoving, his eyes far away, his mind deep in thought.

She prayed he would have a solution. Otherwise, they had no means of protection, no way of escape, and nowhere to hide.

CHAPTER 34

Saturday, 3:35 p.m.

JAKE PULLED UP the stakes and the tent collapsed with a whoosh. He forced out most of the air and rolled up the canvas while Annie rounded up a few basic necessities and hustled the boys from the car. They were the focus of a direct, subtle attack by someone deranged and, if the body in the woods was any indication, highly dangerous.

He knew of a small clearing a short distance away where there was a dip in the terrain, like a small natural valley, the area surrounded by bush and dense forest. They should be able to pitch the tent there and avoid discovery by any intruder until Andy Fletcher came back.

He carried the tent under his arm, the boys following, with Annie close behind carrying a cooler of food.

In a few minutes, they arrived at their destination, where Jake dropped his burden on the ground and unrolled the canvas, and he and Annie began assembling the tent.

Matty came over, a frown in his face, and watched them curiously a moment before saying, "Dad, I know we're in some kind of danger because you and Mom are acting funny."

Jake looked up at his son and struggled to form a response. Finally, he said, "Son, there seems to be somebody around here who's hurting people and I don't want the three of you in any danger. We're being careful, just in case, until the game warden comes back and can take us out of here."

"Is that why we had to stop hiking? Did you see somebody when we were in the forest?"

Jake wasn't sure how to answer that. He'd seen somebody all right—somebody dead, but the last thing he wanted to do was frighten the boys. "I didn't see anyone who could hurt us," he said.

"Then what's the hurry?"

"We're just being cautious, Matty. Just trust your mother and me."

Matty had no more objections. He stood still a moment and watched his parents continue with their task before wandering away and sitting on a log beside Kyle.

When the tent was up, Jake said, "I'll go and watch for the game warden. He should be back soon."

"I'll keep the boys in the tent," Annie said.

Their new camp was a short distance from the narrow road the warden would have to travel when he came by. Jake made his way through the thick undergrowth to the trail, sat on the bank, and waited.

It was more than an hour before Jake heard the unmistakable sound of Andy Fletcher's pickup some distance away. He climbed down the embankment and waited. The vehicle came into sight and stopped, and Andy poked his head out the window.

"I just dropped by your camp," the warden said as Jake approached. "I didn't see anybody there."

"We had to leave camp," Jake said and told him about the body in the woods.

Andy listened intently to the story. "Yer going to have to show me where that is."

Jake pointed down the trail behind the vehicle. "It's back there, and then off the path a quarter mile or so."

"Jump in," the warden said. "We'll take a look."

Jake got in the passenger-side door and the warden turned in his seat to face him. "Where're the kids?"

"My wife came awhile ago," Jake explained and pointed with a thumb over his shoulder. "She's with the boys in a safe place."

Andy pulled the gear shifter into low and the vehicle sprung ahead. "I saw a car at your camp. Is that your wife's car?"

"Yes, and now it won't start. Somebody has sabotaged it."

"Sabotaged?"

"The spark plug wires were taken," Jake said. "It seems like someone doesn't want us to leave here."

"Very strange indeed." Andy frowned and pursed his lips, glaring through the windshield. "How far to this body?"

Jake pointed ahead. "Stop up there by that rock."

Andy drove another fifty feet and stopped the vehicle, and they climbed out. He followed Jake into the undergrowth and in a few minutes, Jake stopped and pointed ahead of them. "Right behind that bush."

Andy moved forward curiously and stepped behind the

wild evergreen shrub. When he saw the body, he let out a low whistle. "Gosh, that's a body all right." He leaned over, wrinkled his face, and examined it closer. "And not dead that long, I guess."

"Do you know who it is?" Jake asked.

Andy straightened and glanced around uneasily. "Afraid I don't. Might be one of those city folk." He looked at Jake. "No offense."

"None taken, but whether or not he's from the city doesn't tell us who killed him."

"Course not. Just makin' an observation is all." He looked closely at Jake. "Have you seen anyone around asides yourselves?"

"Just the teenagers at the other end of the lake."

Andy thought a moment. "I dropped by their camp earlier. Doesn't seem like their work. They're a bit messy and rowdy but not the type to be killin' a man."

"There's no ID on the body," Jake said. "I checked already."

Andy crouched down, lifted the bloodstained shirt, and squinted at the wound. "Appears to be a knife done this," he said. "Looks like maybe a huntin' knife to me." He tugged the shirt back into place and dug around in the pockets.

"I already looked in his pockets."

"Just checkin' is all," Andy replied. "There's nothin' there, but you never know, you mighta missed something." He stood, scratched his head, and looked at Jake. "I think we best get the law in on this. Let them handle it. Not really my specialty. I can track an animal but this is a whole different can of worms. Wouldn't know where to start."

"The boys saw a cabin a mile or so from our campsite," Jake said. "They said it looks like somebody is staying there. Maybe it was him?"

The warden chuckled. "Nah, that's Otis. Harmless guy. Been there for a couple years already. Gave him a visit a time or two in the past. It weren't him, I can tell you that much."

"The police'll want to check him out anyway," Jake said.

"Yeah, maybe." Andy glanced down at the body. "Ain't nothing we can do fer this fellow. We best leave him right here where he lies and be going."

Jake followed Andy to his pickup and they climbed in. The warden backed up a few yards, made a cramped three-point turn, and the vehicle bumped ahead.

The warden peered through the windshield, working the vehicle over the rough terrain. "Been thinking," he said as he hugged the steering wheel. "That guy back there—the dead guy—he musta seen something he shouldn't have fer him to get killed like that. Whoever did the killin' didn't harm you folks or them kids at the lake."

"Don't forget," Jake said. "He sabotaged our vehicles."

Andy's head bobbed up and down. "Yeah, that's so. That's so." He looked at Jake and shrugged. "If it were the same guy. Maybe not."

"It's too much of a coincidence. I'm sure it all ties together in one way or another."

Andy's head bobbed some more. "Guess you're right." He touched the brakes and the vehicle stopped. "You best see 'bout your family."

Jake jumped out, eager to get Annie and the boys to safety. "We'll be right back," he called as he crossed the trail behind the vehicle and sprung up the grade.

The engine roared behind him. Jake stopped short and spun around. The pickup had sprinted ahead and gathered speed.

Jake charged down the grade and raced after the vehicle. His shouts went unnoticed as the pickup continued on, Jake losing ground, no chance to catch up. He stopped and watched as the vehicle disappeared from sight.

Andy had left them behind. The half-baked warden was so eager to bring the police, he'd ignored their safety.

CHAPTER 35

Saturday, 4:59 p.m.

VARICK LUCAS wasn't surprised the Lincolns had left their camp. They were now a part of his little game and he had them on the run.

He prowled around their vacated site, enjoyed the ice-cold soda left behind in the cooler, and stood staring at the abandoned vehicles. He had no use for either one of them. Eventually he would leave this place, commandeer a car, and find a more comfortable spot to hang out. He was having the time of his life right now, but was getting tired of this god-forsaken wilderness.

Later, he might go and visit those kids camped at the end of the lake, but right now, he wanted to find the Lincolns. He liked to keep tabs on everything—keep control of the situation.

The tent was gone, so it seemed obvious they had plans to set it up again—somewhere they assumed was safe. Not far away. What they didn't know was, nowhere would be safe. He was going to make sure of that.

It took him but a few minutes to stumble on their hideout, tucked down in a little valley, safe from all prying eyes. All but his.

He lay down on his stomach behind a bush, rested on his elbows, and observed the camp. The tent was set up like he presumed it would be. The kids weren't around; perhaps they were in the tent, but the two adults were clearly visible, their back to him as they sat on the grass, chatting away as if nothing had happened.

The woman looked almost as good fully clothed as she did in her swimming suit. Almost. He saw her profile as she turned to talk to her husband and again he was reminded of his mother. He brushed the thought aside and backed from his hiding place, still considering whether or not to kill the guy.

Maybe later. There was lots of time.

~*~

ANNIE STOOD AND looked around the new campsite. "We should be fine here until the police come. I heard Andy's truck when he came by before, so we should be able to hear the police when they come."

Jake looked up. "I'm rather concerned about the teenagers camped at the end of the lake."

"Maybe you should drop over there and warn them," Annie suggested.

"And leave you here alone? Not a chance."

"And why not? They have mothers too, and I think it would be irresponsible of us not to do what we can."

Jake seemed to consider that. Finally, he said, "I guess you're right."

"Of course I'm right. It'll be awhile before the police come, and who knows what could happen by then?"

"You're sure you'll be okay while I'm gone?"

"We'll be fine."

"Don't start a fire."

Annie gave him a disgusted look. "I know better than that."

"Yeah. Course you do," Jake said with a crooked grin. He turned and went across the clearing, calling back before he disappeared from sight, "I won't be long."

Jake made his way through the trees and exited the forest, landing on the beach two hundred feet short of their old camp. He moved up the grade toward the site carefully. Someone had been there since they'd left. Things were disturbed. The cooler was tipped over. Perhaps it had only been a bear, looking for treats, but he wasn't convinced of that and wasn't taking any chances.

He went back down to the lake and strode along the beach. The pair of tents at the backpackers' camp stood in the same place as before. As he drew closer, he made out four figures sitting near the tents. Holly and Rosie huddled across from each other, the two guys a little further away, leaning against a tree. One of the boys sported an unkempt mass of red hair, which, along with the color-coordinated patch of sparse whiskers on his chin, made him look comical. The other one held his long hair in place with a baseball cap pulled low, and sat with his arms crossed and eyes closed.

Rosie smiled and pointed Jake's way, and Holly turned and waved, a welcoming look on her face.

"What brings you here?" Rosie said as Jake approached them.

"Just wanted to check on you," he said and nodded at the guys. They looked at him curiously and disregarded his greeting.

"You're always welcome here, Jake," Rosie said and jerked a thumb toward the male companions. "You're better looking than them lumps of coal."

Holly gave Rosie a look of disapproval and Jake smiled politely. "I'm not really here on a social visit," he said as he crouched down. "I came to warn you there might be someone dangerous lurking about."

The guy wearing the cap opened his eyes, leaned in, and listened as Jake continued, "We found the body of a man some ways from our camp."

Holly's mouth dropped open. Rosie's eyes widened. Both boys gave their full attention as Jake continued, "It looks like he was murdered."

"Murdered?" Red Hair asked.

Jake nodded grimly. "Yes, and recently."

The boy stood and came closer. "How do you know he was murdered?"

"I'm the one who found the body. He appeared to have been killed by a knife."

The other boy wandered over and pushed his baseball cap back on his head. "So what makes you think we might be in danger?"

Jake stood and looked curiously at the boy. "Is it worth it to take a chance?"

"Dunno."

"Why didn't you go for the cops?" the boy with the cap asked.

"Our vehicle has been sabotaged. It won't start. The game warden has gone for the police, but in the meantime, I think you should find another place to camp or get out of here entirely."

Rosie and Holly stood and the four of them huddled around Jake. "I think we should leave," Holly said.

Red Hair frowned. "I don't think there's anything much to what this guy says. Why would he want to do anything to us? We didn't hurt anyone."

Rosie gave him a slug on the shoulder. "Didn't you hear what Jake said? A man has been murdered."

"You guys can do whatever you want. I'm staying." He waved it off, turned, and went back to his spot by the tree. The other boy followed and sank down beside him.

Jake sighed, frowned at them, and shook his head. He turned to Holly. "You can do whatever you want. I'm just warning you."

Rosie smiled. "Thanks. We'll try to talk some sense into those guys. I don't want to go anywhere without them. They might be useless, but there's safety in numbers and I say we all stick together."

Holly glanced at the boys, and then at Rosie. "You might be right. I prefer to leave, but I'm not going alone."

Jake had done what he could. The rest was up to them and he hoped they would make a sensible decision. "I have to get back to my family and wait for the police," he said. "Just be careful." He turned to go.

"Thank you, Jake," Rosie called. "Come back and stay the night some time. You can sleep in my tent."

As Jake walked away, he could tell by the tone of Holly's voice she wasn't too pleased with Rosie's comments. Under different circumstances, he would've enjoyed a good laugh.

CHAPTER 36

Saturday, 5:15 p.m.

RCMP SERGEANT LANCE BREWER was sick and tired of getting the runaround. He'd sent a pair of detectives to give Lucas's cellmate a little visit and they'd turned up empty. Stephan Padre was tightlipped and stubborn.

He realized, if they were going to get anything useful from Padre, he would have to do it himself.

He'd spent most of the afternoon making the long trip back to Haddleburg, and as he pulled into the maximum-security penitentiary three miles dead west of town, he was determined not to leave until he had some information that would nail Lucas.

He pulled through the inner security gate of the ten-acre walled enclosure, flashed his ID for the second time, and was let into the main staff area. His eyes roved over the modern facility, recently built to take the place of an outdated establishment that stood empty a hundred miles away.

The notoriety of this new institution's predecessor had grown over the years, fueled by many prisoners' accounts of daily beatings at the hands of wardens, brutal riots, and extended periods in "the box." In contrast, this prison was the epitome of modern punishment and humane rehabilitation.

They were expecting him, and when he strode into the administrative office of the state-of-the-art facility, the deputy warden had already been apprised of his arrival and welcomed him with an offered handshake, introduced himself, and said, "Welcome, Sergeant. As you know, I've interviewed Padre extensively, as have your two detectives, and we can get nothing from him."

Brewer shook his hand, disregarded the youthful and green deputy warden's statement, and got right to it. "I need to see Padre immediately."

The younger man hesitated. "Don't you want to talk in my office first? I can show you what we have."

"You just told me you have nothing, and I'm not here to chat with you. I'm here to talk with Padre and I don't have time to waste."

The deputy cocked his head, taken aback by Brewer's abruptness. He shrugged one shoulder and said, "Very well, then. He's ready for you."

"Lead the way."

Brewer followed the deputy warden through a series of secure gates and they stopped in front of a metal door. "Here we are. Padre is already inside."

Cell doors clanked around him. A large tempered-glass window was the only barrier between him and the common room. Inmates milled about on the other side of the glass, well within his view. And they had a clear view of him.

Brewer scowled. This was not what he'd expected. He

opened the door and stepped inside, followed by the deputy warden.

The interview room was modern, clean, and roomy, but bare, and not much different from an inmate's cell. There was a table in the middle of the room, bolted to the floor. Padre sat on the other side of it, on a stainless steel bench, also bolted to the floor. He was handcuffed and securely chained to a ring in the table. Two comfortable chairs, presumably for the investigators, were on the near side.

A camera hung in one corner of the room, facing Padre. Its red light glowed, always ready to capture any important comments from whoever was unfortunate enough to sit on the hard bench. Brewer gave it a cursory glance.

Padre glared at the sergeant, hostile and unmoving.

This was far from the ideal surrounding Brewer wanted in order to conduct a successful interview. He turned to the deputy warden. "This won't do."

"This is all we have. This is where we conduct all our interviews."

"Then I'll use your office."

The young man stared at Brewer as if the sergeant had lost his mind. "My office? That's ridiculous."

Brewer stepped outside the door and the deputy warden followed him. "What do you mean, my office? I can't allow that."

Brewer moved in close. "Deputy, I'm here to get some information from Padre. You failed and I don't plan to. Do you think he'll tell the truth when he can hear cell doors slam and knows the first thing he'll face once he leaves the room will be the eyes of other inmates?" Brewer waved his hand impatiently. "I might as well interview him in his cell."

"What's the difference?"

"The difference is ..." Brewer raised his voice. "The difference is, I want to get him away from bars and barred prison cells. You can do whatever you want with him when I'm done, but I want your office."

The deputy backed up a step and spoke meekly. "It's highly irregular."

Brewer had calmed down. "And what's wrong with irregular? I've had a successful career in this business and I don't do regular."

The warden thought a moment, then said, "He'll have to remain handcuffed."

A smile touched the corner of Brewer's mouth and he shook his head. "Deputy, I don't mean to usurp your authority, but look at the size of him, and now look at me. Do you think he could ever get the best of me?"

The warden shook his head.

Brewer put a hand on the deputy's shoulder and spoke softly, but firmly. "Just leave a pair of guards outside the door. We'll be fine."

The deputy took a deep breath and let it out slowly. "All right, we'll give it a try." He raised a finger. "But just this one time."

"Just this one time," Brewer said. "Take me there first. Remove Padre's handcuffs outside the office, then bring him in."

"Will do."

"And the leg cuffs too. I want him relaxed."

The deputy frowned at Brewer and let out an impatient sigh. "We'll remove the leg cuffs too."

The warden led the way and Brewer followed. He smiled to himself. He wouldn't likely have gotten his way with the other warden—God rest his soul—but he knew what he was doing.

They arrived in front of the warden's office. The young deputy opened the door and motioned with his hand for Brewer to enter. Brewer did, and after glancing around briefly at the luxurious surroundings, he said, "This is perfect. You can leave now."

The warden scowled and left the office. Brewer examined the warden's desk, opened his cigar box, removed a cigar, clipped the end, and lit it. It was a fine smoke.

Brewer took a seat in a stuffed leather chair facing a matching couch. He dropped his arms on the armrests and smoked the Cuban in the former warden's honor.

Five minutes later, Padre appeared in the door. The inmate's scowl had softened, but the stubbornness remained in his eyes. He stood at the doorway a moment, looking around curiously, his eyes finally coming to rest on Brewer's face.

The sergeant stood and motioned toward the couch. "Have a seat."

Padre sat on the edge of the couch, his back straight, and frowned at Brewer.

"Relax, sit back," Brewer said, leaning over and offering a hand. "My name is Sergeant Lance Brewer."

Padre disregarded the offered hand and sat unmoving, his eyes scanning the office. "Nice cell," he said.

"Yes, it is," Brewer agreed. He sat back down and crossed his legs. "It's not fair the staff get all the perks while you guys have to put up with nothing but iron bars and crappy food all day."

Padre nodded his head uncertainly.

Brewer uncrossed his legs and leaned forward. "I can make your life a lot easier in here."

"I'm not a snitch."

"We don't like to call it that," Brewer said. "Confidential informant is a better term."

"Still the same thing."

"Maybe, but confidential informants get better treatment. We protect them."

Padre studied Brewer's face. "How?"

"How? I'll tell you how. You're in here for murder. Is that right?"

"That's right."

"That's a pretty serious thing, but other than the unfortunate events on Wednesday, which I can make go away, you've been a model inmate. No trouble, right?"

"Nope."

"You never killed the guard when Lucas escaped, did you?"

"Nope. It was all Lucas. He planned it all."

Brewer smiled. "That's what I thought. You're not such a bad sort, and I think I can get you moved to a medium-security facility. Away from all these guys who would like to cut your heart out as soon as look at you."

Padre's eyes narrowed. "I still ain't no snitch."

"Now, Stephan, I would sure hate to hear something happened to you in here. I mean, rumors spread fast, and as soon as they found out you cooperated with us—"

"They can't find out if I don't cooperate."

"I'm afraid they can, and they will." Brewer motioned toward the door. "Some of the guards here have a habit of talking just a little too much." He sighed. "And there's nothing I can do to stop that. You know how it is."

Padre dropped his eyes and brushed at the leg of his orange jumpsuit. Only the ticking of the clock could be heard until finally the convict looked up and took a breath. "You'll get me out of here?"

"I will."

"Medium security?"

"Yup. Better food. Better terms, and better everything else. Away from certain people who might want to kill you."

Padre hesitated, looked around the room, and then sat back. "He's gone north."

"North where?"

Padre's brow wrinkled, his eyes narrowed. "Not exactly sure."

"I need you to be sure."

Padre picked at his fingernails a moment. "He's got a cabin up there."

"Where?"

"You'll keep your word?"

"If you tell the truth and we get Lucas, then yes, I'll keep my word."

"Will you put me in the bucket right now? Keep me safe until you move me?"

Brewer nodded. "Absolutely."

Padre looked at Brewer as if trying to decide whether or not he could trust him. Finally, he said, "He's gone to Algonquin Provincial Park. He's got a cabin there. That's one hundred percent truth and that's all I know."

"Think Stephan. It's a massive park. What area is he in?"

Padre looked Brewer straight in the eye. "I swear to you, that's all I know."

Brewer had done this kind of thing many times before and he knew when someone was telling the truth. "I believe you, Stephan." He stood and went to the desk, opened the warden's cigar box and selected a Cuban. He clipped the end, handed it to Padre, and held the lighter while the inmate sucked eagerly on the smoke.

Brewer sat back down. "I believe you, Stephan, and I appreciate your help. Enjoy the smoke."

CHAPTER 37

Saturday, 5:31 p.m.

VARICK LUCAS had watched the big guy leave their campsite. He followed him through the woods for a few minutes, stopped as they neared the beach, and saw him head toward the kids at the end of the lake.

He saw their tents from where he stood and wondered why the guy would be going there, especially when the game was well underway and his family was left alone.

He stood a moment and watched, adapting his plans. He would kill the big guy eventually, but just as it had been in the past, right now it would be too easy. No challenge. The end result would be much sweeter if there was more thrill to the hunt and the game was drawn out to its logical conclusion.

The backpackers might fit in later—if they were foolish enough to hang around—but right now, he had better things to do.

He turned and retraced his steps back to the camp, approaching it from a different angle. The woman sat by a tree, her knees up, reading a book.

She flipped back and forth through the pages, often resting the book in her lap, and appeared to be having trouble concentrating. Her mind must have been on other things.

One of the kids had come from the tent earlier and she had shooed him back with a wave of her arm and a stern look. The boy ducked back in. He was remarkably obedient, unlike any kids Lucas had known.

And now it was time to make his move.

He backtracked, circled around again, and approached the camp at her back. He paused thirty feet from her, removed the hunting knife from the sheath at his leg, and grinned.

He crept forward, choosing his steps carefully, avoiding twigs and dead leaves, attempting to tread only on the soft-carpeted areas of moss and soil.

Carefully now. Carefully. Quietly.

Three feet from her he dropped to his knees, swung his left arm around her neck, and brought the right one in front, displaying the sharp blade of the knife gripped in his hand.

She gasped. He covered her mouth and bent his head toward her ear. "Shhh."

The book fell to her lap and, obediently, she stayed still.

"Slowly now, stand up," he hissed in her ear. "Don't make a sound."

With the help of his arm around her neck she eased to her feet. He brought the knife closer to her throat, the razor-sharp blade touching her skin.

He spun her around slowly, turning his body with hers, staying behind her. "Now walk," he said, prodding her forward.

They moved slowly, very slowly at first to avoid rousing the kids, and then he removed the knife from her throat and pushed her gently from behind. "Keep moving."

She turned her head to one side as if to catch a glimpse of him. "Where ... where are you taking me?"

He laughed. "Not far. Just keep moving."

She moved obediently as he continued to prod her forward. Her husband could be back any time and they had to get out of the area before then.

The big guy would be a bit confused at first, thinking she'd wandered off, then find the boys in the tent, and perhaps panic. At least, that was the hope—the plan, as it were.

He didn't want to traumatize the boys in any way, but alas, certain things couldn't be helped in light of the bigger picture. And if they ended up seeing their father dead in front of them, they would get over it. Boys always did.

He remembered the day he'd seen his father dead. Lying there, stone cold, taking the easy way out. Drank himself to death. And Lucas had recovered. He got over it. Boys always did.

There would be a bright side. A silver lining. When life hands you lemons, and so forth.

They walked in silence for some time. The woman was being remarkably compliant with his demands, so far, and then she stopped abruptly and whirled to face him.

He held the knife close to her cheek and glared at her. She glared back.

Her eyes grew wider and her mouth dropped open, a glint of recognition in her pretty blue eyes. In a hoarse whisper she managed to say, "It's you."

"Do you know me?"

She nodded carefully, aware of the knife teasing her cheek. "You're ... Varick Lucas, the escaped convict."

He laughed out loud. "You're very attentive. How did you know?"

"It's your eyes," she said. "I know you by your eyes."

She was a smart one, and didn't seem to be all that fearful of him, just cautious.

"What do you want with me?" she asked.

"I'm afraid you'll have to wait and find out."

She put her hands on her hips. "Are you the one who sabotaged our vehicles?"

Oh, she was being obstinate now. He had some respect for that. She was feisty—careful, yes, but standing up to him. Just like his mother did when his father got out of control.

He laughed aloud again, a short laugh, more like a cackle, and ended in a grim smile. "It might've been me."

Her eyes flashed in anger. "It was you."

He held the knife poised just in case she got too brave.

"The police said you went east," she said.

"Part of my well-planned strategy. That's what I wanted them to think."

Her eyes narrowed and she lifted her head defiantly. "You'll never get away with this."

He was beginning to like her more and more. "I have so far."

"My husband will find you."

"He might be big and strong but I've got something that'll stop him dead in his tracks—literally." He lifted the front of his shirt, exposing the pistol behind his belt. "My friend here will take care of him."

She looked at the weapon and laughed. "He's taken care

of bigger guys than you, carrying bigger guns than that."

Now he was really beginning to admire her. Another place, another time, maybe in different circumstances, she could have been just like him. Brave and strong, smart and well mannered—under normal circumstances, that is.

And that could be a problem. He knew deep in his soul, he would find it hard to hurt her. Maybe a little bit, just to keep her in her place, but he seriously doubted if it could go much further than that.

He would have to be careful. He couldn't let her know how he felt. That would ruin everything.

He touched the tip of the knife to her pretty little nose. "Let's go," he said. "Turn around and walk, straight ahead."

She flashed her eyes at him again but turned quietly and walked forward. He followed, careful to keep her at arm's length as he prodded her through the forest.

CHAPTER 38

Saturday, 5:45 p.m.

AS JAKE MADE his way back to their campsite, he was still worried about the teenagers at the lake. Except for Holly, they didn't seem to be concerned about any danger that might be nearby. He feared for their safety, but his primary consideration was his family; the teenagers would have to make their own decision.

The situation he and Annie had found themselves in was unlike anything they'd encountered before. There were no witnesses to question, no forensic team to gather evidence, and no suspects to investigate. To make matters worse, the two boys were with them, and if danger was nearby, his and Annie's priority had always been to shield Matty from any possible risk.

He stepped from the trees, walked down the grade, and peered around their campsite. Annie must be in the tent with the boys.

He pulled back the flap and poked his head inside. Matty and Kyle sat on the mattress playing a board game. Annie was not in the tent.

Matty looked up. "Can we leave this place now? We're

kinda bored." He poked his friend's shoulder with a finger. "Aren't we, Kyle?"

Kyle looked up from the game, his eyes pleading. "Yes, we're bored. Can we go for a hike?"

"Not right now," Jake said and looked at Matty. "Where's your mother?"

Matty shrugged a shoulder. "She was outside. She made us stay in here."

Jake held up a hand. "Stay right here," he said and pulled his head back. His eyes roved around the site. Everything looked okay. Hopefully, she'd just gone for a short walk and would be back in a minute. He sat on the grass by the tent and waited.

When she didn't return in a few minutes, he felt a growing concern. Something wasn't right. It wasn't like her to wander away from camp for long and leave the boys alone.

He didn't dare call her name. If the prowler was in the area he would be sure to hear. He stood and glanced around the site again. His eyes stopped when he saw a book, lying at the foot of a tree by the edge of the clearing. He went over, looked closer at the book and frowned. It wasn't closed with a bookmark tucked neatly inside like Annie always did. She was particular when it came to respecting the written word, and she would never have left the book opened up, face down, and lying in the dirt.

Something was terribly wrong.

His worst fear had come true. He clenched his fists, angry with himself. He should never have gone to the other camp to warn them of danger, when danger lurked right here at their own camp.

He dared to hope she would come walking out of the trees any second, humming quietly to herself, a smile on her face. But he knew in his heart it wasn't going to happen.

He looked around in desperation, glaring at the dense forest in all directions. Had someone come and taken her away by force?

He glanced at his watch. Andy Fletcher had gone for help almost two hours ago. He should be back soon, bringing the police with him. But he couldn't count on them. He had to do something—anything. And he had the boys. He wasn't going to leave them alone, but how could he possibly search for his wife and bring them along?

Did he dare leave them at the other camp and trust Holly to watch them? Maybe that wasn't a good idea. They wouldn't be any safer there than here.

His one consolation was in knowing Annie was quick-witted. She'd been in perilous situations before and always pulled out of it, one way or another. But he couldn't count on that. Someone dangerous lurked about and at least one person was already dead. He shuddered at the thought of losing Annie. That would be impossible to take.

He had no choice. He had to take the boys with him and find his wife. But where would he start? He was surrounded by three thousand square miles of wilderness. And what if the game warden came back while he was gone?

He inspected the ground under the tree and leading into the forest. There were no visible prints in the leaves, moss, and hard-packed dirt of the forest floor, and no other evidence anyone had been there.

He dropped his head back and stared unseeing into the cloudless sky. Unless she'd known her abductor, which would be highly unlikely, the kidnapper would never have approached her from the opposite side of the clearing. It seemed likely he'd crept up from behind as she leaned against the tree. In which case, did they leave in the same direction he'd come? Possibly, even likely, but that wasn't proof they'd gone that way. They might have circled around.

The abduction—and he was certain now it was an abduction—must have taken place mere minutes before he arrived. He wasn't gone for long, and unless the boys had obediently stayed in the tent without a word, they would've poked their head out from time to time and noticed her missing.

Perhaps they were still close by, but which direction? Surely not the direction of the lake where he'd been. They would've headed off some other way to avoid crossing paths with him. Was the kidnapper watching them all the time? Had he waited until Jake left, and then taken Annie? If so, they might've been gone longer than he'd first assumed, perhaps ten or fifteen minutes. Plenty of time to get far away.

He was faced with unanswerable questions. Whatever he did, and wherever he searched, it would be like looking for a needle in a haystack thousands of square miles in size.

He recalled the cabin the boys had discovered earlier. Andy had said a guy named Otis lived there and he was harmless. Perhaps he wasn't so harmless. Someone responsible for the body in the woods, and if his fears were correct, the abduction of his wife.

The cabin was his only lead. He couldn't sit around waiting for a ransom note. There wouldn't be one. This had nothing to do with ransom. This was the action of a madman and he had to search for Annie. He had no choice.

He went to the tent and ducked inside. "Matty, I can't find your mother and we need to look for her."

CHAPTER 39

Saturday, 6:01 p.m.

ANNIE SAW THE weathered gray exterior of an aged log cabin through the trees. Varick Lucas prodded her directly toward it, and she assumed it was their final destination. What she didn't know was, why was he taking her there, and what was his end game?

She knew from news reports she'd seen and heard that Lucas was a violent killer, yet during their trek through the forest, he'd somehow seemed less than that, almost friendly, or at least as friendly as someone with a knife at your throat could be.

He gave her another push and she stumbled into the clearing and faced the cabin. It was old, very old, but the rough-hewn logs of which it consisted would easily stand another hundred years. If he intended to keep her prisoner there, it would be an almost impossible task to escape. The building was like a small fortress.

"Keep going," he said. "Inside."

He was still behind her, his hand gripping her shoulder, assuring she didn't make a run for it at the last moment. She would never be able to outrun him, and it was pointless to resist and put herself in further danger. She would bide her time for now, but when the time was right ...

He held her at arm's length, her back to him as he fumbled in his pocket for the key. He snapped open the padlock. The door creaked forward and thumped against the inner wall of the cabin.

He pointed inside. "Go."

She obeyed, stepping carefully over the doorway and into the dimly lit room.

"Sit there," he said, pointing to a sturdy wooden chair in front of a stone fireplace.

She sat and faced him as he pulled the door closed and latched it securely. He turned toward her and grinned. "Welcome to my home."

She didn't answer. What was the use? She glanced around the ancient cabin. The air was stuffy and stale, but the small room was clean and organized. A bearskin rug lay by the fireplace, tattered and worn. Fishing rods and nets decorated one wall, a small canoe balanced in the rafters.

He dragged a matching chair across the floor, set it in place a few feet away, and dropped into it with a sigh, facing her. She avoided his eyes as he sat quietly and watched her. Finally, she looked at him, stifled a tremble in her voice, and asked, "What do you want with me?"

She felt his eyes on her as they moved up and down the length of her slim frame. Then he said, "I thought maybe I wanted what every man wants." He shrugged. "I haven't decided yet."

Though she trembled, she didn't feel herself to be in

imminent danger. She feared more for Jake and the boys. Did this lunatic's plan involve them? She knew Jake would be constantly on his guard, especially now that she was missing, but he would be handicapped by the presence of Matty and Kyle.

Jake had assured her the game warden had gone for help. Surely he would be back soon and the police would find her. It couldn't be long now.

"I have plans for your husband," he said.

Just what she feared. "What kind of plans?"

He shrugged. "That depends on him, and maybe on you. I can't say yet." A strange look came over his face. "Too bad about the boys, though." He sighed. "Collateral damage, you might say."

Annie leaped forward but Lucas stood and pushed her back into the chair, his hands on her shoulders.

She glared up at him as he stood in front of her, his arms crossed, legs spread.

"You leave the boys alone," she said in a defiant tone. "They never did anything to you."

He cocked his head. "You're rather protective of your boys."

"I'm a mother," she said flatly.

He nodded slightly. "And that's what mothers do, right? Protect their children?"

She clenched her jaw, her brow in a tight line, and spoke firmly. "Above all else."

He glanced toward the small window in the back of the building. His eyes glazed over, his mind somewhere far away.

Finally, he turned back to her and spoke almost gently. "I had a mother once." His shoulders slumped and Annie thought she saw pain in his downcast eyes.

"What happened to her?" she asked.

"She died," he said, almost inaudibly.

"And your father?"

"Dead."

She whispered, "I'm sorry."

The fireplace whistled as an early evening breeze tickled the chimney. A mouse skittered through the rafters. The cabin was otherwise quiet and still.

Lucas raised his head slowly.

Then with a sudden rush, the hardness returned to his eyes—the glint of evil that had softened somewhat reappeared, and he exploded from the chair. "I don't want to talk about it." He stood and stormed about the cabin, mumbling unintelligibly.

Annie stayed unmoving, her head bowed, not wanting to antagonize him further. Her best hope was when he exhibited some semblance of humanity. She would have to wait for him to calm down.

She chanced a careful look in his direction. His back was to her as he bent over the table, his head in his hands. She heard him moan, as if in pain—emotional pain, no doubt.

Now was the chance she was waiting for. Perhaps her only chance.

She prayed the floorboards would remain silent as she crept to the door. Her hand touched the latch and she lifted it cautiously. The door squeaked as she tugged on the heavy wooden portal.

He shouted as she sprang through the doorway and across the hard-baked soil and grass of the clearing. The forest was but a few steps away. He was but a few steps behind.

She often jogged in the morning, and she was lithe and fast, but no match for him. He roared like a savage as he pursued her, now close behind and coming closer.

He touched her shoulder and she wrenched away, taking a hard turn. She'd evaded his grip for now. If only she had a weapon. She spied a fallen branch to one side, the perfect size. She dove for it, gripped it tight, and rolled to her feet.

He was right in front of her, and she swung the weapon with all her strength. The branch whipped through the air as he ducked, straightened up again, and grinned. "You can do better than that."

She swung again. His hand shot up and the weapon smacked into his palm. He wrenched it from her grasp and stood glaring at her, slapping the free end of the weapon into the palm of his hand. Finally, he tossed it aside.

"I must say, I admire your spunk," he said and chuckled. "But you're just not spunky enough. Nice try, though."

She looked at him, panting for breath a moment, and then turned to run. She'd taken a chance, given it her best shot, but now as his hand gripped her arm and pulled her to the ground, she knew her best shot hadn't been good enough.

She fought in vain as he dragged her back to the cabin and threw her on the cot by the wall.

"That wasn't very ladylike," he said. "Unfortunately, I'm going to have to tie you up now."

CHAPTER 40

Saturday, 7:16 p.m.

THE SUN DIPPED in the western sky, scarcely visible above the treetops, as Jake trudged wearily through the forest, the boys following behind. It would be dark soon. The moon would barely penetrate through the thick greenery above, and his desperate search for Annie would be almost impossible to continue.

He couldn't stay still and wait for the game warden to return when his wife was in danger. He had to do something, anything, but with only a vague idea of which way to go, he was afraid his pursuit was futile.

They had searched the area around the campsite in ever-widening circles and had accomplished nothing. They now hunted for the cabin the boys had discovered earlier. Jake felt it might hold the key to Annie's disappearance, and was desperate to find it.

Matty was uncertain of its exact direction, only that it lay somewhere west of their original campsite. When the boys had been lost, they'd followed the sun back, but now in the impending darkness, it would be easy to miss the cabin. A few degrees to the right or left could lead them miles in the wrong direction.

He ducked at the last moment, narrowly missing an overhanging limb across the path. He came to a stop and peered through the trees. The growing gloom of the forest made it hard to see more than fifty feet ahead.

"What is it, Dad? Did you see something?" Matty whispered.

Jake tried to keep the desperation from his voice as he answered, "No, I'm just trying to get my bearings."

"I think the cabin is that way," Kyle said, pointing to the left.

Matty shook his head and pointed in another direction. "No, Kyle. It's that way."

Jake looked down at Matty. His son was trying to be brave, but Jake knew the boy was aware his mother might be in danger. "We'll look in every direction," Jake said. "We'll find her soon." He didn't feel as optimistic as he tried to sound. It would be easy to get lost in the darkness with only the moon and a patchy sky of stars to guide them.

He was startled by the flutter of wings from nearby as an unseen bird took to the air with a screech. The occasional whine of mosquitoes, creaking tree trunks, and the crackling undergrowth with each step, were a constant reminder of the vast wilderness surrounding them.

The faraway howl of a wolf caused Kyle to cling to Matty in fright. He looked around him, his eyes growing large.

Matty soothed his friend. "It's all right, Kyle. It's a long way from here, and besides, wolves aren't usually dangerous. That's only in fairy tales."

Kyle looked at Matty, trying to decide whether or not to

trust him. He finally released his grip, but continued to keep a careful eye.

"I should've brought the flashlight," Jake said, more to himself than anyone else. "We'll go back for it." He turned and went in another direction. "This way, guys."

He led them to their old campsite, unlocked the door of the SUV, dug around in a box in the cargo area and removed a Maglite. He tested it. It was growing dim. He should have brought fresh batteries.

They returned to the forest, continuing on the route they'd previously taken. He used the light sparingly, illuminating the way through and around the thick foliage, hope in each weary step, coupled with a fear he might find his wife's lifeless body, discarded like the unfortunate victim he'd discovered earlier that afternoon.

His hope was that if there was a cabin somewhere in the vicinity, a light might be visible, glowing from its window.

If there was a window, if there was a light, if there was a cabin, and if they were in the right area.

It seemed hopeless, maybe futile, but he continued on, scanning the forest in all directions.

The flashlight flickered; it was dying. He had no choice but to turn back now before they got lost and his desperate search became impossible.

He dreaded leaving Annie to the unknown and he felt helpless. Reluctantly, he stopped and turned to the boys. "It's too dark to see. We have to go back and try again in the morning."

They turned without another word and picked their way

back to the new site. Jake hoped, by some miracle, Annie had returned and it was all a joke. The camp appeared to be undisturbed since they'd left, and Annie wasn't there.

He was sure the game warden hadn't returned yet with the police. If he had, there would've been some evidence of their presence. Was it possible Andy's vehicle had broken down somewhere during the long ride back to the main gate?

As evidenced by the disappearance of his wife, he knew the intruder was well aware of this site, and their own safety would be compromised if they stayed here. "We have to move camp again, boys. Matty, get the sleeping bags. Kyle, you help him."

"What about the tent, Dad?"

"Leave it."

The boys ran to the tent and returned with the sleeping bags and pillows, Kyle struggling with each step as the bags dragged behind. Matty hefted his backpack on his shoulder and picked up the straggling ends. Jake hoisted the cooler under one arm and grabbed one of the sleeping bags with the other.

He led them through the trees for several minutes until finally they approached the beach. He stopped at the tree line, where tall shadowed pines stretched like arrows into the sky. He set the cooler down and spread out the sleeping bags on the soft forest floor.

"We'll be safe here until morning," he said. "Try to get some sleep and I'll call you when the sun comes up."

Matty and Kyle lay down obediently and crawled inside their bags. They whispered together for a few minutes but soon became quiet, sound asleep, exhausted from the day's adventures.

Jake glanced across the lake to the far end, where a campfire on the beach lit up the sky. By the light of the fire, he could make out three or four figures milling around. The backpackers were safe for now, and so were they. It was Annie he was worried about.

He dragged his sleeping bag over to the foot of a large tree, sat down, and leaned against the trunk.

He had no plans to sleep that night. He was sure he would be unable to fall asleep anyway, knowing Annie was out there somewhere and he was powerless. He would keep watch all night, and tomorrow he would find his wife.

CHAPTER 41

Saturday, 8:40 p.m.

ANNIE WATCHED from her seat on the cot as Varick Lucas removed the sizzling rabbit from the spit and dropped it on the table. He slipped the hunting knife from the sheath on his leg and sliced the meat into bite-sized pieces, setting each piece carefully onto a plate.

He stood back, admiring his work in satisfaction, and then reached into a small cupboard and removed a loaf of bread and two more plates. He dropped two slices of bread onto each plate along with several pieces of meat, and carried them over to the cot.

"I hope you're hungry," he said as he handed her a plate. "I'm sorry I have no butter for the bread, and it might be a little stale, but it's all I have."

She reached up with her loosely tied hands, took the offered meal, and looked at it dubiously.

"Try it," he said.

She held it close to her nose. It smelled a little gamey, but not bad.

"It tastes like chicken," he said as he popped a piece of meat into his mouth. He chewed vigorously, swallowed, then bit a chunk from his bread. "Go ahead, try it."

Her legs were tied tightly, but she managed to swing them in front of her and lean against the wall. He watched as she sat the plate in her lap, picked up a piece of the meat, and took a nibble. It didn't taste like chicken to her, but she was hungry and it was pleasant enough, so she ate, avoiding the bread.

He smiled at her as if pleased, then sat in a chair nearby, held his plate with one hand, and ate with the other. He seemed to be enjoying it, scarcely stopping to chew as he devoured the meal. She watched him from the corner of her eye. Besides the constant smacking of his lips, the only other sound was the occasional sputter of an oil lantern, hanging on a hook by the fireplace.

"If you let me go," she said at last, "I won't tell anyone about you. I'll just say I was lost in the forest." She looked at him, hope in her eyes, but in her heart she knew her request was futile.

He stopped eating and looked up at her. She held his gaze until finally he said, "I might let you go. I haven't decided yet." He popped the last piece of bread into his mouth, swallowed, belched, and set his plate aside.

"I've had enough," he said as he dropped his head back and closed his eyes. "But you can have more if you want, when you're done with that."

"This will be enough." She finished the meat and set the plate on the cot beside her.

He opened his eyes, stood, and took the plates over to the table. "Do you want a drink?" he asked. "I have water or beer."

"Water will be fine."

He dipped a glass of water from a pail on the table and brought it to her, then found a beer in the cupboard, popped the top, and took a long swig. He sat down again and looked at her.

"The police will be looking for me," she said. "I think it might be to your advantage if you let me go now."

"They won't find us here."

"How can you be sure?"

"Because," he said, "no one knows about this place." He pulled a pack of cigarettes and a lighter from his shirt pocket, lit one and took a drag. "Besides, I'm not planning on staying here much longer."

"Where will you go?"

He laughed. "You think I would tell you that?"

His question told her a lot; he might let her go after all, and it might be soon. But what about Jake? Lucas said he had plans for him.

She tried to reason with him. "Maybe you should get out of this area soon. I think they might be looking for you here."

"I'll go before long. A few days, maybe. Or perhaps I'll die here." He shrugged. "But right now... I have things to do."

"We found a body in the woods," she said, watching him closely.

"A body?" he asked. "A person's body?"

She nodded. "A man."

"Really?" he asked. "Do you know who it is?"

"No," she said. "Do you?"

"How would I know? You just told me about it."

"I think you're the one who killed him."

He looked at her curiously and puffed on his smoke.

"Why would you assume that? Because I'm an escaped convict? So I'm guilty already?"

"Who else would it be?"

He shrugged. "Maybe a bear got him."

"Bears don't carry knives."

He frowned at her and said flatly, "It wasn't me. It was likely somebody nosing around where he didn't belong. I've heard that happens up here sometimes. There are a lot of people protective of their territory and don't like it when city people come nosing around."

She didn't pursue the point. She assumed he was lying, but if not ... was there another killer around?

He looked at her curiously. "I don't even know your name. You know mine, but we haven't been formally introduced."

"It's Annie," she said flatly.

"Nice to meet you, Annie." He took another drag from his half-smoked cigarette and flicked it into the fireplace. "Those things'll kill you," he said, blowing the smoke into the air.

Her eyes moved toward the ceiling at the faint sound of a helicopter somewhere nearby.

Lucas held his breath and listened intently, unmoving, until the sound faded away, then stood and went to the window. "It's getting dark outside, and it's getting late. Tomorrow's another day and I want to be up early." He turned to face her. "You can have the cot. I have a sleeping bag."

The noise of the helicopter sounded again, this time closer. It gave her hope. Maybe they were searching for her. Perhaps the game warden had finally returned in full force.

The sound vanished again, but Annie's hope remained.

Lucas jumped up, grabbed a poker by the fireplace and stirred the fire, separating the logs. The fire dimmed. He grabbed the pail of water from the table and doused it. It fizzled and died. "I can't take a chance they'll see the smoke," he said.

"They're looking for me," Annie said.

"It's too dark for them to see, and besides, they're gone now."

"Perhaps."

He crouched down and pulled a sleeping bag out from under the cot, unrolled it, and laid it on the floor near the door. "Get your beauty sleep now," he said as he blew out the lantern. Through the sudden darkness, she could still make out his outline as he crossed the floor and climbed in the sleeping bag.

He was making sure she didn't try to escape. She would have to climb over him to do so, and even then, the door wouldn't open with him blocking its path.

Perhaps if she had a club she could beat him senseless first, but she'd checked around earlier, and there was nothing that would serve as a weapon. At least, nothing she could get to easily. There was a pair of oars in the rafters, but she would never be able to get to them with Lucas around.

"I'm a light sleeper," he said as if he had read her thoughts. "I wake up at the slightest noise."

She was exhausted, physically and mentally, and no choice but to try to rest. She lay down, pulled the blanket up to her chin, and eventually drifted off to sleep, her troubled thoughts of Jake and the boys slipping from her mind.

CHAPTER 42

Sunday, 5:45 a.m.

JAKE HAD NODDED asleep on a few occasions during the night, but thoughts of Annie would always startle him awake. It had been a long night and he finally dozed awhile just before dawn.

The sun peeked over the trees and, like a blaring alarm, jolted him awake, bringing thoughts of Annie foremost in his mind. He shook his head and jumped to his feet, angry with himself. If he hadn't slept, he would have been awake with the sun and already searching for his wife. He shuddered to think what could have happened to her during the time he'd slept.

In an attempt to stay awake during the long hours of the night, he'd wandered up and down the beach. Near the out-jutting rock where he'd sat fishing two days before, he'd found a small natural cave, possibly worn into the limestone in ages past, but now dry, well away from the lake waters, and large enough for his purpose.

His plan was to hide the boys there while he searched for Annie. Maybe not a perfect plan, but they would be safer there than wandering into possible danger with him.

He'd given up hope of seeing Andy Fletcher or the police anytime soon, sure now the game warden had fallen into some trouble, possibly even an encounter with the savage killer, and now it was all up to him.

He gently shook Matty awake. The boy moaned and opened his eyes, looked up, and spoke in a hopeful voice. "Is Mom back yet?"

"Afraid not, son. But I'll find her today." He had to keep his hopes up; that's all he was running on, and he was determined not to tell Matty how worried and afraid he was.

Kyle raised his head, rubbed his eyes, and looked around as if trying to get his bearings.

Matty spoke. "It's time to get up, Kyle. We have to look for my mom."

Jake helped the boys to their feet, rolled up the sleeping bags, and picked up the cooler. "This way," he said as he started down the beach. Matty grabbed his backpack and the boys trudged along behind, still rubbing the sleep from their eyes.

When they reached the cave, Jake ducked inside. The space was only a few feet square with no room for him to stand, but plenty of space for the boys to move about freely. Matty followed him into the cavern and watched curiously as his father set the cooler down, unrolled the sleeping bags, and laid them out neatly on the floor of the cave.

"I want you boys to stay here while I'm gone," he said. "You'll be safe here and I'll come back to get you after I find your mother."

Kyle was looking at the lake. "Can we go swimming while you're gone?"

"No, Kyle. I want you to stay in here."

Kyle dropped down onto a sleeping bag. "It's awful boring."

Matty sat down beside Kyle and turned to face him. "We'll be okay, Kyle," he said. "My mom is lost and Dad's going to find her. It won't be for long, and we can tell stories."

Jake pointed to the cooler. "There's some food in there if you get hungry." He turned and ducked out of the cave. "I have to go now. I'll be back."

He strode down the beach, climbed the grade to their original campsite, and looked around. Everything seemed to be the same as it had been the evening before. He examined the vehicles. They were still locked up, apparently untouched.

After another quick glance around, he hurried through the forest to their newest campsite. The tent still stood, but the small cooler containing drinks had been knocked over, its contents spilled. Not likely the work of a killer, more like the evidence of bears or raccoons snooping around, looking for treats. Nothing else appeared to be disturbed, and he wasn't sure if that was good news or bad.

He turned back and headed into the forest, hoping to continue on from where they'd left off the night before. It was easier going now; he saw his way clearly, and he had a distinct plan. He made his way to the clearing where the boys had encountered the bear, arriving there in a few minutes. According to Matty's blurred memory, the cabin was somewhere west.

A mile or two is a long way in the forest, and still uncertain whether or not he would stumble across the cabin, he set out due west. Twenty minutes later he gave up in disgust, sure he'd gone too far. He cut to his left a hundred feet and backtracked.

His route took him past the spot where they'd found the body. It still lay in the same spot, yet undisturbed by wild animals, but insects crawled over the decomposing remains, flies buzzed around, and the face was now barely recognizable. The undignified sight made him angry at whoever had done this, and more fearful for Annie. A distinct odor choked him and he held his breath and turned away in disgust.

He continued on and in a few minutes ended up back at the clearing. A pair of squirrels chased each other through the weeds, free and unaware of the torture in his soul.

He was getting nowhere, still unsure the cabin was what he should be searching for, but he had no other ideas, and no clues to guide him. He had only his gut instinct and sheer perseverance to drive him on.

He started through the trees again at a different angle, when a sudden movement to the right caught his eye. His heart slammed against his ribs when a clump of bushes shook, branches thrashing and snapping. Taking each step slowly, not daring to breathe, he skirted around the bush, being careful where he trod as he crept soundlessly closer. He stopped short, his breath left his body, and his jaw dropped at the sight of a black bear, ambling away, paying him no attention.

He didn't know what he had expected to find and he sagged against a tree in disappointment, his face against the rough bark, the ridges biting into his skin. He leaned there a moment, breathing a soft prayer, unable to continue.

Finally, he raised his head, took a deep breath, and went on, dragging himself through the wilderness, each step growing heavier, unsure whether those steps brought him closer to, or farther away from, the love of his life.

CHAPTER 43

Sunday, 6:29 a.m.

MATTY SAT IN THE cave with Kyle, staring out at Lake Wendigo. The lake shimmered in the sunlight, calm and undisturbed, the morning mist catching the rising sun and reflecting shades of blue and orange onto the waters below. Unlike the peaceful lake, he grew restless, his mind in turmoil. He was tired of sitting in one spot, telling stories, and above all, he was deeply concerned about his parents.

He knew his father was worried, more than he'd seen before, and was attempting to cover it. Matty had tried not to let his father know how anxious about his mother's whereabouts he was as well. His dad had enough on his mind, and Matty wanted to help out.

He thought long and hard about the cabin—the cabin his father had so desperately tried to find the night before and was scouring the woods for even now. Dad likely assumed his mother was there. Otherwise, why would he be so eager to find it?

He and Kyle had been there once before; why couldn't they locate it again? There must be a way. He sat still, contemplating the idea, attempting to work out a solution.

Then something popped into his mind—something that just might work.

He turned to Kyle, flat on his back, staring up at the low ceiling of the cave. "I've got an idea."

Kyle turned his head and waited for Matty to continue.

"I think I know how to find the cabin."

Kyle sat up. "Your dad told us to stay put."

Matty nodded and looked at the floor of the cavern. "I know he did, but he's been gone a long time and I'm getting worried about him."

Kyle whispered, "But what if we get lost again?"

"We won't. Even if we don't find the cabin, the compass will guide us back safely." He slapped a hand on his backpack sitting nearby. "It's in here."

"So, let's go, then," Kyle said eagerly.

Matty sat still a moment, reconsidering the idea. He didn't want to go against his father's wishes and get them all into deeper trouble. His mother had often called him "responsible." Matty wasn't exactly sure what that meant, but he thought it had something to do with doing the right thing.

He remembered his father had once told him that the best thing you can do is the right thing, but the worst thing you can do is nothing.

He found it hard to do nothing when he had an idea that might help his parents. He hoped he was doing the right thing now. He decided he was.

He grabbed his backpack and the boys scrambled to their feet and crept from the cave. Matty pointed down the beach. "We need to start this way, from the old camp. That's the easiest way for me to remember where we're going."

They started across the sand and grass when Matty stopped. "Wait a minute," he said and turned back. He found a short stick, went to the mouth of the cave, and carved a message in the dirt. "Back soon. Don't worry." He stuck the stick in the sand so his father would be sure to see it if he returned before them, and then stood back.

"That should do it," he said. "Let's go." He led the way across the beach and then stopped and held a hand up in his friend's direction. "Keep quiet, in case anyone's around."

He turned and crept up the grade to their old campsite. He wasn't going to take any chances. If his mother was in danger, and someone was responsible, he might be lurking around. They moved cautiously toward the site, staying behind trees and bushes.

The camp was deserted. He glanced around, and then pointed. "This way," he said and headed into the trees.

Kyle followed him awhile before asking, "What's your idea? How're we going to find the cabin?"

Matty kept on, picking his way around low branches, clumps of bushes, and fallen trees. "First we have to find the clearing where we saw the bear."

"What if the bear is around?"

"He won't likely be there." Matty hoped he was correct on that point. The last thing he wanted right now was a run-in with a crazy bear. They'd been lucky the first time, but he decided to be cautious just in case.

He was certain he could find the clearing. He had been there twice before and he was pretty sure it was dead ahead.

"I'm hungry," Kyle said.

Matty stopped and looked at his friend. "Yeah, me too. We should've had something before we left. We'll just have to wait, that's all." He continued on and, in a few minutes, pointed ahead. "There it is."

He moved carefully through the trees, memories of their frightening encounter with the bear foremost in his mind. He stepped slowly into the clearing and looked around. The awful creature wasn't there. "This is it, Matty," Kyle said." He pointed. "That's where the bear was."

They stood still a moment, Matty with his hand on the flap of his backpack, Kyle glaring toward the spot the bear had appeared, listening in case the fearsome animal lurked close by.

"I think it's okay," Matty whispered.

Kyle stood straight, cocked his head to one side, and squinted at Matty. "Now what?"

Matty pointed. "The bear was there." He moved his hand. "And we were standing there." He spun around, pointing again. "And then we ran like crazy that way."

"So?"

"So, we do it again."

"Run like crazy?"

"Yup."

"How far?"

Matty thought a moment, doing some quick calculations in his head. "After we found the cabin last time, it took us about half an hour to get back to camp." He looked up and frowned. "So it's about a mile from here."

Kyle shrugged. "I'm ready if you are."

Matty adjusted his backpack and poked a finger to his left. "Watch out for the bear," he shouted, and charged into the forest, Kyle right behind.

Matty tried not to pay much attention to the route they took, rather to run by instinct like they'd done before. He was positive they would find the cabin soon.

"Are you sure this is the right way?" Kyle asked after a few minutes, panting out the words as he followed his friend.

"I'm sure," Matty said and waved a hand. "I recognize that fallen tree over there. We ran right past it before." He was growing tired as well, but didn't dare stop. He had to keep on; he had to find that cabin and, if possible, get back to the cave before his father returned.

CHAPTER 44

Sunday, 6:35 a.m.

VARICK LUCAS had been up early, polished off the rest of the rabbit meat, and smoked a cigarette from the dwindling pack, and now he was eager to get his plans for the day underway.

Annie had awakened a few minutes earlier. She lay on her side on the cot, watching him as he went about his morning business.

He flashed her a smile. "Did you sleep well?"

She rolled to her back and didn't answer.

"Just trying to be friendly," he said.

Silence.

"Do you want some breakfast?"

"No, thanks." She turned to face him. "I would like a glass of water."

He brought her a drink and she swallowed it eagerly. "Thank you."

"More?"

She shook her head.

"I have to go out," he said. "The crux of the game has just begun."

Annie didn't comment.

He rummaged around in a box in the corner and came up with a length of nylon rope. He was going to lock her in the cabin when he left, but he wanted to be safe, and tying her up would make her doubly secure.

He carried the rope over to her and held it up. "This is for you."

She turned her face to the wall.

"Just for a while," he said. "I'll take it off again when I get back." Then in a stern voice, "Sit up."

She rolled over, dropped her feet on the floor, and sat on the edge of the cot. She gave him a look of disdain and said, "You don't have to tie me up. If you padlock the door, I can't get away."

He smiled. "One can never be too careful. Now please stand up and turn around."

She stood, raised her nose in the air, and spun around. He tied her wrists together securely, pushed her onto her back on the cot, and then tied her ankles. "I guess I won't have to gag you," he said. "Only the birds and the squirrels will hear you, and they don't care." He laughed at his own joke and stood back.

"Do you need anything before I go?" he asked.

"A knife would be nice."

He chuckled. "The knives are well out of your reach, unfortunately. So you'd best just stay put until I get back."

"Don't hurry back," she said.

He crossed his arms and looked at her. "I'm glad you still have a sense of humor."

She turned her head away and stared at the ceiling.

He opened the cupboard and found a pair of padlocks, the

keys in them, then fastened the hunting knife to his leg, checked the pistol tucked behind his belt, and left the cabin.

He padlocked the front door, went to the side of the building, unhooked the shutters from the outside wall, swung them closed, and fastened them securely with one of the padlocks. The back window got the same treatment. The solid shutters would make it dark in there, but they would guarantee she stayed put.

He dropped the keys into his pocket, turned, and strode into the woods.

~*~

RCMP SERGEANT LANCE BREWER had been awake into the wee hours of the morning, waiting to hear whether or not his team had found the location of the cabin where Varick Lucas was holed up. He had hoped Padre would've been more precise, but even with the sketchy information they had, he expected his men to zero in on Lucas's position before long.

Immediately after interviewing Padre, he'd spoken to the chief of intelligence and surveillance and was advised a pair of Air-1 service helicopters, each complete with sophisticated surveillance equipment and an expert team, was at his disposal.

By the time he had the operation assembled, their short window of opportunity had dwindled with the daylight and they were forced to put the bulk of their efforts on hold until daybreak.

A renewed push was now underway. Up in the air, RCMP

officers were in the cockpits with the pilots, passing information to constables on the ground by radio. Meanwhile, RCMP commanders in the situation center watched images relayed by satellite.

Three thousand square miles was a lot of space to cover with just two units, so existing aerial photographs were consulted, pored over, and scrutinized.

Brewer was now on the phone with Special Constable Dunkirk. Brewer had remained in the Haddleburg region and sent Dunkirk to oversee the gathering of intelligence.

"I don't have anything promising to report," Dunkirk said. "As you know, it's a large park, and we have narrowed the possibilities to fifty-six locations."

"Fifty-six?" Brewer roared. "Is that the best you can do?"

"I believe it is, sir."

Brewer paced the floor of his hotel room. "That'll take weeks to cover with a ground approach. I don't have that kind of time."

"I can assemble three task forces and cover it in two weeks."

"Not good enough." Brewer bit the end off a cigar and spat it across the room. "Can you narrow the possibilities down more than that?"

"I'm afraid not, sir. With nothing else to go on, as far as location is concerned, that's the best we can do."

"What about thermal imaging?"

"Sure, but in a heavily forested area, the thick trees block video cameras as well as limit the capability of thermal imaging devices." Dunkirk paused a moment before patiently continuing, "Thermal imaging picks up heat. There're thousands of campfires at any given time and thousands of campers throughout the park. We can eliminate the ones in known camping spots, but thermal imaging is not the way to go, sir."

"What else do we have?"

"Without a more precise location, all we can do is send in tactical troop members to investigate possible targets one at a time."

Brewer swore. He didn't have that kind of time to waste but he had no other choice at the moment. "Start the ground search. I'll let you know if we come up with anything further here. And keep me posted." He hung up, tossed his phone onto the bed, went to the window, and gazed over the small town spread out before him.

He chewed impatiently at his cigar. He wasn't optimistic about the ground search. Lucas was volatile and could move his location at any time. He needed something else, and he needed it now.

His team had confirmed Lucas's parents were dead, and the whereabouts of Otis, his one known friend, was undetermined. There was no other information forthcoming as to the location of the cabin where Lucas was allegedly hiding out.

His men still questioned possible acquaintances of Lucas in an attempt to come up with some information, but to date it was a dead end. Lucas had been transient, never spending more than a couple of years in any one place, and his trail of friends was sparse.

Brewer needed a break soon, something to go on. In the meantime, there wasn't much use in hanging around Haddleburg.

At first, he'd planned to head north early that morning, but the uncertain information Dunkirk had provided was not encouraging. He decided to make the trip to the town where Lucas had been arrested. If any information was forthcoming, he wanted to be there.

It was a good two-hour trip, but it seemed that right now, unless one of the teams in the service helicopters came up with something soon, he had lots of time to get there.

This would go down, one way or another, and when the ground assault on Lucas's hideout by tactical troops was finally activated, he had plans to be present.

CHAPTER 45

Sunday, 6:44 a.m.

ANNIE STRUGGLED at the rope that held her hands. The bonds were tight; not so tight they hurt her wrists, but secure enough to keep them from slipping off. Any attempts she'd made only resulted in chafing her skin, and with her arms behind her back, her movement was severely constricted.

She maneuvered herself into a sitting position, her back against the wall, her feet extending out over the edge of the cot. She had but one concern for herself—to get free from the ropes, and then escape the cabin.

But her chief concern was for Jake and the boys. The maniac, Varick Lucas, had mentioned some kind of game he was playing. She expected its end result would be an attempt on Jake's life, an attempt that might succeed, and she agonized over the thought. She was uncertain how her freedom could thwart the madman's plans, but was determined to get away, thoughts of her family driving her on.

It occurred to her the only reason he kept her alive at the moment was as a pawn in his game. She expected he would eventually use her against Jake. But how? If he wanted to kill her husband, he surely could've done so by now. Why would he need her?

At first, she'd feared he would attempt to rape her, or worse, but as time went by, she realized his plan involved much more than temporary physical pleasure, and certainly not longtime containment of her as a prisoner, but rather something more sinister and immediate.

She'd assumed his first priority as a convict on the run would be to evade the law and remain hidden. In disregarding that, he'd exposed himself as a highly unstable and dangerous maniac, and she was frightened more by the unknown than by what she knew.

The horrific thought spurred her on, giving her determination and a single-minded purpose—freedom. She cleared her mind and squinted through the murkiness at her surroundings.

The cabin was in total darkness other than a small amount of sun creeping through cracks in the shutters, painting a dozen parallel slashes across the wooden floor. Some light came down the chimney, barely enough to illuminate the cold ashes and the stone hearth in front.

She slid forward on the cot until she could bend her knees and touch her feet on the floor. She tried to stand, but lost her balance and fell back onto the bed. Had her abductor not tied the rope from her wrists around her waist, she could've slipped her bound hands under her feet, then out in front.

Her only option was to attempt to remove the ropes from her wrists first, and then she could untie her feet, and then—

She slid off the cot and crumpled to the floor, managing to roll and finally position herself with her back to the fireplace. She rubbed the ropes at her wrists against the sharp edge of the hearth, up and down, up and down.

She paused, raised her eyes upward, and listened intently. The unmistakable sound of a helicopter was barely audible through the thick wooden roof, but it was a helicopter, no doubt. The sound faded, and with it, her hopes they'd finally come to rescue her. She took a deep breath and continued with her task.

It was hard to maintain the steady motion. Her shoulders grew tired, her wrists were sore and her fingers numb, and she rested often. She celebrated silently as each of the dozens of small strands making up the nylon rope snapped. It was slowly wearing through.

She started and held her breath as she heard a thump, then the patter of small feet. She breathed freely; it was just a squirrel on the roof. Perhaps a pair of squirrels, playing in the sunlight, enjoying the freedom she'd taken for granted and now struggled to reclaim.

A final snap, and the ropes fell away, her arms free. Then it was a simple matter to remove the rope from her waist, and she flung the tattered cord across the room and massaged away the pain in her wrists and shoulders.

The cord holding her ankles was next. The slick nylon rope clung stubbornly to itself, difficult to untie. She peeled off a broken fingernail with her teeth and continued her battle with the cord. It took her several minutes until finally it loosened and fell away. She flung it into the corner with the other one and stood to her feet.

In the near darkness, she stumbled to a cupboard near the sink and groped inside. She knew Lucas kept a box of matches in there somewhere; she'd watched him as he'd lit the lantern earlier. She found them and struck one. The light from the match lit up the small room and made it slightly more bearable. She lit the oil lantern by the fireplace and welcomed its warm glow.

She went to the window and pushed against the shutters. They were solid—very solid, intended to keep intruders out rather than prisoners in. The door was likewise sturdy, inches thick, and padlocked securely from the outside. It seemed unlikely she could break through either the shutters or the door without a tool of some kind.

There were a handful of utensils in the drawer, but nothing sharp. Beans and other canned goods occupied the lower cupboard. She rummaged through boxes and trunks, but found nothing to serve as a battering ram or crowbar.

She turned her attention toward the ceiling. Fishing rods and tackle were useless to her. There was a small canoe, holding a pair of oars, but they would snap before the shutters ever did.

The floorboards were solid, immovable. The walls were built to last and none of the strong logs would budge with her desperate attempt. The stones on the well-built fireplace and sturdy hearth were unyielding. Even the flimsy cot was useless.

Her search continued in vain until finally her assurance of escape ended, her determination faded, her hopes now dead.

She dropped onto the cot in despair. She had loosened her bonds, tasted freedom, and yet she still remained a prisoner.

CHAPTER 46

Sunday, 6:55 a.m.

VARICK LUCAS approached the camp of the teenagers with the stealth of a seasoned hunter. He was getting good at this, and starting to enjoy the game, even with its ever-changing rules. But since he'd written the rulebook himself, he was free to change them whenever he saw fit.

And right now, he saw fit.

His plan was to get rid of the two guys there, and that meant killing them, but as he crept toward their campsite, he was disappointed to find it vacated. It didn't appear they'd left completely; the tents were still there. Perhaps they were sleeping the day away.

He stole forward and peeked inside the closest one. A pair of backpacks lay on the floor, right next to their sleeping bags.

The other tent was the same—two backpacks, and two sleeping bags. An empty wine bottle and candy bar wrappers littered the floor. He stepped back. They were likely here somewhere.

He crossed his arms and looked around, unsure what to do. Turning abruptly, he kicked aside an empty potato chip bag, strolled down to the beach, and went to the edge of the lake. He peered left, then right. Nothing. Nobody around.

A small heap of beer bottles lay beside a large, flat rock serving as a makeshift bench. He scowled at a couple of broken ones, the pieces scattered about the patches of sand and grass.

He turned and went back up to the campsite; he would have to come back later. Right now, time was wasting away and life was short. So short.

The sound of a helicopter somewhere above the trees caught his attention. He gazed upward, attempting to spot it through the thickness of the leaves, until the sound faded away. He crossed his arms, frowned, and continued to glare upwards. That was the second helicopter that had flown over, more than a bit unusual. Perhaps Annie was right, and they were looking for her.

He forced the matter from his mind. Maybe he would go see what the rest of the Lincoln family were up to right now. He strode into the forest with the intent to circle around the lake through the trees, and sneak up to their campsite from the far side.

He picked a path carefully around a fallen tree, then raised his head to the unexpected sight of a girl, not ten feet ahead. She was surprised by his sudden appearance and stopped short, her eyes wide, then stepped forward and smiled. "Hi, I'm Rosie."

He avoided the introduction as he scrutinized her. His eyes roved over her skin-tight pants, her revealing blouse, her seductive pose, and a teasing look in her eye that was more than friendly.

He knew who she was, of course; he'd seen her at the campsite earlier. He hadn't liked her then, and he didn't like her now. She reminded him too much of those slutty women he used to hang around with, back when he and Otis were the best of buds and had nothing better to do.

"Were you coming to our site to visit?" she asked.

"No," he said. "I was just in the area."

As she gazed at him, her eyes narrowed. "You look familiar."

He shrugged.

Her hand covered her mouth and she gasped. "It's your eyes. You're … you're the killer who escaped from prison a few days ago." She stood still, unable to move, and then turned to run.

He caught her by the arm and gave it a brutal twist, forcing her around to face him, then grasped her by the shoulders and held her at arm's length.

She trembled and he saw terror in her eyes. She tried to break free, striking at him with her hands. He gripped her arms, forcing her to stop, but she kicked at him, screaming, "Let me go."

He freed one hand and swung a fist. It connected with the side of her head and she went down onto her back and lay still.

She held up her hands as if to ward off further blows. "Please," she begged. "You don't have to do this." She dropped her hands and forced a smile, another attempt to seduce him, this time to save her life. "I can give you much more than you ever hoped for."

Her solicitation only served to increase his anger—furious at the stupid girl who'd recognized him, annoyed at himself for being seen before he was ready, and burning now with a desire to end her useless life.

This new feeling astounded him. He'd never killed a woman before and the impulse to do so now caught him totally unawares. He hesitated, unable to move and unwilling to act on this strange new urge.

She must have sensed his abhorrence of her proposition. Before he could clear his mind and make a decision, she rolled, scrambled across the forest floor on all fours, and then stumbled to her feet.

She was getting away and he couldn't let that happen.

"Come back," he called, striding forward.

She had found her voice again, and as she tore through the trees, the bushes grabbing at her, she cried for help. She pushed through branches and briers, their prickly thorns tearing at her jeans.

He avoided the obstacles she had blindly encountered in her uncontrollable urge to escape, and followed her with long strides.

Now on her hands and knees, she clawed her way up a bank, gaining ground, then sliding back.

He stooped down and caught her by a leg. She kicked at him in vain with the other one as he dragged her backwards. A shoe came off in his hand and he flung it aside, regaining his grip on her ankle. In a moment, she lay helpless and trembling at his feet.

"I can't let you go," he said.

"I ... I won't say anything." She implored him with her eyes. "I promise. Just let me go and I—"

He dropped his right foot onto her throat, cutting off her pathetic words. With both hands, she struggled to remove the heavy boot choking off her air.

He removed his foot and she breathed again, panting for breath, unable to speak. She held up her hands for protection against further onslaught as he knelt at her side, slipped the hunting knife from the sheath, and held it up for her to see.

Her eyes grew wide as she stared at the fearsome weapon. "No." She choked out the words. "No. Please."

He smiled. "This won't hurt."

The perfectly honed knife descended toward her throat, gripped in his right hand while he held her down with the other.

Her arms flailed uselessly toward his face, coming short of their mark. Now weakened and unable to fight, she ripped at his shirt, at his throat, his chest, her nails gouging his flesh, drawing blood.

He didn't feel the pain she inflicted on him as he finished the task, the knife sinking deep into her flesh, her throat severed. He dodged the upward spray of blood and when it finally subsided, he rose to his feet.

The shower died to a trickle, and then stopped, the green moss below her head now stained a bright red.

Her unseeing eyes still reflected the terror and hopelessness she had felt. He didn't like to see it. It disturbed him. He rolled the lifeless body over to hide the face, wiped the knife clean on the back of her blouse, and stood.

He gazed at the body a few minutes, sighed, and walked away.

He hadn't enjoyed that as much as usual. It had made him feel uncomfortable. He shook off the strange feeling and picked up his pace, leaving his troubled thoughts behind him with the fresh corpse.

CHAPTER 47

Sunday, 7:01 a.m.

JAKE STOPPED AND sank down beside a tree, his head in his hands. He was no closer to finding Annie than he had been the night before. The cabin he so desperately sought had evaded him and his hopes faded.

He was in the middle of the wilderness, Annie was missing, and the boys were hidden in an insecure spot. They faced an unknown enemy and he had lost control of the situation. His usual optimism was consumed.

He felt he had no choice but to return to the boys and wait for Andy Fletcher to come back. The warden knew where the cabin was, knew the owner, and he was the best chance they had now.

Reluctantly, he made his way back to the cave where he'd left the boys. He crouched down and looked in. They were gone.

His attention was caught by a scratching in the dirt outside the entranceway—words, "Back soon. Don't worry."

He stood and looked thoughtfully around, wondering where they might have gone. He had fully expected them to stay where he'd left them, but now they had wandered off—

or had they? If they'd run into foul play from an intruder, Matty wouldn't have left a note. At least, not likely.

He felt satisfied they'd left of their own accord. The boys wouldn't leave without a reason. Though his son had said nothing, Jake was certain Matty was aware of something sinister taking place. And whatever it was, now that they were out in the open, he worried they might be exposed to danger. He now feared for the boys as well as for Annie.

He checked out both campsites in hopes they'd gone looking for food or drinks. Finding no indication where they might be, he went back to the cave, ducked inside, and reluctantly waited.

~*~

MATTY SCRAMBLED up a grade, stood on the top of the ridge, and looked ahead. "Yes," he shouted. "There it is. There's the cabin."

Kyle made it to the top and stood beside Matty, peering in the direction his friend pointed.

"Do you see it?" Matty asked. "I can make it out through the trees."

"I think so."

"Let's go." Matty went ahead, but after a few steps, he stopped, turned to Kyle, and raised a finger. "We need to be quiet in case someone's there."

Kyle nodded and followed. They dodged behind trees and bushes, making their way to the edge of the clearing surrounding the cabin.

"We'll circle around first," Matty said. "Just in case somebody's outside."

They stepped back into the trees, and staying out of sight as much as possible, they skirted around the building, returning to their starting point.

"The windows are all covered," Kyle said.

"Yeah, I noticed that. They weren't like that before. Somebody lives here?"

"Do you think he's inside?" Kyle asked. "I don't think he would cover the windows if he was."

Matty scratched his head. "I think you're right, but did you notice the padlocks on the shutters? He's trying to keep intruders out."

"Maybe he went on a holiday."

Matty chuckled. "I don't think so. This place is a holiday. You don't go on a holiday from a holiday."

"Yeah, I guess not."

"He might be out hunting." Matty took a step forward. "Let's go take a look."

They eased toward the building and Matty pointed. "Look, the front door is padlocked too."

"So there's definitely nobody there."

"I guess not."

Kyle dropped his hands on his hips and cocked his head at Matty. "Now what?"

Matty thought a moment. "We should probably go back to the cave and wait for Dad. He said he'd be back soon."

"He might be mad at us," Kyle whispered.

"Don't worry. He'll get over it when he finds out about this place."

"Yeah, I guess so."

Matty turned to leave, then stopped suddenly and held up a hand. "Shhh. Did you hear that?"

"What?"

"A banging. I heard something banging." Matty turned back and frowned at the cabin. "Somebody's inside."

"I don't hear it."

"It stopped," Matty said and hurried forward. "Come on."

He reached the door, tightened his fist around the padlock, and tugged. It was locked securely. He stood back, unsure what to do.

"Maybe we should knock," Kyle said.

Matty thought about that. "But what if somebody bad is in there?"

"I guess we just tell him we're lost. If he looks dangerous then we run away."

"It might be my mom in there," Matty said. "She's missing and you know she's a private detective and always seems to get in some trouble."

"Okay," Kyle whispered. "You knock."

Matty stepped forward, took a deep breath, and rapped on the thick wooden door. Kyle backed up a couple of steps and appeared ready to run at a moment's notice.

There was no indication anyone had heard the knock.

"Knock again," Kyle said.

Matty knocked again and heard a muffled voice. "Hello."

"Mom," he shouted.

"Matty?"

"Yes, it's me and Kyle, but the door's locked with a padlock."

"Can you break the lock?"

Matty leaned and peered at the padlock. "Maybe, but it's a thick one. It looks pretty strong."

"Where's your father?"

"He's … I'm not sure. He's looking for you but he's not here."

There was silence from inside the building for a few moments.

"Mom. Are you still there?" Matty asked.

"I'm still here. I think you'd best go and find your father. I'll be all right until you get back."

Matty didn't want to leave his mother. He was terrified the owner might come back, but horrified at what might happen to his mother. He bit his lip, stepped back from the door and looked around in desperation. He needed something to break the lock. He found a fallen tree branch, but it was rotting and would never do.

Kyle had found a log, a little bit sturdier, and he handed it to Matty and whispered, "Try this."

Matty had doubts, but he wrapped his hands around the end and swung at the lock. Nothing happened. He hammered again and again until his fingers were numb, but the stubborn lock held firm.

"We have to get your dad," Kyle said.

Matty nodded reluctantly. "I think you're right."

He stood still a couple of minutes and stared at the lock, frustrated and unsure what to do.

"Someone's coming," Kyle whispered.

Matty spun around and listened to the distinct sounds of

something treading on leaves and branches. They had to get out of there—fast. He grabbed Kyle by the shirt and tugged at him.

Kyle didn't need further encouragement. He tore behind Matty, across the front of the building, up the side, and into the forest.

Matty glanced over his shoulder as they ran. A man was coming from the trees at the far side of the house. He didn't wait around for a clearer look. They dashed away as fast as they could, tearing through the forest.

When they were a safe distance away, Matty stopped short, Kyle almost barreling into him.

"We're safe now," he said. "But we have to find my father." He turned sharply and jogged through the trees. He was certain he knew the way back now. He needed to find his dad, or somebody else he could trust, and then they would return and free his mother.

CHAPTER 48

Sunday, 7:20 a.m.

HOLLY CHURCHILL had enjoyed her bath in the stream a couple of days prior and had decided to look for the magic spot again and freshen herself. She had savored the invigorating water for almost an hour before she reluctantly stepped from the pool, dressed, and headed back to camp.

This was the last day of their excursion and they would be packing up to leave soon. She felt energized after a night's sleep and early morning bath, and looked forward to going home. It wasn't that she hadn't had an enjoyable weekend, but her companions left a lot to be desired.

As she neared their campsite and dipped over a knoll, she was startled by a bone-chilling sight. A body lay face down in the dirt, and even though it was half-hidden behind a rotting tree, she recognized who it was. It was Rosie.

Even without a closer look, it was obvious Rosie was dead. Blood had spread from her severed throat and snaked across the dirt in a dark red stream. Holly could see the face—the once pretty face, turned to the side, now utterly lifeless.

She stood paralyzed, her heart pounding against her ribs,

unable to breathe for a few moments. Then she drew a quick breath, then another, hyperventilating, and crumpled to the ground, her legs too weak to sustain her.

She tried to call for help but her voice failed. Finally, she struggled to her hands and knees, closed her eyes, and tried to clear her mind.

She recalled how Jake Lincoln had warned them the day before. She'd been fearful, but had only half-believed there was any danger. But this was Rosie—poor Rosie—the one who'd mocked Jake, and waved off his warning.

The girl didn't deserve this. No one deserved this, and it took a few minutes for the horrible truth to penetrate.

Rosie—flirtatious, foolhardy, and carefree Rosie—was dead.

Eventually, she managed to stand. She shuddered violently and turned her back on the scene. She had to warn the others before it was too late.

She approached the camp cautiously in case the murderer still lurked close by, waiting, waiting for another victim.

With a breath of relief she saw Thad and Billy were there, safe, standing by one of the tents, laughing and talking casually. For a moment, she feared they might be the killer, or killers. Perhaps she was safer to make a run for it. She brushed the idea aside. They weren't killers. A bit annoying, yes, but killers?

She stumbled a few more steps, tripped over a root, and almost fell to the ground. She regained her balance and staggered toward them.

"Whoa," the red-headed boy said, taking her arm to steady her. "What's going on, Holly?"

"It ... it's Rosie. She's dead, Thad."

Thad looked at Billy, then back at Holly and frowned. "What're you talking about?"

Holly pointed in the direction of her dreadful discovery. "Back there. Somebody ... killed Rosie. She's dead."

Billy pushed back his baseball cap and leaned in toward her. "Show us," he said, unbelief in his voice.

"I ... I don't want to go back there."

"Then just show us where she is," Thad said.

Holly looked behind her, hesitated, and then turned slowly and headed toward the forest. She beckoned with a hand. "This way."

She wanted to run the other way but felt safer with Thad and Billy, so she led the way into the trees. When she got near the ghastly scene, she stopped and pointed. "Just over there." She could make out a foot—Rosie's foot.

Billy went ahead, easing up to the scene, and Thad followed. She heard them talking as they crept up to Rosie's body. Thad stopped a few feet back but Billy went on.

"Is that Rosie?" Thad called.

Billy answered without taking his eyes off the body. "Sure is."

"Is she dead?"

"Yup. Sure looks that way." Billy crouched down for a closer look, then turned and waved Thad over. "Come and see."

"No, thanks. I've seen enough," Thad said. He turned back and stood beside Holly, watching Billy curiously.

Finally, Billy stood and joined them. "It's pretty gruesome.

Her head is almost halfway off. Looks like he used a knife."

"We'd better get out of here," Holly said, still trembling. "The killer might be lurking around."

Billy shrugged. "Yeah, I think you're right. I wouldn't want to end up looking like that."

Holly turned and scurried back to the site, the boys jogging behind.

"Leave the tents," Thad said. "Let's just get out of here."

"Wait," Holly said. "I need to get something." She went into the tent she'd shared with Rosie. The dead girl's backpack lay near her sleeping bag. She would have to leave it there. It would be too much for her to lug back and would only slow her down.

She grabbed her own backpack, gathered up some of her loose items that were spread around, stuffed them into the pack, and stepped from the tent. She looked around in dismay. Billy and Thad had already left, gone, and abandoned her.

She was miles from the main road and unsure which way was the correct route to safety. She hadn't paid much attention when they'd hiked here, trusting the guys knew where they were going. She could easily get lost if she headed out in the wrong direction. She berated herself for being so mindless. She stood still, distressed and fearful, trying to get her bearings.

One thing was for sure, she couldn't stay here.

She slung her backpack over her shoulder and hurried along the beach. If the Lincolns were still around, she would ask if they would let her stay with them, and maybe they would give her a lift back to town.

She hurried around the beach, shaking at everything that moved, every tree that rustled by the breeze, and every small creature of nature that played among the trees. She was ever fearful the killer was behind her. Or maybe he was ahead. She didn't know who to trust. Even Jake might be the killer, but she had to do something.

"Holly?"

She stopped short and spun around, unsure who called her name.

"Holly. Here, in the cave."

She turned toward the sound in time to see Jake duck out. He looked at her curiously. "Are you all right?"

She studied him carefully. He seemed sincere, concerned. Could she trust him?

"It's Rosie," she answered carefully.

"What about her?"

She looked him straight in the eye, watching for his reaction. "She's dead."

"Dead? How? What?"

"Somebody killed her," Holly answered, looking instinctively back toward the camp she'd just left. Suddenly, the tears came. She dropped her head and sobbed hysterically. She felt his arms around her, patting her hair, comforting her, soothing her as she shook uncontrollably.

Eventually, her sobs diminished and he stepped back, leaned over, and held her by the shoulders. "Where is she?" he asked.

Holly wiped at her cheek and motioned down the beach. "She's back there, near our camp."

"And where are the guys you were with?"

She sobbed again and a tear fell. "They ran away and left me. I had no choice but to look for you." She raised her head. "Can I stay here? Is that okay?"

"Absolutely," he said and glanced around. "I'm not sure how safe any of us are right now, but you're welcome to stay."

CHAPTER 49

Sunday, 7:35 a.m.

VARICK LUCAS raised his eyes and froze, his hand on the padlock. Another helicopter was in the area, its choppy rhythm coming from a distance away. It wasn't as close as the last one, but it made him uneasy. They might be looking for him, and if so, it would be just a matter of time.

He had to get the game underway and get out of here.

He pulled the key from his pocket and frowned at the small chips of wood and bark that clung to the lock. Someone had tried to break in. He glanced around apprehensively and saw a short log a few feet away, tossed aside. He picked it up and examined it, sure now his suspicion was correct.

Someone had definitely been here. He'd suspected it would happen sooner or later, but it was too early. He wasn't ready for them.

Rounding the cabin, he checked the locks on the shutters. They were secure and seemed untouched.

He returned to the front of the cabin, unlocked the padlock, eased the door open, and stepped inside. He ducked as the blade of an oar zipped through the air and crashed into the solid door frame, narrowly missing his head.

His right hand shot up and he grabbed the oar, then stood and glared at his attacker through the dimness of the small room.

"Did you think I wouldn't be ready for you?" he asked as he moved forward, forcing Annie to take a step backwards.

She dropped onto the cot and watched him while he struck a match and lit the lantern, then closed the door.

"Good thing I locked the shutters," he said with a curt laugh.

"You didn't have to come back so soon," she said. "It was rather pleasant here without you."

He laughed again, this time long and hard. When he was done, he took a deep breath and sat on the chair near the cot. He leaned forward and studied her carefully. She was brave, at least on the exterior. It was hard to tell what was going on inside, but she sure put up a fearless facade.

"How did you untie yourself?" he asked.

She didn't answer.

"I rather expected it, anyway," he said offhandedly and stood again. "By the way, we have to move."

She looked at him curiously. "I quite like it here," she said.

"And why is that? So they can come back to rescue you?" He chuckled, evil and low. "That won't happen. I've taken care of them."

Something crossed her face—something like fear, or apprehension, or maybe unbelief. Maybe a combination of all three. That was exactly what he wanted. Keep her guessing. Keep them all guessing.

"Where are we moving to?" she finally asked.

Ah, there it was. She was curious and couldn't help herself.

When he didn't answer, she shrugged, pretending it didn't matter. But he knew it mattered to her, very much indeed.

"You'll see," he said.

He found a six-foot length of cord in a box and stuffed it into his back pocket, then retrieved the pieces of rope she'd tossed in the corner and examined them. He tied the two pieces together, tested the knot, and held it in front of her.

"Afraid I have to tie you up again," he said.

She shrugged. "Do what you have to."

He wondered how long she could keep up that plucky attitude. He saw right through it. If she only knew what he knew—

He stepped closer to the cot. "Lie down."

She lay back and crossed her arms.

"On your face," he said.

She rolled over.

He tied her wrists together—tighter this time, then ran the cord down her back to one ankle, tied it securely, then to the other ankle, leaving a length of several inches between her feet.

Leaning over, he wrapped his arms around her waist, dragged her off the cot, and set her on her feet. He felt her trembling with fear in spite of her brave face.

"Can you walk?" he asked.

She took a short step forward.

"Good enough," he said. "How does it feel?"

"It feels comfortable."

He laughed. "Now I know you're lying. They used to tie me up like that when I was in prison. At first, it was like that all the time, whenever they moved me. Course, they used

240

chains and cuffs, but it was anything but comfortable." He laughed again. "Then they relaxed a bit after that because I became a model inmate."

"You sure had them fooled."

"It wasn't hard. Course, a lot of the screws were always careful, but there were a few you could fool. They thought they were rehabilitating you, and you smiled pretty at them, but they didn't know I was just aching to cut their slimy throats."

She was looking the other way as if not listening. He knew she heard him. "Do I have to gag you, or will you keep your mouth shut?"

"You don't have to gag me," she answered.

He squinted at her, hoping he could trust her, then turned suddenly and blew out the lantern. He spun her around and grabbed the rope at her back. "Enough talk. Time to move."

He prodded her toward the door, opened it, and secured the padlock in place behind them. "Walk," he said, pointing toward the forest.

She hobbled her way across the clearing, her hampered legs causing her to stumble on the uneven ground. He wasn't in a hurry anyway. They were away from the cabin, the coast was clear, and the game continued.

She slipped backwards navigating up a grade, so he pushed her from behind, patiently prodding her upwards and onwards.

In a few minutes, the sound of a stream could be heard in the distance and grew louder as they approached it. This was close to where he'd seen the girl bathing, a little further upstream from here.

He gripped the rope at her back as he prodded her into the stream, then across to the other side.

"In there," he said, pointing to a limestone cave formed in the side of a cliff. "You'll be safe there."

She didn't move, so he pushed at her, forcing her to walk or lose her balance. A trickle of water pooled at their feet as it made its way from the cave, down the cliff, and joined the stream below. He pushed her deep into the hundred-foot-long cavern. The air was damp, the high ceiling dripping with moisture and puddling on the smooth limestone floor.

He pointed toward one of the many stalagmites rising from the floor near the back of the cave. "Sit there and lean back."

She objected at first, so he spurred her forward by a grip on her shoulder. She hit the column and dropped to her knees, then rolled and sat with her back against the tapering rock formation.

He pulled the rope from his back pocket, tied it securely to one wrist, and wrapped it around the column, then tied it back to the other wrist. He tugged on the cord to make sure it was snug. She winced at the pain, but it was necessary to tie her tightly. There were no shutters to keep her in if she got free from the ropes.

"You won't be able to get loose this time," he said. "So save your strength."

He stood back and observed her a moment, then strode toward the entrance. "They won't hear you either," he called back over his shoulder. "So save your voice as well."

CHAPTER 50

Sunday, 8:05 a.m.

JAKE HAD LEFT HOLLY in the cave and had paced the beach for what seemed like hours, keeping an eye out for anyone who might be lurking around, be it friend or foe.

His worry for the boys deepened with each passing moment. With Holly's frightening revelation that Rosie had been brutally murdered, it seemed obvious the killer targeted people at random, and no one was safe.

His heart jumped, ecstatic to hear a familiar voice call his name. "Dad." He spun around to see Matty and Kyle racing down the grade from the campsite.

His displeasure with the boys vanished along with the dread for their safety he'd felt a moment ago. He raced to his son, crouched down, and pulled him close with one arm, the other around Kyle.

"Where've you been?" he asked Matty, the relief in his voice mixed with gentle rebuke.

Kyle spoke up, eagerness in his voice. "We found the cabin."

Jake pushed back and looked at Kyle. "You found the cabin?"

Kyle shook his head vigorously and pointed vaguely toward the forest. "It's that way."

He'd spent hours looking for that cabin, almost given up hope, and the boys had found it.

"Mom's in the cabin," Matty announced in an excited tone. "We talked to her but couldn't break the lock."

Jake's jaw dropped. It took a moment for the realization to sink in. They had found Annie.

"She said to come and get you," Kyle put in. "All the windows are locked and so is the door."

Jake hugged the boys again, his heart racing. He had to get there right away. "Where is it?" he asked. "Is she okay? Is your mother all right?"

"She said she's fine, Dad," Matty said. "We can show you where it is."

Jake had a choice to make. If he dared let the boys take him there, he might put them in danger. On the other hand, they knew where the cabin was and were sure they could find it again.

He made the difficult decision. "I want you boys to stay here. If you can explain to me where the cabin is, I'll go by myself."

Kyle looked at Matty. "Can you explain?"

"Sure, it's easy." Matty reached into his pocket and removed his compass. "You have to go to the clearing where the bear was." He pointed to a spot on the compass. "Then you have to go this way."

Jake looked at the compass. "West-northwest?"

"I think so."

"Are you sure?"

"I'm sure, Dad. Just a few minutes past the clearing there's a big hill, like a cliff. If you see that, you're going the right way. Then just keep going, follow the compass, and watch for it."

He had missed that area entirely. It seemed like he'd searched everywhere but there, always going in the wrong direction, too far south. He was irritated at himself, but eager to get going.

Jake took the compass from Matty, put it into his pocket, and headed down the beach, beckoning to the boys. "Come on, guys, back to the cave."

"Do we have to?" Kyle asked.

"Yes, and there's someone I want you to meet."

They followed him to the cave and ducked inside. Holly sat on a sleeping bag and looked up when they appeared. She gave them a weak smile and said, "Hi."

Matty looked at her curiously and said, "Hello." He looked at his father, and then back at Holly. "You're the girl we met in town the other day. The backpackers."

"Yes, I am," she said. "It's nice to see you again."

"Where are the rest of them?" Kyle asked.

She paused. "It's just me now. The others are ... off on their own."

"This is Holly," Jake said. "They were camping at the end of the lake. The rest of her companions left, and we're going to take care of her until we leave."

Kyle looked at Holly closely. "She doesn't look like anybody needs to take care of her."

Jake chuckled. "Maybe not, but for now, she's going to stay here and watch you while I'm gone."

Jake explained the situation to Holly in as few words as possible, and then raised a finger toward the boys. "I want both of you to remain in this cave until I get back. No excuses this time. Is that understood?"

Matty nodded. "Understood."

"I'll make sure they stay, Mr. Lincoln," Holly said.

Jake hated to leave them alone, but again, he had no choice. His wife needed him, and needed him immediately.

"I won't be long," he said, giving Matty a quick hug. "Remember, do as Holly says."

Matty nodded. "We'll be okay, Dad. Go get Mom."

Jake ducked from the cave and ran from the beach into the forest. He didn't stop to rest, leaping over branches and fallen trees, dodging bushes, running up and down grades, until he finally reached the clearing. He stopped, panting for breath, and rested a few moments before digging the compass from his pocket.

West-northwest. He looked across the clearing, checked his bearings, and started off again.

Matty had given him great directions, and in a few minutes, he came across the cliff the boy had mentioned. Two sets of footprints were visible in patches of loose soil at the base, and more marks where the boys had scrambled up the eroded hill.

He followed Matty's instructions and a few minutes later, his heart jumped when the distinct pattern of the outer wall of a cabin came into view. He had found it.

He crept closer and stopped a few feet back from the edge of the clearing surrounding the building. He listened for telltale sounds indicating that someone else might be close by, but nothing but the constant voice of nature could be heard.

From where he stood, the padlock on the front door was visible. He moved over to his left. The shutters at the side of the building were closed; everything appeared exactly the way the boys had described it.

Annie must be inside.

He strode to the door, pulled at the unyielding lock, and then banged on the heavy wooden panel. He waited but no answer came, and there was no indication anyone was inside. He banged again. Nothing.

"Annie," he called, over and over, to no avail.

He could try to break in but a closer look at the lock revealed it was too sturdy. No amount of whacking at it without the proper tool would do anything. He should've brought a tire iron from the SUV, and he contemplated going back for it. No, that would waste precious time.

He went to the side of the building, checked the shutters, and found the same type of padlock. The hinges were solid and assembled in such a way they weren't accessible from the outside.

He banged on the solid shutters, not expecting an answer. None came.

He considered the situation. Something had taken place since the boys were here. It didn't appear Annie was inside and he concluded if no one was around, then the kidnapper must have taken Annie somewhere else.

Had the kidnapper been aware the boys had found the cabin? If not, why did he take Annie away? But if so, why'd he let the boys go, knowing they would return and tell somebody? Was that what he wanted? Was he lurking around here right now, watching, and waiting?

Jake looked around uneasily. Something didn't seem logical.

His fear for Annie's safety increased and he tried to think clearly. If the kidnapper had meant to harm her, why'd he keep her locked up, rather than killing her immediately? What would be his reasoning?

What was his plan, and where could they be?

CHAPTER 51

Sunday, 8:33 a.m.

ANNIE STRUGGLED against the stubborn ropes that held her firmly to the column. If she could get loose from them, there were no padlocks, doors, or shutters between her and freedom.

She had tried rubbing the ropes against the stalagmite but it was rutted, and the cord seemed to be wedged into a natural groove, not willing to budge in either direction. It kept her from sliding the ropes up the column to attempt a standing position and she was forced to stay in one spot.

She recalled her conversation with Varick Lucas. She'd tried to hide her fear from him, putting on a brave face, but the truth was, she was terrified. His unpredictable actions made it difficult for her to judge what his plans were. But whatever they were, it wasn't something she relished being a part of.

Any attempts she'd made to call for help were futile, only resulting in a hoarse throat. Lucas was right, she might as well save her strength. No one would hear.

She shifted her weight, uncomfortable on the hard stone surface, and then pulled up her knees to soothe her cramping legs. The unyielding bonds allowed little room for movement, and she was starting to ache all over.

Jake, Matty, and Kyle's safety were foremost in her mind. She was comforted by the thought there was no reason to believe any harm had come to them yet. Lucas's game might be underway, but she had confidence Jake was sharp-witted enough to anticipate the lunatic's actions. Surely Jake and the police were scouring the forest, searching for her even now.

~*~

JAKE STEPPED BACK into the forest out of sight of the cabin. He looked around for a sturdy weapon, something he could use against the killer if he was so lucky as to come across him. Everything was rotten, or rotting, and unsuitable for any kind of protection.

He saw a low-hanging branch, wrenched it from the tree with sheer strength, and then snapped pieces off until it was about the size of a baseball bat. He hefted it. It would have to do.

He looked around for a safe place to wait, a spot where he wouldn't be seen from any direction. He found a tight area between two bushes where he could watch for anyone coming, yet remain out of sight.

He hunched down and waited. He was used to stakeouts, but he was up against an unknown enemy, and unsure if the killer would return. If, as he suspected, the brutal murderer was aware they'd found the cabin, he might have vacated the place, planning never to return.

Half an hour later, his suspicions appeared to be true, and

he might be wasting valuable time. He was puzzled. He had no clear plan of action, nothing to go on, and no one else to turn to.

He ducked from his hiding place and circled the cabin once, twice, then several more times in an ever-increasing radius. The unmistakable sound of a nearby stream caught his ear. He followed the sound, ducked through the undergrowth, and stepped onto rich, fertile soil, populated with weeds, wildflowers, and struggling grass.

It was a beautiful spot, and on any other day but today, he would have enjoyed it immensely. But today, it was just one more place in the endless wilderness.

He walked a hundred feet up the edge of the stream, then back the other way, and stopped, frustrated and angry. He was getting absolutely nowhere. He might as well return to camp and see if the police had arrived.

On his way back he stopped at the cabin again. The door was still locked, the shutters were still fastened, and everything was the same.

He made his way back to the cave where he'd left the frightened kids alone, and crouched down by the entrance. He let out a breath of relief at seeing Holly and the boys, still safe.

Matty looked at him expectantly. "Dad, did you find Mom?"

Jake shook his head slowly and crawled inside. Exhausted, he dropped his club near the wall of the cave, sat beside his son, and looked the boy straight in the eye. "Sorry, Matty. I couldn't find her." He felt like he was letting his son down, along with everyone else. "She wasn't in the cabin when I got there."

Matty cocked his head. "But I heard her."

"I know you did, but she's not there now. I banged on the door and there was no answer."

Kyle looked fearful. Holly noticed and put her arm around him, drawing him close. He looked up at her. "It'll be all right," she said in a soothing voice. "We'll find her."

Matty didn't look so sure. Fear showed through his determined exterior. "Where's the game warden, Dad? Why didn't he come back?"

"I don't know, son. I hope he'll be here soon."

Holly spoke in a whisper. "Should we try to hike out of here?"

Jake wanted to encourage the girl to stay, but he wouldn't try to dissuade her from leaving if she was determined. "I advise against it," he said. "It's a long way, but I won't keep you here if you want to go."

"And you?" she asked.

"I'm not leaving without Annie," he answered in a firm voice.

"Then I'll stay too," she said flatly.

Jake saw determination mixed with fear in her eyes. "It might not be safe and we might be here awhile."

"I'm staying."

Jake nodded slowly, his mouth a grim line. The girl was being braver than she looked. "Okay," he said. "We'll stick together."

Holly glanced at Matty, then back at Jake. She looked troubled. "Should we do something about Rosie? I … I don't like to leave her there alone."

"There's nothing we can do," Jake answered slowly. He

hadn't told the boys about the brutal murder and he tried to keep his answer as vague as possible. "She would be no better off here than there."

Holly dropped her head. "I guess you're right." Then her voice took on a tone of sadness and she added, "She wasn't so bad."

"Yeah," Jake said quietly, and then looked dubiously at Holly. "You don't think those boys you were with have anything to do with this, do you?"

Holly thought about the question a moment, then shook her head slowly. "I can't say for sure, but I'm truly convinced it wasn't them. They got along good with Rosie, and I believe they've known her awhile. I'm the newcomer to the bunch. As annoying as they can be sometimes, they're really good-hearted." She paused, then repeated, this time more sure of herself, "No, it wasn't them."

Jake managed a foolish grin. "Yeah, I'm just grasping at straws."

Matty spoke up, giving no indication he'd gleaned anything sinister from their conversation about Rosie. "What're we going to do now, Dad? About Mom, I mean."

Jake's heart ached—ached for Annie and ached for Matty. He didn't have an answer. At least, not one he was satisfied with. "We'll find her soon," he said.

Matty looked dubious. "How?"

That was the question Jake had asked himself over and over. How? All he could say was, "The police will find her when they come. They will bring dogs and they can track every move she made."

For once, Matty looked hopeful.

CHAPTER 52

Sunday, 9:18 a.m.

RCMP SERGEANT LANCE BREWER flicked off his car radio and answered his cell phone in a curt manner.

"We might have something, sir." The caller was Corporal Loy, one of his team, and a dedicated cop.

Brewer straightened up, concentrating on the conversation. "You have my full attention, Loy."

"A hooker, sir. She came forward when she saw Lucas on the news. She said she knew him from way back when."

"What does she have for us? Anything we can go on?"

"Not yet, sir. She just came forward a few minutes ago. They called me and I called you immediately. Figured you'd want to know."

"You figured right, Corporal. Where is she?"

"She's at the local police station. We haven't interviewed her yet."

Brewer looked at his watch. "I'm almost there. Give me about half an hour and I'll interview her myself."

"Yes, sir."

"Oh, and Corporal."

"Yes, sir?"

"Make sure she doesn't leave. Keep her comfortable. Give her whatever she wants."

"You got it, sir."

Brewer hung up and pushed the gas pedal closer to the floor. The tires whined on the asphalt as the car's speed increased.

This could be the break they needed—he needed. The testimony of a hooker was notoriously unreliable, but not always. He had a feeling about this one. Or maybe he was just hungry to get Lucas back behind bars. Whatever it was, he had to get there ASAP.

In a few minutes less than the estimated half hour, Brewer pulled in front of the police station, shut down the vehicle, and jumped out. His car blocked access, but he didn't care. The sticker on his windshield would cover him.

He pulled out his ID as he ran up the steps, presenting it at the duty desk. "RCMP Sergeant Lance Brewer," he said in a gruff tone. "You have someone here I want to interview. A hooker. Came in awhile ago."

The duty officer grinned. "Yeah, we have her." Then he laughed. "All the cops here are eager to lend a hand. Keep an eye on her, you might say."

"I wonder why," Brewer said dryly. "Where is she?"

The officer pointed to the back of the precinct. "Right down that hall. Interview room one."

Brewer offered a quick thanks and strode to the indicated room. The door was open and he stepped inside, holding his ID up.

The three cops in the room paid no attention to the

newcomer. One leaned against the wall, his arms crossed, while the other two sat forward, their full attention on the girl in front of them who lounged seductively in a comfortable chair. They were laughing, as if someone had told a joke.

"Out," Brewer commanded in a brusque tone, cocking a thumb back over his shoulder.

The cops looked his way, saw the badge, and reluctantly left the room. Brewer closed the door, kicked one of the chairs away, and pulled the other one back a couple of feet and sat down.

The girl looked like she'd just stepped off the street corner. The typical look—short skirt that left little to the imagination, a revealing top that left even less, and shoes with heels that made her long legs even longer.

He showed his ID and introduced himself. "Sergeant Brewer," he said.

She held out a hand. "You can call me Modesty."

He gave her hand a quick shake and got right to it. "Modesty, I understand you knew Varick Lucas."

She brushed back a strand of dyed blond hair. "I might. I came here on my own time, Officer. I'm a busy lady and my time is money."

"Don't worry about it. Call it advertising," Brewer said, with a gesture toward the door. "You'll probably pick up a few good customers here."

Modesty giggled. "They're mighty handsome." She looked Brewer up and down. "And you look good yourself, Officer."

"I'm not an officer," he said. "I'm a sergeant."

"Yes, Sergeant," she said, with a smile and a mock salute.

Brewer sat back. "You can call me anything you want. Now, can we get down to it?"

Modesty wiped away her smile with the back of her hand. "What do you want to know?"

"You knew Lucas?"

"Yes. A long time ago."

"How long ago?"

"Before he went to prison."

"How do you know him?"

She smiled. "He was a customer at first, and then we became friends. He actually wasn't a very good customer. Didn't like to pay, but as a friend, we always had lots of fun." She frowned. "Not just sex."

"So you hung out?"

"Sure. There was always a party somewhere, and we were together a lot. He was okay. I never, ever thought he would kill anybody." She shuddered. "Who knows, maybe he would've killed me some day."

Brewer ignored the extraneous comments and leaned in. "Did he ever tell you about a cabin up north?"

Modesty laughed. "Sure. I went there once with him, a guy named Otis, and another girl. It wasn't much of a time. I never went back." She picked at a fingernail. "I prefer the city life, if you know what I mean."

Now for the vital question. "Would you know how to get there again?"

She shrugged. "Maybe."

"Maybe yes or maybe no?"

"I think so," she said. "Is it important?"

"Very important. We think he might be there now."

The girl's eyes widened. "You don't say." She leaned forward a couple of inches. "Is there a reward?"

"Don't you think doing the right thing is reward enough?"

She thought about that a moment. "It's a start."

"How about this?" Brewer said. "I'll guarantee you those cops leave you alone and you can do business all day and all night if you want."

"You can do that?"

"I can do that."

She paused a moment, and seemed to be deciding whether or not to trust him. Finally, she sat back, uncrossed her legs, crossed them the other way, and said, "I remember exactly where it is because we stopped at a little town along the way, and it's just past there."

Brewer leaned back and smiled. "What's the name of the town?"

She looked at the ceiling. "San ... Sanderson or something like that."

Brewer jumped to his feet and leaned in. "Sanridge?"

"Yeah, that's it."

Brewer pumped a fist and sat back down. "Where is it from Sanridge?"

"We went about two miles or so past the town, then we hopped the fence and hiked into the forest for an hour or so. Maybe more. Maybe less."

That was good enough. The helicopters and the existing maps would pinpoint the exact location, and then specially trained ground troops would do the rest.

And he was going to be there when the operation went down—when Lucas went down.

Brewer stood and grinned at Modesty. "You've been a big help. If we catch this guy, you'll never see the inside of a holding cell again."

She saluted once more. "Happy to have been of help, Sergeant."

He chuckled, then howled with laughter, the sound filling the small room. He was still laughing when he exited the precinct and made his way to his car.

He dug out his cell phone and called Corporal Loy. "Get me a copter," he said. "I'm heading north."

CHAPTER 53

Sunday, 10:15 a.m.

JAKE RAISED HIS head and listened intently. He was sure he'd heard a sound, something not made by nature—the distinct sound of an engine.

He dove from the cave, spun around, and held up a hand. "Stay here," he said. "I think I heard somebody coming."

Without waiting for an answer, he raced along the beach and up the grade. The rough road was not far from their original campsite and the sound was coming from that direction.

As he topped the knoll, he saw the distinct outline of Andy Fletcher's pickup. His heart jumped at the sight. They could finally get some help. Hopefully, the police were right behind.

Andy stepped from the truck, came around the front of the vehicle, and waved a hand as Jake drew closer. "Howdy," he called.

Jake approached the warden and stopped, his emotions a mix of anger at the officer's lack of a quick response and relief at finally seeing him. "Where've you been?" he asked, exasperation in his voice.

Andy pushed back his sunglasses and peered at Jake. "Sorry. Couldn't get back any sooner. Hope everything's okay here."

"As a matter of fact, it's not. My wife is missing, another person has been killed, and the kids are frightened."

The officer looked stunned. "Your wife is missing? How long ago?"

"Since yesterday." Jake looked anxiously down the road. "Are the police on their way?"

"They'll be here before long," Andy said. "Almost had to drag the chief out of bed to get him to come here."

That wasn't a good enough answer for Jake. "What about yesterday?" he asked, his voice tinged with frustration. "Why didn't they come then?"

Andy shrugged. "It's a small town. Nothing ever happens here and the station is pretty much closed on the weekend. Only one cop hangs around and he said he couldn't leave the station. I finally got ahold of the chief and he said he'd come."

Jake shook his head in unbelief. "And the people at the park entrance?"

"They don't get into any criminal stuff. Said they leave all that up to the police."

Jake took a deep breath to calm his rising anger. "You could've at least given us a lift back yesterday instead of leaving us here."

"Figured you'd be okay all set up in a safe place. Thought nobody would find you there." Andy's voice took on an apologetic tone. "Guess now in hindsight I should have, but I was in a hurry to get the police here. Had that man's body on my mind."

Jake leaned in and raised his voice. "You could've come back for us."

Andy took a step back. "Careful there, friend. I'm here now. No need to get ourselves out of control."

Jake pointed toward the forest. "My wife is missing."

"I'm sure the police will find her."

Jake found it hard to calm down, and the casual attitude of the game warden added to his frustration.

"Are they bringing dogs?" Jake asked.

"Could be they'll send out for some. We don't have any tracking dogs 'round here."

"I know who you're looking for," Jake said. "That lunatic from the cabin, the one you said was a good guy."

Andy cocked his head. "What makes you say that?"

"Because my boys were at the cabin and my wife was a prisoner inside. When I went back, nobody was there."

Andy scratched his head. "Don't seem right to me."

"Whether it seems right or not, it's a fact."

Andy gazed into the forest in the direction of the cabin. "Ain't Otis," he said. "Maybe somebody else has taken the cabin and did Otis some harm."

Jake glanced at the pistol strapped on Andy's thigh. "Whoever it is, we can't wait for the police to take their sweet time about getting here. I need you to come to the cabin with me. You have a gun and we're up against a killer."

Andy shook his head. "I ain't a cop." He tapped his weapon. "And this here ain't for police work. Sorry, friend, but you're gonna have to wait fer them to show."

Jake wasn't confident when the police finally showed up, it would be any more than one cop, no more capable than the game warden.

Andy looked at Jake, his brow wrinkled. "I clean near forgot. You say there's another person killed now too?"

"Yes, one of the girls from the backpackers' camp. Her throat has been slit."

Andy whistled. "That's a shame. Just young girls they were too." He shook his head slowly and gazed toward the lake. "And the rest of them, they still here?"

"The two boys ran off. The other girl, I have her stashed away with my boys."

"Maybe you should show me the body."

Jake took a deep breath and let it out slowly. He was irritated, but he tried to remain patient with the slow-witted warden. "I don't see what good that would do. You already said you're not a cop, so I think it would be best to leave the girl's body there and let the police handle it."

"Yeah, guess you're right about that one. No use messin' around. Can't do nothin' for her anyway."

Jake looked carefully at the warden. "Andy, I need a favor."

"What's that?"

"Lend me your gun?"

Andy shook his head adamantly. "Nope. No way. Can't do that."

"I need to find my wife and I need some protection."

"Can't do it, friend."

"What about a rifle?" Jake motioned toward the pickup. "You have a rifle in your truck?"

"Sure do, but same thing. Can't let you use it. That's my own neck on the line."

Jake kicked at the dirt, trying to come up with something. He'd run out of ideas and the warden wasn't much help. He wasn't confident he could find Annie's whereabouts either way. It looked like he had no choice but to wait for the police.

Andy glanced at his watch. "Well, I guess I should get going. I got other places to go. I'll see if I can hurry up the police on my way through."

Jake held up a hand. "Wait. I want you to give Holly and my boys a lift out of here."

"Sure. Guess I could do that."

Jake turned. "I'll go and get them." He took a few long strides and turned back. "Wait right there." He didn't want the warden to leave this time like he'd done so foolishly before.

"I'm waiting. Get the kids."

Jake hurried to the cave and crouched down. "The warden has finally come. He's going to take you guys away from here."

Matty grabbed his backpack and hurried from the cave. "What about you, Dad?"

"Not until I find your mother."

Kyle and Holly had scrambled from the cave. The four of them hurried up to join the warden.

"Let's go," Andy said, leading the way to his pickup. You

boys get in the back seat there, and Holly, you can get in the front." He opened the doors and they climbed inside.

Jake came around to the driver side as Andy got in. "Are you going straight out?"

"I am now," Andy said. "Wasn't going to, but I guess I should take these kids away from here first."

Jake watched as Andy backed the vehicle up, spun around, and headed away. He felt relieved they would be safe, but he still had to find Annie.

CHAPTER 54

Sunday, 10:22 a.m.

ANNIE WAS FEARFUL, frustrated, and angry. Even worse than the physical pain of remaining bound in a damp cave in such an agonizing position was her uneasy anticipation of the horrifying plans Lucas had for her and her family. Her only comfort was in knowing, as of two or three hours ago, when the boys had discovered her in the cabin, they were still safe. It was what might have happened since then that caused her the most anxiety.

Surely the police would bring tracking dogs and she listened in vain for their eager barking, but the only sounds were the quiet whistle of the breeze in the cave, and the constant drip, drip from the ceiling of her tomb. Each time she called for help, her own voice echoed back, mocking her attempts to be heard.

She raised her eyes to a different sound—a light repetitive thump, but as it grew louder, she realized it was the reverberating sound of footsteps drawing closer. Someone was coming.

A silhouette appeared against the brightness of the cave opening. She dared to hope it was Jake. Her illusion was crushed when the shadowy profile moved closer and revealed itself as Varick Lucas.

He grinned at her, the now familiar glint of evil flashing from his eyes. "Ah, you're still here. I suspected as much, but one can never be too sure about these things." He moved behind the column and gave the ropes a tug. "Still secure. I thought you would at least have made some headway in getting loose."

Annie ignored his comments as he crouched in front of her. "You don't look comfortable," he said, with pretend concern.

"It's okay," she said. "It gave me a chance to catch up on some sleep."

He laughed, long and hard. His laughter echoed throughout the cave, fearful and eerie, resonating with pure evil.

His laughter died away and he spoke. "I have some good news for you. You'll be happy to hear we're moving back to the cabin."

Annie was mystified. He'd just brought her here a couple of hours ago, and now was taking her back. What had transpired in the meantime?

"You're not safe here," he said. "There are wild animals and all kinds of crazy creatures inhabiting this forest. Something could happen to you, and we wouldn't want that."

She rolled her eyes at him. "Thank you for your concern."

He stood and shook his head slowly. "You're a tough broad, aren't you? Anyone else would be pleading for mercy right now." He paused. "You're not at all like the one I had begging this morning. In fact, I might've let her go if she'd been more like you."

Annie narrowed her eyes. Who was he talking about? If what he said was true, the only females she knew about were the backpackers. Had one of them, or both, become a victim of this lunatic?

He liked to boast and inflict emotional pain, and she dared believe if he had harmed Jake or the boys, he would be bragging about his dreadful feat. But he wasn't, and she forced herself to assume they were safe. Maybe they'd gotten a ride back, but no, Jake would never leave her.

He continued, observing her as he spoke. "I haven't killed your husband yet."

She studied his eyes, getting no indication whether or not he spoke sincerely. She knew he was watching for her reaction as well and she struggled to remain quiet, responding neither with her voice nor her actions.

She wanted to believe he spoke the truth, and whether or not he did, his words revealed his clear intent. He had plans to kill Jake sometime soon.

Lucas leaned over and withdrew the hunting knife from the sheath at his leg. He bent over her, bringing the tip of the blade ever closer to her face until finally, she felt it touch her cheek. It pushed against the skin. She closed her eyes and held her breath, tensing her face muscles, her teeth clamped tight. She heard him breathing and she waited.

She felt the blade slide down her cheek, then a sharp pain. Her eyes sprung open and she drew a quick breath, responding to the suddenness of his voice. "Oh, I've cut you."

A single drop of blood trickled down her cheek and dripped off her chin. She dropped her head and watched it stain her shirt.

"Time to go now," he said. He went behind and cut the ropes with a quick slash, and her hands fell free.

She touched her cheek and looked at her finger. There was little blood, but her face stung where he'd pierced the skin. She wiped her face with the palm of her hand, and then massaged her wrists in an attempt to increase the blood flow.

Lucas held out a hand, offering to help her up.

"I can manage on my own," she said.

"I insist." He gripped her by the wrist, pulling her to her feet.

She wrenched her arm from his grasp but dared not look him in the eye. Her courage was slipping away and she didn't like the feeling. She couldn't let him win, couldn't let him see her growing fear.

She summoned her dwindling inner strength and forced her eyes upwards, finally glaring into his. "Will you loosen the ropes around my ankles? They're numb."

He stood back, crossed his arms, and squinted at her thoughtfully.

"Please?" she said. She saw a hint of a smile on his lips. Or was he gloating?

He crouched down and severed the ropes at her ankle, then selected the longest piece and tied it around her waist. He gripped the end of the two-foot-long leash, giving it an abrupt tug from behind. She staggered backwards and almost lost her balance.

"That should hold you," he said in a low voice, more to himself than to her.

He prodded her from behind. "You know the way. You lead, I'll follow."

She walked toward the exit, shuffling her feet as she went. She was regaining the strength in her legs but didn't want him to know that.

They went down the bank, crossed the stream, and entered the forest on the other side. Yes, she knew the way, and she'd remembered every dip in the terrain, every hill, and every bush, and she would use that knowledge.

As they approached an embankment, she leaped, her full weight propelling her forward and down, dragging him with her as she tumbled and rolled.

But she was free. He'd lost his grip on the rope during the fall.

She scrambled to her feet and dashed forward, dodging trees, vaulting obstacles, and tearing through bushes, branches, and hanging vines.

The strength she'd regained soon waned. Her valiant attempt ended as he dove from behind, bearing her roughly to the ground. She hit her head on a stump and lay stunned, unable to fight as he straddled her, bringing her into complete submission once again.

CHAPTER 55

Sunday, 10:36 a.m.

JAKE WAS AMAZED at the negligent and casual attitude the police had displayed toward his predicament. They'd been slow in responding, and even when they had, were taking their sweet time about getting here.

Since Andy had left, Jake had paced up and down the trail, stopping each time to peer ahead, then returning to sit on the bank and wait some more.

Finally, he heard the sound of a vehicle in the distance. He hoped it wasn't the game warden returning for some unknown reason, and was overjoyed to see a mud-spattered red pickup coming his way. The vehicle whined as it rolled over the rough terrain, spinning its wheels, jolting and jumping toward him.

He stood and waited until the truck ground to a halt in front of him, the driver-side door opened, and a figure stepped out.

Jake's heart fell as Bob walked around the front of the truck and approached him. What was the game warden's nephew doing here? And where were the police?

Bob walked over to Jake, touched his worn-out baseball

cap, and grinned. "Hey, Jake. Thought I would find you here." He offered a hand.

Jake shook the boney hand. "I'm waiting for the police. Did you see them on your way in?"

Bob wrinkled his face. "The police? No, I haven't seen them. I'm looking for my uncle. Figured he might be round here somewheres."

"Your uncle was here not too long ago. He's on the way out now. You didn't meet him coming in?"

"Nope. I just wanted to find him. There're a bunch of rowdy campers a long ways back. I saw them fightin' and drinkin' and disturbing other campers something terrible. I thought maybe Uncle Andy should drop by and give them the heave-ho." He shook his head and frowned. "We don't like to see that kind of stuff going on."

Jake looked at the aspiring game warden in amusement. "You didn't feel qualified to give them the 'heave-ho' yourself?"

"If I had a badge maybe I could. But I ain't got any authority." He gave a crooked grin. "Tried it already one other time. They wouldn't listen to me."

Jake thought he understood why.

Bob scratched at a pimple and looked around. "So, what's all this about the police? Something happen?"

Jake filled him in quickly with a few facts, leaving out the part about Rosie and the other backpackers. "My wife's been missing since yesterday and everything I've done to find her has turned up a dead end. I've been waiting for the police ever since."

Bob looked at Jake in unbelief, his mouth hanging open a moment. All he could manage to say was, "Sheesh." He looked around uneasily. "Sure hope the cops get here fast. For the sake of your wife, that is."

Jake hoped so too but said nothing.

"I met your wife when she was coming in," Bob said. "She stopped at the store. Bought some snacks and stuff. Said she was coming here to join her husband. I put two and two together and knew it was you. Nice lady, your wife."

Jake wasn't in the mood to exchange a lot of small talk, his concern for Annie being foremost on his mind. He would be more than pleased if the youth left.

"So, nobody knows who the dead guy is?" Bob asked.

"Your uncle took a look, and he didn't recognize him. There was no ID on the body either."

"Must be another camper. Sometimes they wander around, bring their dirt bikes and stuff."

"There was no dirt bike there, and he didn't look like he had been riding one."

Bob rubbed at his chin. "Well, far as I know, there's nobody reported missing in town. Small town, you know. Word would get around real quick if there was."

"Do you know if the police have access to any tracking dogs?" Jake asked.

"Don't think so. They could send for some, I guess. Far as I can remember, nobody ever had any call for anything like that round these parts."

Jake wasn't surprised at the revelation. When it came to the local police force, nothing surprised him anymore. He pointed a finger toward Bob's truck. "You wouldn't have a rifle in there, would you?"

"Sure enough do."

"And ammunition?"

"Yup."

"I want to borrow it."

Bob removed his cap and scratched his head. He looked at his truck, and then back at Jake. "Don't know if I can do that."

Jake leaned in a bit, glaring down at the youth. "I'm not asking."

Bob stepped back and squinted up at Jake as if considering the demand.

Jake held his gaze.

Bob rubbed the back of his neck and stared at his truck. Jake didn't want to press him too much—unless Bob made the wrong decision. Then he would have to change the young man's mind for him.

"Well, I guess it would be okay," Bob said. "But if there's a problem later, you gotta say it was your idea." He waited for an answer.

"Whatever you say. I only want to borrow it."

"All right, then." Bob beckoned and led the way to his vehicle. He opened the passenger door, removed a rifle mounted above the rear window of the cab, and handed it to Jake.

Jake took the rifle and examined it—a semiautomatic with a fully loaded magazine.

Bob dug around under the seat, removed a box of

ammunition, and held it out. "Plenty of ammo here if you need more."

Jake put the box into his pants pocket and pointed off to the right of the trail. "Do you know anything about a cabin a couple of miles that way?"

Bob had removed a hunting knife from the glove compartment and was fastening it to his belt. He looked up and shook his head.

"That's where I'm heading," Jake said. "How much further does this trail go?"

Bob shrugged. "Not far. Maybe a half mile or so, then there's no getting through. But it don't go in the direction you want to." He nodded toward the trail. "Goes to the left just up there."

"Then I'll have to hike it," Jake said and looked down at the young man. "Are you coming with me or not?"

Bob looked at Jake, then down the trail, then at his rifle. "Guess I best go with you," he said.

~*~

THE HELICOPTER SCREAMED to a halt, flinging dirt and dust across the asphalt. The door opened and RCMP Sergeant Lance Brewer stepped out.

His cohesive team of tactical unit officers, wearing full camouflage and wielding assault weapons, streamed out behind him. The group of four was highly trained in the employment of specialized weapons, equipment, and tactical methods.

With an armed suspect on the loose, and many bodies left in his wake, getting close to Lucas from the air was a risky proposition. With the help of aerial photographs, Brewer had zeroed in on the precise location of the target, and they would approach the cabin by stealth.

He wasn't taking any chances.

The helicopter took to the air. Rather than block the highway, it would land in an empty field a little further on and remain in radio contact, returning when necessary. A car would be dispatched to escort their intended prisoner.

"This guy's a cop killer," Brewer said, his no-nonsense voice commanding immediate attention and respect from his men. "Emotions are a little high today, but let's keep it professional. You all know what to do."

Brewer consulted the aerial photographs. If Modesty was correct, and he had every reason to believe she was, the cabin where Varick Lucas was holed up was slightly more than two miles due east of their current location. There was some rough territory, but his men were trained to adapt to all types of terrain, locations, and weather conditions.

The cabin itself would be easy work. They could penetrate just about any barricade or stronghold, but they had to know what was going on inside. There was always a possibility of hostages, and the mobile thermal imaging system would aid them with that.

Lucas was undoubtedly armed and known to be dangerous; any possible hostage situation, if not handled correctly, could soon escalate into a nightmare. Brewer had proven himself an expert negotiator, but wanted to avoid an armed standoff at all costs. The last thing he wanted was for civilians to be caught in a crossfire.

A car slowed as it approached the group gathered by the shoulder of the road, its occupants craning their necks. Brewer waved them on. Maybe they would find out what happened on tomorrow's news, but right now was not the time for public relations. The car picked up speed and disappeared around a bend in the road.

Brewer watched his team finish last-minute preparations— checking their weapons, donning protective gear, and readying themselves for the hike into the forest.

His team was ready. "Move out," Brewer said, taking the lead. "Let's get this guy."

CHAPTER 56

Sunday, 10:59 a.m.

JAKE HELD THE rifle in his right hand, the safety off, ready to bring it into action at a moment's notice. He led the way through the forest, Bob following behind.

He was uncertain what he would find. When he'd been to the cabin earlier, it was empty, but he fully intended to persevere this time. The boys were safe and he was determined to pursue Annie's abductor wherever the chase might lead. All he had to do was find him.

Whether or not his quarry was armed, Jake didn't know. Both of the known victims had been killed by a knife, but he wasn't about to rule out the presence of more lethal weapons.

"Ain't never been in this area before," Bob said from behind.

Jake stopped, turned around, and spoke quietly. "Keep your voice down. We have no idea where this guy is, and if he sees us first..." He didn't finish the sentence. The implication was clear.

Bob looked uncomfortable and glanced around. He whispered, "You're sure you don't want to wait for the cops?"

"Look," Jake said. "You're free to turn around any time you want."

Bob licked his lips. "I'll come along."

"Then keep it down. And keep an eye on our flank."

"What's a flank?"

"Just keep watch on both sides of us."

Bob nodded. "Okay."

Jake turned and continued on, careful where he placed each foot, keeping a close eye in all directions, ready to react to any potential danger. Maybe he should have left the young fellow behind; he wasn't going to be of much use.

The occasional small creature of the forest rustled leaves on the ground or overhead, darting through bushes or rooting in the underbrush, and Jake paused each time, moving on only when he knew it was safe.

He glanced back at Bob. The youth was diligent about watching their flank. His head moved back and forth in a comical, rhythmic pattern. Jake wasn't sure about the boy's ability to be a game warden one day, but he couldn't be worse than his uncle.

Branches slapped together in a sudden breeze, causing Bob to jump, then grin foolishly when he realized what had startled him. Jake shook his head and continued on.

In a few minutes, the outline of the cabin became visible through the trees. Jake pointed and held a finger to his lips. Bob's eyes grew large and the young man didn't appear to be breathing. Then he swallowed hard, his eyes narrowed, and his hand dropped to the knife at his belt.

Jake became doubly vigilant as he moved to the edge of the clearing surrounding the cabin. He held up a hand of caution to Bob and listened intently. Other than the young man rustling his feet nervously in the leaves, no other sound caught his attention. Everything appeared to be the same as before.

Except one thing. Jake peered closer and his heart jumped. The padlock, now unlocked, hung loosely on the wide-open clasp.

Someone was in the cabin.

He turned back to Bob and whispered, "Someone is here now, so don't move, and don't breathe."

Bob took a shallow breath and nodded, looking bug-eyed toward the building.

"Stay here," Jake said and paused a moment to make sure the young man understood.

Bob remained frozen as Jake crept across the hardened ground to the corner of the cabin. The shutters at the side of the building were still closed and locked.

He needed to take a look inside. He checked the rear window, but the shutters were secure, without so much as a pinhole to allow a peek into the building.

Jake weighed his options. He could wait until someone came out of the cabin before making his move, or he could barge in the front door with his rifle ready and hope for the best. He decided both options were dangerous and could endanger Annie—if she was in there.

He decided on a third possibility. He would find a way to draw Annie's abductor out of the building, and then overpower him, either by brute force or by deadly force, whatever best insured Annie's safety.

He returned to Bob and prodded him behind the trunk of

a large tree, out of sight of the building. "I need your help," he said to the trembling youth.

"Uh, okay. Sure," Bob said, looking hesitant.

"I need you to knock on the door."

Bob's bulging eyes bulged even more. "Uh." He licked his lips, swallowed, and blew out a long breath. "Are ... are you serious?"

"Deadly serious." Jake realized he should've used a different choice of words. "I have a plan that should work."

"Should?"

"Will. It will work. Trust me."

Bob swallowed again and nodded slowly. "Okay."

"I'm not forcing you. It's your choice."

The youth's head bobbed up and down. He took a deep breath. "I can do it."

"You're sure?"

"Yup."

"Then let's go," Jake said with a thumbs-up. He moved toward the cabin and took up position to the left of the door, out of sight, the rifle ready. He had to do this right; he would only have one chance. Not only was his life at stake, but possibly Bob's, and certainly Annie's as well.

Bob stepped in front of the door and raised his hand, ready to knock. He bit his lip and looked hesitantly at Jake.

"Knock and stand back," Jake whispered, offering the terrified young man encouragement with a nod.

Bob took a deep breath and stared at his trembling hand, then at the door. He leaned in and rapped twice, then stepped backwards and looked at Jake.

A muffled voice came through the door. "Who is it?"

"Tell him your name," Jake said quietly.

"It ... it's Bob," the frightened young man called.

The latch rattled and the door opened a couple of inches. Jake tensed and gripped the rifle, his finger tightening on the trigger, ready to make his move.

The door creaked fully open and Bob's eyes bulged. He made a gasping sound, then turned and dashed away.

Jake stepped out in full view and raised the rifle. He stared hard, frowned, and lowered the weapon.

Andy stood in the doorway, a raised pistol in his hand.

"Andy," Jake said. "What's going on?"

"Hi, Jake," Andy said with a warm smile. "My name is Varick Lucas, and I've been expecting you."

CHAPTER 57

Sunday, 11:40 a.m.

ANNIE WATCHED IN horror as Jake stood in the doorway of the cabin, a confused look on his face. Lucas stepped backwards and kept the pistol trained on her husband.

"Drop the rifle," Lucas said.

Jake's eyes roved over the group huddled on the cot—Matty and Kyle, one on each side of Annie, one arm around each. Holly sat on a nearby chair.

"Andy, what's this all about?" Jake asked, his voice mixed with confusion and dread.

Lucas laughed. "You can stop calling me Andy now. He's dead."

The truth dawned on Jake. "The body in the forest … that's Andy."

"Yup."

"And you took his place, his clothes, everything, pretending to be him."

"Yup again."

"How did you know I'd never met Andy before?"

"Simple. Our dear warden dropped by and he happened to mention he hadn't made his rounds yet this weekend." Lucas waved the gun. "Now, drop the rifle and go sit on the cot."

Jake hesitated and continued to stare at Lucas. Annie saw

him weighing his options. Finally, the rifle clattered to the floor as Jake released it from his grasp. He stepped inside, took a seat on the cot beside Matty, and leaned forward.

Lucas kept the pistol trained on his hostages while he bent to pick up the rifle. He inspected it, then grinned, pulled up a chair, staying a few feet back, and sat down. He laid the rifle across his knees and held the pistol in his right hand.

"Why're you doing this?" Jake asked.

"It's just a game," Lucas said. "Something to pass the time."

"And what's the end result?"

Lucas raised the pistol, stretched it out, squinted one eye, and aimed at Jake's head. "Bang, bang."

"Why?" Annie asked, her voice hoarse with fear.

"Because you mean nothing to me." He waved the pistol. "Any of you."

"So you killed the game warden just to play your sick little game?" Jake asked.

Lucas seemed offended. "You have to admit, Jake, it's been quite a game. It's been a challenge for both of us. You have no idea what I went through to orchestrate this whole thing—to make everything work together, and time it just right."

Annie glanced down at Matty. He seemed to be putting on a brave face, but Annie could tell how frightened the boy was. His eyes never wavered from Lucas, his face almost expressionless as he hugged his backpack. Kyle had snuggled in tightly, his eyes closed, and Annie drew him even closer.

Holly sat with her head down, her hands clasped tightly in her lap. Occasionally she glanced toward her captor, and then dropped her head again when his eyes fell on her.

Jake seemed unruffled but Annie knew he wasn't. She could tell by his tight voice. "Why don't you let the children go?" he asked.

Lucas shrugged. "Why should I? What's so special about them?"

"They're innocent kids," Jake said, his voice raised.

Lucas moved the pistol toward Jake. "Keep your voice down."

Jake sat back and glared.

Annie spoke up. "Your mother wouldn't want you to harm the children."

Lucas's jaw clenched, his eyes becoming wild. He leaned forward and pointed a finger at Annie. "What do you know about my mother?" His face flushed, his voice now intense. "I told you about my mother in confidence and you have no business repeating what I said."

"You told me your mother was a saint."

Lucas gritted his teeth. "She was."

"Then she's in heaven now, and she's watching you."

Lucas exploded to his feet. "I know what you're trying to do, and it won't work." He strode behind his chair and leaned over the table, slamming his fist on the hard wooden top. He stood still a moment, then raised his head toward the ceiling, closed his eyes, and took a deep breath.

He opened the cupboard and removed a glass, then picked up the water pail. It was empty, and he tossed it into the corner and found a beer in the cupboard, took the top off, and took a long drink.

"I have one beer left," he said calmly. "Anybody want it?"

Nobody answered.

He left the half-finished beer on the table, went to his chair, and sat down, his face returning to normal, his rage expended.

He smiled with his lips, but Annie saw the same evil as before. He sat still for a minute or two, the smile remaining, breathing quietly to regain his composure as his eyes flickered over the hostages.

"And now it's time for the next phase of our game," he said quietly. "Which one of you wants to play first?"

When no one spoke, Matty slid forward and said, "I will."

Annie glanced down at her son. His face was unsmiling, and she could tell he knew it was much more than a friendly game. "No, Matty," she said frantically.

"It's okay, Mom."

"The boy has volunteered," Lucas said as he reached back, grabbed another hard-backed chair, and swung it forward. It slid toward the cot and stopped. He motioned to Matty. "Sit there."

Matty attempted to slide off the bed but Annie held his arm.

"Let him go," Lucas said, pointing the gun in her direction.

She held on to her son. Matty touched his mother's hand and peeled back her fingers gently. "It's okay."

Her hand slipped away and she watched in horror while Matty sat in the chair, hugging his backpack, five feet from the insane murderer.

Annie calculated the odds. If she sprang at Lucas, he would more than likely shoot her, but Jake would undoubtedly act fast and tackle Lucas before he had a chance to harm anyone else. Especially her only son.

Lucas swung the gun toward Matty. "Thanks for volunteering. It makes my life easier."

"No," Jake shouted and leaped to his feet. He seemed about to spring at the madman.

Lucas paused and pointed the pistol at Jake. "Do you want to take his place? I had hoped to save you for last."

Annie leaned forward slightly and tensed up. If Jake made a move, she was ready to spring off the cot and help him subdue the crazed killer. If he got shot, she was still determined to do all she could for the sake of her family.

"I'll take his place if you let him go." Jake waved toward the group of terrified hostages. "If you let them all go, you can do whatever you want with me."

"That's sporting of you," Lucas said. He touched the pistol to his cheek and frowned. "But that would require a change in the rules."

"It's your game," Jake said. "You can change the rules any time you want."

Lucas glared at Jake. He seemed to be considering the proposition.

"I'm the one you want," Jake continued.

Lucas laughed. "That's just the point. I don't want any of you." He moved the pistol, pointing it one by one toward each of the hostages. "I don't want you, or you, or you—"

He laughed loudly again before continuing. "It's not a matter of who; it's a matter of who's first." He looked at Matty. "And the boy volunteered to go first."

CHAPTER 58

Sunday, 11:56 a.m.

RCMP SERGEANT LANCE BREWER stood on the knoll, a hundred feet from the rear of the cabin, his field glasses trained on the building.

The only window in the back of the aging structure was shuttered and padlocked. He motioned for one of his men to move forward and take up position by the rear wall. Brewer moved in behind him, keeping low.

"Can you get a look in there, Shears?" he asked.

Shears inspected the window and replied. "There's no place to fit a camera, but I might get some sound."

Brewer motioned for Shears to stay and he circled around to the side of the building. Another window, shuttered and locked. They wouldn't be able to get any sight through this one either.

Brewer motioned to another of his men. "Wilton, watch the corner."

Wilton moved out to a position where he could see both the side and front of the structure and crouched down, his weapon drawn, safety off and ready.

Maynard and Collins had already taken up position in the

288

trees at the front of the building. Maynard sighted through the scope of the modified Winchester, trained on the only door of the cabin.

Brewer instructed him, "Take the shot if necessary. Use your discretion."

"Yes, sir," Maynard said. He was trained to target the body's center mass or upper torso to stop the threat. Brewer knew it was difficult to aim, particularly under stress, with the accuracy needed to hit extremities. Maynard might need to shoot to kill.

Collins removed the portable thermal imaging system from his pack. The sophisticated piece of equipment looked like a small camera, but was capable of detecting heat given off by objects and persons. The portable battering ram he'd carried, capable of producing eight hundred pounds of force, lay beside him, ready for use at a moment's notice.

Brewer crouched beside Collins. "What do we have?"

"It's hard to tell precisely," Collins answered. "It appears there are several individuals inside." He pointed to the display. "Maybe three or four right there." He moved his finger. "And another one right there."

Brewer's face was grim. "Could be hostages," he said.

"Pssst."

Brewer spun around, his SIG Sauer semiautomatic pistol drawn and ready. The sound had come from behind them, a few yards away.

"Over here." The voice was a little louder, and a hand waved from behind a bush.

"Come out of there," Brewer demanded, his weapon trained on the spot.

A young man crawled out on his hands and knees, then sat on his heels and raised his hands. Brewer squinted. It certainly wasn't Lucas. He moved in, his pistol ready.

The lad stood up, his hands still raised.

"Who're you?" Brewer asked.

"Bob." The young man's voice shook, his eyes fixed on the deadly weapon. He cowered as Brewer towered over him.

"And what're you doing here, Bob?"

"I ... uh."

"Spit it out, boy."

Bob swallowed hard. "I came here with Jake and ... there's a guy in the cabin with a gun. He captured Jake and I ran."

Brewer frowned. "Who's Jake?"

"They ... uh ... they were camping here and I think the gunman has his wife in there too."

Brewer turned and glanced at the cabin. It made sense. He turned back to the frightened youth. "Put your hands down."

Bob's dropped his hands in front of him, wringing them nervously.

Brewer twisted sideways and pointed to a patch on his shoulder. "RCMP. We'll handle this," he said. "Stay back out of sight, but don't go far. We'll need to talk to you after we get this guy."

Bob nodded vigorously, stepped back a few feet, and hunkered down behind a tree trunk.

Brewer followed him and pointed a finger. "I don't have the manpower to watch you. Are you going to stay put?"

Bob nodded again.

Brewer returned to where Collins crouched, watching the heat images. "It appears there's at least one hostage, likely more." Brewer said. He pointed to the monitor. "This looks like the gunman, and these are the hostages."

He removed a megaphone fastened to his pack, flicked it on, and raised it to his lips.

His voice filled the forest. "Varick Lucas, this is the RCMP, come out with your hands up."

CHAPTER 59

Sunday, 12:08 p.m.

JAKE'S HEART JUMPED and he celebrated silently when the megaphone blared outside the cabin. It was the RCMP. They must have been tracking Lucas since his escape, the local police perhaps still unaware of the situation.

The rifle clattered to the floor as Varick Lucas cursed and sprang to his feet. He looked in confusion toward the door, then at the rifle, then back at the door.

Jake contemplated diving for the weapon, but reconsidered. Lucas was waving the pistol, apt to fire at the slightest provocation.

The killer stooped, picked up the weapon, and backed up, the rifle in his left hand, the pistol in his right. He looked at his prisoners with wild eyes.

"You'll never get away," Jake said.

Lucas pointed the pistol at Jake. "It doesn't matter. If I die, I'm taking every one of you with me."

The megaphone blared again, repeating the same message.

Lucas tucked the pistol behind his belt and switched the rifle to his right hand. He took a deep breath and closed his eyes. When he opened them again, he looked calmer. He moved to the door and shouted, "Save your breath. I'm not coming out."

A muffled voice came through the door. "Lucas, my name is Sergeant Lance Brewer. We have you surrounded. Surrender now and nobody gets hurt."

Lucas yelled back, his voice remarkably calm, "Stay back or everyone dies." He glared at his hostages and lowered his voice. "All of you."

"How many hostages do you have?" Brewer called.

"Plenty."

"I've been authorized to negotiate with you. What do you want out of this?"

Lucas paced the floor, never taking his eyes off his prisoners. He returned to the door. "I want a helicopter out of here."

"I can do that, Lucas, but I need a show of good faith from you. Send me two hostages."

"The only thing you're going to get is a dead hostage," he shouted, and then leered at Matty, lowering his voice. "And it might be you."

Matty looked up bravely. "I'm thirsty."

"Shut up, kid," Lucas said. "All I have is beer, and you're too young for that." He laughed at his own comment.

Matty held up his backpack. "I have some Coke in here."

"Stay still and be quiet." Lucas scowled at the boy. "You're starting to annoy me."

"Are you there?" Brewer called. "I can get you out of here, but I need two hostages."

"I've changed my mind, Brewer. I'm not leaving."

"We don't want to break the door down, Lucas," Brewer called back. "That won't go well for anyone."

"I'm thirsty," Matty whined, looking ready to cry.

Annie leaned forward and touched her son's arm. "Matty, just wait."

Matty turned in his chair to face his mother. "But I'm thirsty."

Lucas gave Annie a black look. "Let the boy have a drink. It might be his last request."

Matty dug in his backpack. He removed a can and fiddled with the top. "I can't open it," he said, his lower lip quivering. He wrapped his hands around the container and held it toward Lucas. "Can you open it, please?"

Lucas cursed and took a step forward. He held the rifle steady and reached for the can with his left hand.

A sudden shower of bear spray shot from the nozzle as Matty gritted his teeth and pressed his thumb down.

Lucas staggered backwards, screaming with pain. Blinded by the spray, he stumbled against the table and fell to his knees, still retaining his grip on the rifle. The weapon fired and a bullet pierced the canoe over his head and embedded itself in the ceiling.

Annie ducked to the floor, taking Kyle with her, as Jake sprang forward and pulled Matty off the chair, dropping beside Annie. Holly had reacted by diving toward the wall, where she lay prone.

There was a sudden crash and the door burst inwards, splinters of wood spraying across the room.

Lucas blindly raised the rifle in the direction of the sound and pulled the trigger. Three shots sounded, then four more as Brewer knelt in the doorway and emptied his pistol into Varick Lucas.

Lucas howled—a horrible shriek that slowly faded as he wavered, and then crumpled to the floor. He lay still and lifeless, the blood from his wounds puddling on the rough wooden floor.

EPILOGUE

Sunday, 8:55 PM

ANNIE WAS EXHAUSTED, still shaken from their harrowing experience, and glad to be home. The coziness of her overstuffed chair made her sleepy and she snuggled in deeper.

Jake slouched on the couch opposite her, his feet resting on the coffee table, his head back, dozing. Matty seemed to have recovered remarkably well and was sitting on the floor, content to read a comic book.

When the doorbell rang, Jake blinked, stood, and went to the door. It was Hank. They were expecting him. The cop followed Jake into the living room and stopped to tousle Matty's hair before dropping onto the other end of the couch.

Matty closed his book and looked up. "Hey, Uncle Hank."

"Hey, Matty."

"Did you hear about our weekend?" Matty said as he climbed onto the couch and snuggled up next to Hank.

"Your father gave me some details on the phone, but I didn't get everything." He turned to Jake. "How'd you get home so fast?"

"After the RCMP interviewed us, they were good enough to help get our vehicles up and running. They brought the parts by helicopter and got us out of there immediately."

"And what about the girl?" Hank asked.

"Holly? They gave her a lift home. She was pretty unnerved."

"Who wouldn't be?" Hank said as he looked at his watch. "By the way, you might want to turn on the nine o'clock news. Amelia called me on the way over. There'll be a story on Varick Lucas coming on just about now."

"Lisa Krunk has been trying to call us," Jake said as he grabbed the remote from the coffee table and switched on the television. "We didn't answer the phone."

On the TV, teasers for upcoming stories ran. Then, the familiar station logo flashed on the screen, and the anchor took his cue, shuffled his papers, and looked at the camera. It was the Channel 7 Action News.

"Our top story. Escaped convict Varick Lucas has been shot dead by the RCMP. In an exclusive report, here's Lisa Krunk."

The scene flashed to a view of Lisa in front of a large building.

"I'm standing here in front of RCMP headquarters. Earlier this morning, the RCMP raided a cabin in Algonquin Park where escaped convict, Varick Lucas, was thought to be holed up."

The view switched to a highway panorama. Police cars lined the road, their lights flashing. A helicopter was seen touching down, and a stretcher, covered by a white sheet, was loaded into a waiting ambulance as Lisa continued.

"A team of tactical unit officers surrounded the building where Lucas was allegedly holding hostages. Attempts were made to negotiate, but when gunfire erupted from inside the cabin, officers entered by force, killing the armed Lucas, and freeing the five hostages."

Jake sat forward when a picture of him and Annie flashed on the screen.

"In a surprising turn of events, it appears the hostages were citizens of Richmond Hill. Private detectives Jake and Annie Lincoln, whom I've had occasion to interview several times in the past, were vacationing in Algonquin Park and taken hostage by Lucas. I've been unable to reach them for comment and details are sketchy at this time, but sources have confirmed their eight-year-old son, Matty, was responsible for setting about the chain of events leading to Lucas's defeat."

Lisa came back on the screen, hugging the microphone.

"I'll bring you more on this story as information becomes available. For Channel 7 Action News, I'm Lisa Krunk."

The anchor appeared.

"Tune in tomorrow night when we'll bring you an exclusive look at the life of Varick Lucas, along with further details of the RCMP manhunt culminating in his death."

Jake switched off the television and looked at Hank. "Next time I ask you to come vacationing with us, maybe you should. It would have come in handy to have a cop there."

Hank chuckled. "Why would you need me when you have Matty around?" He glanced down at the boy. "Isn't that right, Matty?"

But Matty didn't hear. He was fast asleep.

###

CPSIA information can be obtained at www.ICGtesting.com
Printed in the USA
LVOW10s1428050616

491307LV00012B/791/P